MEXICO DAYS

MEXICO DAYS

A Novel

Robert Roper

Weidenfeld & Nicolson
New York

Published by Weidenfeld & Nicolson, New York
A Division of Wheatland Corporation
841 Broadway
New York, New York 10003-4793

Published in Canada by General Publishing Company, Ltd.

Library of Congress Cataloging-in-Publication Data

Roper, Robert, 1946–
Mexico days / Robert Roper.—1st ed.
p.   cm.
ISBN 1-55584-073-6
I. Title.
PS3568.O69M49   1989
813'.54—dc20   89-5717
                                                         CIP

Manufactured in the United States of America

This book is printed on acid-free paper

Designed by Paul Chevannes

First Edition

1   3   5   7   9   10   8   6   4   2

For Mady

For Mady

This book was written partly with the aid of a grant from the National Endowment for the Arts; and largely with the aid of grants from the BWR Foundation, may they prosper.

MEXICO DAYS

M Y SISTER DID poorly at Stanford. She arrived just when politics became a big attraction, an area of effort much more promising than mere studies, and I doubt she took a single grade the last semester she attended.

By then (fall of 1968) she was a third of the central committee of No Pasarán, the determined and rather vicious little group that out-lefted all others at Stanford and elsewhere in northern California for a time, by following through on a policy only much-discussed in other circles. All black prison inmates being *political* prisoners, by virtue of their skin color and the oppressive mechanisms of Amerikan society, it followed that the white cadre who, because of their position of racist privilege, were on the outside, should do their damnedest to liberate some soul brothers.

Accordingly, in February 1970, two black cons serving

long sentences at Soledad were busted out of a prison lorry en route to the medical facility at Vacaville. One of these men, Peter Jarings, was recaptured just hours later, but the other stayed free for a good six months and had a passel of armed robberies and two rapes to his credit when eventually reapprehended. His name was Buford Wilson (later, Yamaan Ali Mustafa). Wilson was the one who snitched on No Pasarán; not that I blame him, but as a result of his tale-tellings my sister and some of her comrades became fugitives for a while.

I was then living in Berkeley. I had had my own brief college career at the university there, and was engaged in criminal activities of my own, involving many visits to Mexico, when my sister and two friends showed up. My sister, Sylvia, only wanted some money from me; not then, and never before or since, did I doubt her perfect competence. But the two friends were in a state of agitation that made it likely they would use the heat they insisted on carrying either on themselves or on the first unlucky cop who pulled them over for a taillight infraction. I argued, to no effect, that Sylvia should separate herself from these fools at the earliest opportunity; seeing that she was determined to be their nursemaid, I drove all four of us north in the Chevy panel truck I owned at the time, my vague plan being to stash them temporarily on a farm that some friends had in Trinity County.

Well, this turned out to be a fateful move. Not in the sense of trouble with the law—there was none, nor did anyone in No Pasarán, with the exception of my sister, ever do so much as a day in jail for the big break-out—but in the sense that my sister and I, finding conditions at the farm uneasy (her friends irritated mine enormously, and v.v.), went out and rented a nearby property, a run-down, timbered-over spread with just the shell of a farmhouse on it. This meandering, ex–cow-and-alfalfa operation, a mere thirty acres or so, with the special feature of being adjacent to a national forest, has been my home ever since. In 1973 I moved up full-time, and in 1977, with a girlfriend serving as purchaser of record, I bought it outright.

My sister went to jail because she refused to play the game in either of the two most likely ways. By the time of her capture, about a year after we went north, she was so sick of her comrades that she wouldn't join their collective defense effort, which, as seemed to happen a lot in those days, was successful in the end, productive of so many mistrials and reversals of decision that everybody walked. Nor would she accept legal help from our father. A lawyer himself (though, as far as I know, never admitted to the bar in California), he could have arranged the dismissal of all charges against her in a matter of minutes, I'm sure, but Sylvia, hating him as she did, would sooner have gone to the chair than return his calls. So she did twenty-two months. When she got out she had no one, no more political friends (who had turned against her, as she had against them), hardly any personal friends, either; after a brief stay in Mexico—where we ran into each other, almost by accident— she went back home (L.A.), enrolled in a community college, and after a year of that went to nursing school. Until just recently she was working as a hospital administrator in El Segundo.

I'm writing this in Mexico. Let me be no more specific about my whereabouts than that, since the people I'm staying with, old friends from my *contrabandista* days, might suffer otherwise. In any case, I won't be here long.

It will be sad to return to the States. I love Mexico, but I need to kill someone, and after I accomplish this task I won't be able to come back. Also, what awaits me in the U.S. is my sister in a physical and emotional condition that it distresses me to contemplate, let alone confront. I'll be going back mainly to be with her, to take her up to the farm.

I started loving Mexico early on. My father, the late Gerson Sanders, having a certain amount of money that he needed to put to work (but anonymously, and not in his own country), formed a partnership with some Mexican nationals in the late 'forties, and it was partly to inspect his investments, partly just to get away that he took to traveling south every now and then, sometimes bringing me along. We often stayed in Cuernavaca. Here, in a house that was indeed a palace (owned by his principal partner), I can remember understanding Spanish for the first time: a kitchenmaid, who was giving me lunch, asked if the hot peppers 'bit' me (*"¿Te pican los chiles . . . ?"*). I was four or five years old. Up till then I had been a fairly quiet child, I'm told, the sort who looks up at the adults with a blank and hungrily absorptive expression, who seems to be storing away experience as if it were film footage, to be edited later.

With Spanish, though, I became (somewhat) different, much less stiff and withheld. As best I can remember, I was under the impression that this other language was for 'fun,' that anything you managed to say in it was all right, was sure to be applauded and found humorous. No doubt this is because the kitchenmaids, the other servants, Gerson's partners, and all the other Spanish-speaking adults were trying to encourage me. But I think also that some quality peculiar to Spanish is also peculiar to me, that it 'fits' in my mouth in a happy way. English, on the contrary, though my mother tongue, has an edgy quality, or a boniness, that shocks me on those occasions when I suddenly become cognizant of it.

Gerson's partner, the one who owned the Cuernavaca palace, was Martín de Onis y Guzmans. He was customarily referred to as the richest man in the state of Morelos. When he died, in 1954 (during one of our visits—I was then eight years old), his wife, Marcela, became in form what she had always been in fact: head of the various family interests. This woman was very beautiful, in a corseted, heavily made-up way, and I remember her as somewhat cool, never very 'present' to me.

They had twin daughters, Marcela and Marta, a year or so younger than I and a little older than my sister. When they were small these girls looked like spiders, or I should say, spider monkeys, with fantastically long and skinny arms and legs. They were dark, secretive, and sneaky. For all their parents' pretensions to being 'one hundred percent' Spanish-blooded, the girls came out looking exactly like Aztecs; that is, like a million other pure-blooded, breathtakingly beautiful Indian girls to be encountered in the villages of the central plateau. Their hair was black, thick, and coarse; their eyes were large, Asiatically slanted, and in Marcela's case, slightly protuberant; they had moderately beaky noses, strong, absolutely horizontal cheekbones, and softly cleft chins, around large mouths of bright teeth and purplish lips, which gave them a disturbing, fundamentally grave appearance mitigated just slightly by the inexplicable comedy of its being doubled. I'm speaking now of how they looked in their teens, or in Marcela's case, later (Marta died almost exactly on her twentieth birthday); when they were girls, in the years when I first got to know them, not only weren't they beautiful, they were positively strange-looking, even ugly, and the standing joke, invoked each time my father and I came to visit—that I was destined to marry one or the other—disturbed me on more than the ordinary grounds.

Both were playful, but Marta evinced a great interest in me and, even though I was older and bigger, led me around and completely dominated our choice of games and where to play. Marcela, I think, evinced a similar interest in me, and likewise dominated me—something I would never have tolerated back home—but not so much from a natural inclination as in a spirit of competition with her sister. I was a curious object with a natural value in the eyes of the one, a derived, backhanded interest for the other. I'm trying to remember how things actually were with us, on those afternoons almost thirty years ago, and the persistence of this impression, occurring to me now, is all the evidence I have that such a thing was really the case; it may be that I'm reading something in, on the basis of later developments, but I think not (at least not entirely). In any event, there was something magical, strangely fascinating and promising, in the way we got along. I was conscious—even then—of being stood on my head to a certain extent, of having some other, previously unsuspected side of myself called forth by these little spider-girls. They played convoluted, somehow electrifying tricks on me, which I always fell for like a clod. Yet my dignity was never at stake with them—for reasons I still can't explain—and I sometimes connived at my own victimization, so thrilling did I (secretly) find it.

Later on, when my sister got included in a few Mexico trips, her reaction was the same; but Marcela was the one for her, never Marta (or Marta only 'artificially'). Right from the start there was a powerful, deeply gratifying mutual attraction, of the sort that makes those left outside of it (Marta and me) feel stupid, dismayed to realize that all along there was the possibility for feeling on a vastly more significant level. They were inseparable, they spent all their time together laughing (or hiding, doing 'mysterious' things together in secret); well do I remember how my little sister, who had never before been any sort of puzzle to me, would seem fundamentally strange after time with Marcela, her very features, her whole way of standing, of attending, subtly altered, inwardly transformed by the contagion of this exciting attachment. I probably wouldn't have cared—and certainly I tried never to *seem* to—except that this change ran in a direction counter to my own interests. My masculine authority, what there was of it, was somehow challenged by the spirit of what these two concocted between them; and I remember, at age ten or so, turning briefly against Marcela, striking out in some crude way that she pretended not to notice.

I MAY HAVE given the impression that we spent all our childhood, or even a big part of it, in Mexico, but we didn't; almost all the time we were back home, growing up in strange circumstances in Bel Air.

Our father owned a large house on Dolores Court. Now a 'personal manager' lives there, a man whose name means nothing to me or to anyone else outside the business. I'm told that he takes a sort of pride in occupying Gerson Sanders' old digs, to the point of implying that Gerson's much-storied, industry-wide influence, as well as his famous way of doing business, somehow belong to him as well, were left behind the way a previous tenant might leave an unwanted piece of furniture. In this way do some people find romance in even the most sordid human material.

Actually, my father's life was sordid only at heart, only in its essence; all its visible manifestations were pretty slick, up to the end, and the circumstances of my sister's and my upbringing were such as I've never been able to make myself dislike. My sister, on the other hand, had a revulsion that started in her early teens and that designated the house, the actual physical structure, with its expensive interior appointments, as the living symbol of all that was wrong, all about my father and his life that was deserving of hatred.

Accordingly, after about the age of sixteen or so she never set foot in his house. She maintained that she would have gotten physically sick to go there, that just being inside those walls, where our mother staged her long decline; where our father conducted his business (in the 'library,' the leather-bound book-lined sanctum we children were rarely allowed to enter); where Boteros, de Chiricos, the few good Ben Shahns ever drawn (in my opinion), as well as a superb collection of 'green-dream' Chagalls, were lightfully and unostentatiously displayed, would have been too much for her. Nor did she ever see my father, himself, again, from the time she went away to college until the last day, the very last minutes of his life. He, too, had become an unendurable symbol, a physical reminder in whose presence she couldn't trust herself.

Yet I never had this reaction, either to him or to his house; to me it was just a house, and my father was a man I was somehow able to get along with, notwithstanding the bad times and my fundamental, 'adult' opinion of the sort of person he was.

In the early 'fifties, when my father's position became even more formidable than previously, my mother was already a drunk. *Pace* my sister, but I think a drunk is a drunk either by volition—that is, by desire leading to conscious choice—*or* because alcoholism is a disease, she can't help herself, etc. In other words, what I can't hold with is the idea that someone else drives you to the sauce. But this is what my sister maintains, or used to, that our poor, fey, lovely, and darling mother, she of the short but noteworthy cinematic career, of rare—but therefore searingly memorable—gestures of tearful tenderness toward her children, was made to be a drinker by her awful husband.

This theory, superficially attractive, and remindful (as so much about my mother is remindful) of the plots of movies (in this case, a silent two-reeler starring Mae Murray, with gobs of eye shadow), has the disadvantage of making her into even more of a cipher than she may have been. I've always preferred to give her the credit at least of choosing her own end. However, it's true that, after the first couple of years of marriage, Gerson reverted to his customary manner as regards the companionship of women. (I have this on the authority of Ray Narciso, his bodyguard and longtime friend, general factotum, procurer, and ardent worshiper, whose inconsolable sadness it is these days to have survived him.) Additionally, it may be that the vague idea my mother had of who he was and how he made a living was not something she could go on supporting very long, not with all the more eloquent evidence that soon accumulated, and the 'shock' of this delayed recognition may, indeed, have made her want a drink. Even a lot of drinks.

But this presupposes a certain obtuseness on her part, and though I know it's customary to think that people back in the old days were a lot more naive than we, somehow I can't quite feature the young, bright-eyed Sandra Styles, the same one I saw in *The Red Queen* (a small part, but fascinating, if only for the feeling of a funny, complicated existence led before the camera happened to catch her in its lens), the same one I fell in love with in *Viking Ships* (*not* the Kirk Douglas movie, and not even about Vikings; she played the daughter of a Baltimore shipbuilder, the period was pre–Civil War, and the story was vaguely a clone of *Gone With the Wind*, done on the cheap and on a different lot), somehow I can't believe for a minute that this glittering, teasing screen presence, or rather, the woman behind it, would have let herself be fooled by anyone. I don't see her marrying my father, I don't even see her getting in a car with him, or letting him bring her a drink at a party, without complete intuitive (not to mention extensive evidential) knowledge of who he was. No way that this woman—the one I 'read' behind her screen projections—could have been gulled. But this raises the possibility, which my sister always angrily dismissed, that she married him for what he was, wanted him even on those terms; if she wasn't a deluded drunk at the start (and I'm fairly sure she wasn't), if she wasn't stupid, either, then she must have been responding to something like the actual Gerson.

M Y FATHER GREW up in Chicago. His father, Louis, after whom I'm named, owned a kosher butcher shop and then a series of moderately successful restaurants. Sadie, his mother, was an immigrant from Lemberg (Lvov) in the Pale of Settlement, and from what I hear she spoke only Yiddish till her dying day.

Louis, my namesake, came from Odessa, the Black Sea port, where the Jews lived a relatively cosmopolitan, unshtetlized existence. He spoke Russian, German, Yiddish, Hebrew, and even a crude, telegraphic sort of English (gotten entirely out of books), and during his years in the Moldavanka, the Jewish ghetto of Odessa, he followed many careers: journalist, butcher, loanshark, landlord, restaurateur, and even violinist of the kind hired to play at low-rent weddings. One of the few stories my father ever told me about my grandfather, whom I never met, had to do with this fiddling; it seems that he used it as an excuse to get out of the house, that he would announce he had a bar mitzvah to play at, would go off on a Saturday morning, fiddle case under his arm, and not return for a week or two. The purpose of these excursions, I gather, was to womanize (Gerson once or twice referred to him as "my *handsome* father," in a certain snide, half-admiring tone, in which I later thought I could trace a modicum of resentment, the faintest residue of childish hurt).

In the Moldavanka, according to the stories of Isaac Babel, the greatest and artistically most unimpeachable source on turn-of-the-century Odessa, the Jews had progressed so far in the direction of enlightenment as to be known for their criminal gangs. Benya Krik, the most famous of gang leaders, was a well-known extortionist and murderer. Even the gentiles, including the Russian authorities, feared him, and in the course of the state-sanctioned pogroms that swept the Moldavanka every few years, only those shops enjoying his protection went untouched.

My grandfather, being savvy, never lost whole businesses in a single afternoon; never found himself playing the role, ascribed by Babel to his own father, of blubbering, glove-kissing supplicant before the figure of a mounted Cossack captain, who, contemptuous beyond words, accepts tribute yet allows his troops to go on looting. Even so, America seemed a better place to be for the long run, and my grandfather came over in 1896. Not the standard immigrant by any means, who pawns everything just to pay for his passage in steerage, he had the butcher shop, a new wife, and a little house on the West Side within weeks of arrival, and from all I can gather, his business career in the New World was a series of modest, ever more comfortable–making advances.

Business smarts alone might account for this, and probably do, in part; certainly the history of his co-religionists is not lacking in examples of solid, honest, yet economically adven-

turous individuals, makers of tidy, self-perpetuating little for-
tunes, but something makes me doubt that, in my grandfather's
case, this is the whole story. The fiddle player, the womanizer
(and incidentally, also a big bettor on the ponies) is not, at least
to my mind, the same man who runs a kosher butcher business, who finds time and opportunity to open three restaurants, each more successful than the last; the man who can
disappear for weeks at a time, who reads four newspapers a day
(according to my father), each in a different language, who
quotes Byalik and Chernikovsky 'by the yard,' isn't the one to
end up in life with a paunch, a gold watch, and half a million in
the bank.

In the case of most people's personal histories (and I suppose that, in the end, what I'm mainly writing here is my own),
such incongruities remain unresolved; the lack of hard evidence
and an understandable laziness about forcing our ancestors
through the conceptual wringer make us happier leaving them
as found. I don't mind if my grandfather, a man I never met,
contained 'multiple potentialities,' was a rake as well as a canny
shopkeeper; I might even take pride in him, find him more
interesting on this account, but the fact is that I've always half
suspected that the fix was in. For reasons having nothing to do
with him per se, I believe he was what Ray Narciso, speaking
out of the side of his mouth, would have called a 'wise guy'—
that is, a wised-up, on-the-take sort of individual, someone
who knew the right people, who progressed by means of his
connections rather than, shall we say, the sweat of his brow.

Attachments formed while he was still in Russia, arrangements of convenience that continued to be convenient, dictated
all his major moves. This was why he settled in Chicago (rather
than Toronto, Brooklyn, Pittsburgh, or wherever); this was
why the tremendous uprooting, the journey of thousands of
miles, the leaving behind of one rich, familiar culture for something hopelessly strange, threw him off not in the slightest.
Exactly what the nature of his arrangements was, I can't say; no

doubt it had to do with his charm, with 'friendship,' as much as with lamb-chop dinners on the house. There is a kind of legitimate-seeming businessman who gets along largely on the basis of his 'act,' the sheer audacity of his pretension to being something he isn't, which awakens in other pretenders a desire to back the show; and I think that this is who my grandfather was.

My father was born in 1904. He had an older brother, Moses, who became a history teacher and died a long time ago. Moses was an amateur boxer, as was my father. They both went to the University of Chicago.

All the stories I've heard about my father's earlier (as well as later) years are suspect, considering that my informants in every case have had an ax to grind, motives of either friendliness, or hatred, or fear, or some other sharply defined, unmistakable feeling; no one has ever spoken about him to me in an offhand, objective-sounding way, which may not be such a great disadvantage, but my real deprivation (if that's what it is) results from his own habit, cultivated over the course of a lifetime, and amounting finally to something like a first principle of his personality, of revealing nothing that he didn't absolutely have to, avoiding the topic of himself with an unexampled rigor. Other fathers, no matter how closemouthed by nature, or primly opposed to 'unmanly' exposures of the self, let drop a fairly substantial amount of information over the years. But Gerson never did. He was born with an instinct for avoiding indictment, and his professional behavior, I've been told, was so impersonal, so uncluttered with telltale signs and traces, that 'God Himself' couldn't sniff out his presence behind a deal.

I have it on the authority of several people—some who hated him, at least one who still worships him—that he was a 'tough kid,' that, notwithstanding his intellectual gifts, he took no shit from anyone and cut a fairly wide swath through the neighborhood streets. He was always tall for his age, good-looking, and well built, and he was mean. His brother Moses, a scrawny specimen destined to be no bigger than a welter-weight, took up boxing in self-defense, after years of being pounded by the Polacks, Ucks, Irish, and even the tougher Jewish kids. Gerson, on the other hand, started going to the gym because he liked to, because he liked to hit, because he could get a fight there whenever he wanted. In college, since they had no boxing team at the U. of Chicago, he fought for Sy Bennett of the Mayflower Club. He had over two hundred fights as a light heavyweight. I don't know how many he won.

After college, he went to law school at De Paul. As soon as he got out he went to work for Jacob Vanarsky, whose small, but influential, office handled labor problems for some big Chicago-based corporations, among them Spiegel, Inc., Armour Products, and National Arts, the latter a movie-theater chain. Vanarsky later became Democratic party chairman for Cook County. In 1963 he died in prison, crushed in a bizarre accident involving a printing press.

Vanarsky was an old friend of my grandfather's, and here may be the simple explanation for the course my father's career was to take: if Vanarsky had been, rather than a notorious, mobster-friendly labor fixer, a corporate counsel of impeccable credentials and stainless reputation, then perhaps Gerson would have ended up a corporate lawyer with a specialty in taxation. But I shun such explanations. I sincerely believe that the bad penny seeks its own kind, turns up, ultimately, where it belongs, there and only there. If Vanarsky had been stodgy and good, then Gerson would have passed on the job offer.

Besides, several of my sources, my variously motivated Gerson experts, say that he knew gangsters in college and before, that he liked them, found their style, their colorful company to his taste. Maybe he first knew bookmakers, bootleggers, bone-crushers, and the like at his father's restaurant, admired the way they wore their hair, the way they talked and tipped; or maybe his two-hundred-some fights at the May-flower Club, all those afternoons spent smacking some other guy in the face, were enlivened by side bets, complicated ar-rangements about going down in a certain round, or giving his opponent a cut of a certain type.

I remember first learning about my father quite by acci-dent, as I read up on mob history in one of those tomes that masquerade as hard-hitting, morally repulsed studies even as they deliver a ton of titillating detail. I was then about fourteen. So ignorant was I of my father's past that when I first came across the name 'Gershom Shavelson' no bells rang. I knew that he had grown up in Chicago, that he was a lawyer, even that he used to practice something called 'labor law'; beyond that, however, I knew nothing, nothing about my grandfather or grandmother, certainly nothing about any Anglifying name changes.

It was while reading one of the later chapters in this estimable exposé, an account of the career of Willie Bioff, who had recently (and in the implied opinion of the authors, de-servedly) been blown into a bloody sludge by a bomb attached to the starter of his Oldsmobile, that I first became suspicious:

> I was staying [Willie told the authors, and I quote from memory, having read the relevant pas-sage probably a hundred times] at the Blackstone. This was the fall of '28. Frank Fischer had a room down the hall. One afternoon this *pisher* comes in, a tall kid with black, wavy hair, and Frank imme-diately gets up and gives him his chair. The kid says, "Willie, I'm pleased to meet you. I have a message for you from the boys."

"Oh, yeah?" I says.

"It don't look so good," the kid says. "They can't get the judge. They got the prosecutor, but they can't get the judge."

"Oh, yeah?"

I knew what this meant. But I didn't like hearing it from this kid.

I says, "And who the ———— are you? I don't know you from any other little ————."

The kid says, "Willie, no one can predict these things, but in a year or so this judge may get sick. He might develop a lung condition. If so, I think we can get a better decision, something we can all live with."

"Oh, yeah?" I said.

But that's exactly how it happened. I was out in ten months.

The point of this reminiscence was the pull that the 'organization' had had, in the 'twenties, with the Illinois judiciary, and Bioff went on to retail a few other anecdotes, nowhere mentioning Gerson (or 'Gershom') by name; and yet I somehow knew. I think it was the phrase ". . . Frank immediately gets up and gives him his chair." Anyway, I leafed back through the book looking for all the earlier references to 'Shavelson,' whom the authors identified only as "a lawyer," "a young mob attorney," "an associate of Vanarsky," "a some-time mob mouthpiece," and so on. This must be the first time I came across Vanarsky's name, too.

I can't remember how I felt, how my 'discovery' affected me. No doubt I was shocked, horrified, and secretly pleased all at the same time, stirred down to my fourteen-year-old toes to have an associate of killers for a father. What I do remember clearly is going to the library (*not* going to my father), taking out a whole raft of similar mob studies (*The Dirty Secret of Las Vegas, They Know No Law, Windy City Confidential*, etc.) and beginning that bookish program of learning about my paternity

that probably says something terrible about my essential nature, how I prefer inert, inhuman, controllable sources of information to living-breathing people every time.

Aside from the fact that this isn't really true, I can explain
my behavior, which does seem a little strange to me now, in
terms of my father's secretiveness. I probably half suspected
that he wouldn't own up, that he would have fended me off with
one of his mildly disgusted, ironic half-smiles. Even more pertinent, I think, is how deeply I was then under his influence
(and may still be), how enormously, pathetically eager to play
the game by his rules. One simply didn't (if one wanted to be a
man, were in training for that high vocation) go right up to
someone and baldly ask for information, since this was a kind
of double insult, a frank admission of one's own stupidity and a
confession of faith in the other guy's, too. Only a boob would
tell you what you really needed to know, something valuable,
for no good reason, and even at the age of fourteen I knew this,
I had imbibed it as with my mother's milk (father's?).

What I learned from these books was nothing very useful,
or specific. Yes, 'Shavelson' was mentioned here and there,
always in the same capacity, as a kind of behind-the-scenes,
supremely efficient legal adviser, a 'Chicago boy' with ties to
gangsters going way back. But none of these studies, even those
most recently published (I was reading them in '60 or '61),
carried Shavelson up past 1940 or so, and certainly none connected him to the Gerson Sanders who was then living in
California, practicing what I'd heard described as 'entertain-
ment law,' and collecting Chagalls and the odd Arshile Gorky.
My investigation into my father's identity stalled, temporarily,
at this point, since I really didn't know how to proceed with it; I
was probably just as happy leaving it where it was, in a sort of
fertile limbo.

O<small>N</small> A<small>PRIL</small> 8, 1961, my mother died. She had taken a few too many of her 'favorite purples' (some kind of barbiturate, whose name I've blocked out; her writing doc, Arnold 'Ari' Benbow, of Beverly Hills, had been prescribing them for her for at least a dozen years by then) combined with a few too many vodka-tonics, and slipped away. She left no note. This fact, plus the TV that she left on, and the new Agatha Christie on her bedside table, led me to believe that she hadn't intended to kill herself, at least not that particular evening.

Possibly the worst aspect of her death was that all of us were home when it happened. My twelve-year-old sister was in her bedroom, I was in mine, and our father, who was often out of the house in those days, happened to be downstairs in his library, entertaining some business friend or other. But we had so read my poor mother out of our lives (and had been read out of hers) that it was nothing for us to pass a whole afternoon, evening, night, the next morning, and most of the next day without any contact, with only the dimmest, slightly irritated consciousness of her continued existence. In this case, of course, her existence wasn't continuing, and only by a sort of fluke did I happen to go up to the third floor, which was entirely hers (my father slept in a small room off the library, when he slept at home), being in need of a fresh washcloth or some other bath item that I thought I might be able to find in one of her closets.

Her TV was on, and I went into her bedroom jabbering in that way I often used with her. Either you joined her already talking, already having launched a sort of preemptive talk-strike, or you succumbed to her own manic monologism, which was distressing and impossible to escape from to the extent that you were worried about hurting her feelings. For some reason, I found it impossible to walk out on her, simply couldn't cut her off once started. To deprive her of my respect-ful attention was beyond me, involved me in a strange syn-drome of guilt calculations based on the altogether false idea that contact with her reasonably normal son had a curative effect, might even be that crucial input that kept her going.

Anyway, I entered her bedroom jabbering, going on about some nonsense or other, and getting no response from her, turned off the TV and made as if to tidy up. You have to imagine me talking all the while, free-associating with a certain tone of eager desperation, and now, finally turning to confront the inevitable disarray of her huge, satin-sheeted bed, the cus-tomary spectacle of her sad, small, slightly bloated figure tucked up in a million pillows, I find her staring back at me with but a single eye (the other one shut tight), one of her still beautiful, if mildly edemic, hands thrown up against a pillow in a gesture of surprise. In her other hand (I see as I come a bit closer, having finally stopped winking back at her) is a plastic pill bottle. The top is off, and as soon as I jog her rigid elbow two capsules come out of her fist.

By now I understand that she is 'gone,' her spirit flown, and all that, but even so I keep jabbering as if to control the new meaning of our encounter, the device that served me in the past, the means by which I overrode her own divagations, coming immediately to mind as the most likely way to get us through this awkward experience. It may seem strange—I think it *is* strange—but my strongest impression is of the moment's stilted, or formulaic, quality, how everything is just as it would be if say some bad movie director were to have sent me up here; like this bad director myself, I view the proceedings from just off-screen, a little above and beyond myself, conscious in a 'new' way of the appropriateness of every detail, how those two pills, resting next to each other in a fold of the peach-colored counterpane, how my mother's carmine-painted fingernails (the tips chipped), and even more so, her wedding band, for years now unremovable due to the fattening of her finger, add each a certain telling note to the proceedings.

I do want to get this right, though—how this all seemed to me, its immediate effect on me—so I should add that even as I felt myself a little above this spectacle, safely apart from it, I was also aware of taking this mental step for purely self-defensive purposes, that is, that I was fooling myself. Because the *real* meaning of having stepped into a movie (one in which you find your mother dead) is that your personal magic is suddenly deflated, a much larger, more potent, more sharply resolved system of understanding has suddenly swallowed your own, that 'system' which will have as one of its manifestations, certainly, an article tomorrow in the *Herald-Examiner* ("SANDRA STYLES, SCREEN-STAR OF THE FORTIES, DEAD OF A STROKE"), which will require you to say for the rest of your life, in tones variously offhanded, flat, wry, snide, or heartfelt, but never completely natural, "She died when I was fourteen."

I don't mean to say that I saw all this, or foresaw it, in that couple of minutes I spent with her corpse. A certain large percentage of my thinking was, indeed, just about how her hair looked (thin and disordered, but still of the color of sun-bleached wild wheat), about the freckles on her exposed chest, etc. Her housecoat had fallen open, and for the first time I really saw one of her nipples. It was small, hardly colored at all, pink sort of by default. At just about this time—as I was looking at her breast—I became aware of an anxious, semi-insane jabbering (my own voice, of course); I decided quite logically to turn it off, to squelch this pathetic line of drivel, which hadn't ever meant anything to my mother (I suddenly felt), which certainly wasn't a comfort to her now, and by dint of a prolonged, slightly frantic inward effort, I finally did manage to cut it off.

I went downstairs, found Ray Narciso (my father was gone from the house by now) and explained that Mother was dead, that she'd probably been in bed like that for days. Doctors were called, and so on.

❊

This untoward event, which, nonetheless, we all took very much in stride, has 'echoed down the years,' turns out to have been a turning point in all our lives.

In the immediate sense, it meant that Gerson took a new approach to raising my sister and me, wavered for the first (and only) time in his basic commitment to the project; I was sent to the Point Pedro Academy, where I learned to salute and wear a uniform (and actually had a pretty good time for three years), while my sister, always a more nervous and explosive quantity, was disastrously sent to a boarding school in Santa Barbara, a horsey and Episcopalian sort of place. I mean to say nothing against either horses or Episcopalians, but Sylvia, never very close to our mother before (in fact, much less able to bear her company than I was), had a sort of nervous breakdown at Miss Petty's, expressed her grief, or whatever it was, in ways that her teachers and counselor mistook for wanton offenses against decorum. Sent home in punishment, she began to pester Gerson to let her go to Mexico, to get her into a school in Cuernavaca, the famous *escuela bilingüe* that Marta and Marcela attended. Gerson finally did so, even though relations with the elder Marcela, the twins' mother, were different now, less friendly than before (for reasons I could have had no idea of at the time).

In Cuernavaca my sister boarded at first with a family chosen by the school staff, probably the family of one of her teachers, but as might have been expected (and was certainly her intention all along), she spent all her time with Marcela, and soon she was living at the 'palace,' had her own room and took all her meals there.

I've always been guardedly curious about what went on during those years (spring of '62 till '65). As I've already mentioned, these Mexican spider-girls had a certain hold on my sister and me, and we on them (I think), so I was already interested, to some extent, in how they were getting on. My father's visits to Mexico having slackened off considerably, I hadn't had occasion to check up on 'my Marta' (and Sylvia's Marcela) in a long while, but what with Sylvia coming home on vacations, and the single brief visit I made (spring break, 1964), I now had the opportunity.

Or *should* have, but the strange truth is that a combination of reticence on my part (or rather, reluctance to show an unseemly interest) and secretiveness on my sister's made it hard for me to ask. She had borrowed wholesale Marta's (and Marcela's) maddening way of always seeming to be on to something, some powerful mystery, and this confirmed me even further in my reluctance. I couldn't let her see that I cared at all, and while this may seem a fairly typical sort of impasse, the average thing to have gone on between a teenaged brother and sister, actually it was a symptom of something important, of her willful, angry drifting away from my father and me (and of my stiff, snooty, older-brotherish acquiescence in such a split).

So aside from a few offhand questions about how 'they'

were—to which she hardly bothered to respond—we let the matter hang. My sister was now about fourteen, surely a rough age for any girl (or boy); in her case, a really alarming, impressively rapid onset of physical maturity made things harder than they might have been, and her way of dealing with this—which shows her to be my sister in truth—was to ignore it, just act as if nothing special were going on. In June of 1963 she suddenly appeared to me fully formed, after having been her normal bony, freckled self in January. The resemblance to our mother was uncanny, from the hair, to the freckles across the bridge of the nose, to the long, pretty hands; she had our mother's swollen, yet precisely outlined, mouth, those puffy lips that nonetheless looked incapable of any imprecise contact, and even if her eyes were smaller, farther apart, and of a different color, they had the same sad tilt (down at the outside corner, especially the right one). Our mother, however, was a fairly small woman, just five-three or so. Sylvia already stood five-nine, and her shoulders were almost perfectly square, which made them seem unusually wide.

Even these days, when I see a girl of a certain age, one seemingly unaware of her great good fortune (that of all possible outcomes in the genetic lottery, she should end up looking like this), one who carries her charming, inspiring, perfectly harmonized physical self like a garbageman hauling a half-full sack, I think of my sister. Some girls may come to this attitude naturally, or even out of self-defense (the 'burden' of being beautiful, of being like honey to man-bees, forcing them into acts of camouflage), but I felt at the time, and still feel, that she concocted this largely out of her head, and there was even at that time a perverse emanation from her performance that set my teeth on edge. However, I lacked the words and concepts— and we both lacked the habit of communication—that would have let me go into it with her.

But I think my father's personality had something to do with this. I had learned from him to reveal nothing I didn't have to, and my sister had also learned this, in her way, and was especially inclined to apply the lesson where I was concerned. From our mother, of course, we got more or less the same 'message,' though negatively demonstrated: a sick, empty talkiness, the point of which was never self-revelation, nothing like real sharing, but simply relief from a sort of chronic toothache of the soul.

But forgive me, please, this digression into sensitive psychologizing; I disbelieve it, myself, even as I write such things down, the unspoken assumption being that all might have turned out differently, that, if only we had gotten something different from our parents, exposure to some more humane model of how to go about making contact, everything would have turned out well. But in that case, I wouldn't be myself; Sylvia wouldn't be Sylvia; our parents become other people entirely, figures in some completely different story, and the whole thing falls apart.

I'VE JUST CLAIMED that my sister and I were strangers, that nothing was going on between us at that time, and now I have to amend this: in Mexico, for a period of about ten days once, all channels were open and richly, dangerously overloaded.

Taking a break from my studies, at my father's insistence, I had flown to Mexico City and from there driven to Cuernavaca, following the down-the-mountain route that the Aztec kings also used to take. I was just seventeen. In another couple of months I was to be eighteen, and this age shortfall was significant in a number of ways; for one thing, I had had to lie about my age in order to rent a car. Nor did I have the international certificate normally required of foreign drivers; somehow I lied my way around that, too, and these, I think, were my first 'larcenous' actions, spontaneous untruths called forth, in some mysterious way, by my being once again in my beloved republic, my Mexico of the colorous, euphonious tongue, which so happily 'fit' in my mouth. For another thing, being seventeen, not yet eighteen, meant the end of boyhood to me, boyishness on its last, already hairy, but still somewhat spindly legs. In another two months I would begin to feel, or at least try to act, like the college freshman I was soon to be; but for the present, especially since this was Mexico, the scene of wonderful childhood memories, I could relax.

In my mind Las Casuelas, home of the Señora and of her twin daughters, and lately of Sylvia, too, was a little larger than I now found it, more imposing just in terms of the height of its ceilings and the number of its rooms. Even so, the feeling of magical possibility I had always gotten was still here, a property (it seemed to me) intrinsic to the very walls, the polished floors, the equilateral arches giving onto the courtyard.

I suppose it was nothing more than a Colonial-style *hacienda*, but a grand one, a vast, carefully restored and maintained one. Built and first occupied in the late eighteenth century, by an *intendente* of the viceroy of New Spain, it must always have sat upon its slight rise, commanded its spread of subtly landscaped, hilly acres, with a feeling of perfect sufficiency and justice. From those acres (reduced in modern times to a mere forty) a visitor, pausing in his happy progress along the cool, secret, sand-paved paths, looked up and saw the house, always turned, by a kind of magnetic inevitability, in the direction of the ruling structure.

I was admiring this view, peering back at the house, when I first ran into Marta. It was the afternoon of the day of my arrival, and though I had taken lunch with the Señora, Marcela, and my sister, no one had spoken to me about the missing twin (nor had I asked). I had assumed, probably, that she was gone somewhere, that my arrival was of so little moment to her that she hadn't bothered to cancel some prior engagement, or I might even have thought that she was playing with me, absenting herself intentionally to show indifference. She had often done this sort of thing in the past. But here she was, stretched out on her back on a concrete bench, reading a book. It was *The Fountainhead*, that piece of noxious crap that was then enjoying a certain vogue. Unlike my sister and Marcela, who had mildly shocked me with their identical short haircuts, their baggy dungarees, and their 'private language' (mostly gutter Spanish and knowing looks), Marta had let her hair grow very long, and she looked the very type of a Joan Baez-y sensitive maiden, with bare feet (though I saw sandals under the bench), a deep blue, heavily embroidered Guatemalan skirt, and a peasant blouse with puffy sleeves. I stood silently under a tulip tree a few yards off. I wasn't exactly embarrassed to come on her this way, nor was I so thunderstruck by her mahogany-skinned loveliness as to be rendered speechless; I was just trying to think of something unusual to say.

"Oh, come over here," she finally spoke in English, her face still partly hidden by the book. I obeyed, and after finishing a page and bending down the corner, she lay for a long moment with book and hands crossed over her abdomen, idly gazing up at me.

"You weren't there at lunch"—this was the unusual statement I finally came up with.

"I haven't been feeling well. I have a sickness of some kind on my stomach." She lapsed into Spanish on the word 'stomach,' and I heard no more English from her that day or at any other time during my visit. "How tall you've gotten. I don't like boys to be so tall, if they're as skinny as they said you are. Well, it's good to see you. Sylvia said that you had gotten ugly. And that you joined the army. Is that right? I expected you to arrive in a tank, wearing khaki, and holding a machine rifle. Come on, sit down. You don't have to stand there at *alerta* all afternoon," and she laughed.

I was strangely tongue-tied, but I managed to stammer something about military school being different from the army. Of course she knew this already, and by her expression she made me feel dumb for having taken her seriously.

"Come on, come on." Now I did sit down. Although she
had stopped looking me over in that frank, casual, and distinctly unimpressed way, I was stiff through and through,
unrelaxably so, devastated to have heard the word 'ugly' used in
reference to myself. This was a big concern of mine, due to
recent changes in my complexion and an ongoing thickening of
my features; in the end I got a face I could live with, even be
fairly happy about, but at the time I was secretly terrified of the
process, sure that the outcome would be awful. I had been a
pretty, girlish-looking boy, and though I had therefore been
extra-determined to demonstrate manliness, now that I was in
fact becoming a man, secretly I wanted to turn the clock back. I
had never admitted this to anybody, concern about how one's
face was 'turning out' being distinctly unworthy (I felt).

Marta, however, seemed to understand, and with a naturalness that disarmed me (but which could as easily have made
me terminally uptight), she said, "If Sylvia thinks you're ugly,
she's got a head like a brick wall."

We were sitting next to each other. We were in that part of
the grounds that had been planted, probably thirty years before, with many species of tropical tree, mahogany, lignum
vitae, sapodilla, and various kinds I couldn't identify. Other
parts of the garden had been landscaped to suggest the high
deserts of Sonora (candelabra cactus, agaves, creosote bush)
and the tropical savannas of the Yucatán (saw-edged grass,
opuntia, mesquite), but here the growth was so tall and rank,
complete even to trailing liana and half-uprooted banana trees,
that you could hardly see the sky or house. The feeling was
much like a real Chiapanec rain forest, with a man-made creek
in the vicinity and mosquitoes as big as hummingbirds, which
were also numerous. Had she chosen this place (I secretly
wondered), intentionally set herself down in the most remote-
feeling, secluded corner of the property? I hoped that she had,
though my low opinion of my value as a romantic figure argued
against a too-optimistic interpretation. Probably the desire for
privacy, pure and simple, had directed her to this spot, a

privacy from which I was meant to be excluded, as well. I suddenly rose up.

"Where are you going?"

"Don't you want to read your book?"

"My book?" She found it in her lap; seemed surprised it was there. "Ah, my book. Yes, of course. I should read my book."

"I've already read it," I said. "It makes an interesting, but flawed, argument."

She had continued to look at the book, a paperback edition with a steely-looking hero and voluptuous heroine on the cover, and now she tore it in half down the spine, a hard thing to do in a single pull.

I was mortified. My value system at the time, the usual collection of liberal tendencies combined with a premature judgmentalism, must have included strictures against the damaging of any books, even paperback editions (and certainly, anything assigned for a class). I remember standing there, openmouthed, for a long moment in that glen full of mosquitoes and bananas, but as Marta never lifted her head, I was able to look down on her immaculate, matte-black hair, parted just off center, and then also to admire the smooth red-brown of her bicep where it emerged from the white of her sleeve. When she finally did look up, it wasn't into my face; looking superbly like some graven image on a pre-Cortesian stele, one of those Aztec visages that seem, above all, not to care about you or anyone else, she merely gazed off into the bush, idly chewing the inside of one cheek.

Some minutes later we were running down a path, going really fast, and a kind of choked, half-embarrassed laughter welled up out of me, a sound surprisingly like the braying of a donkey. Marta, however, either didn't hear or didn't care, so intent was she on flying away on her bare feet. We never did this when we were kids (I remember thinking); our garden games, especially in the rain-forest section, had always been of the

stealthy, creeping-up-on-somebody sort, but we were undeni-
ably 'hurtling back into childhood' now, letting go of any pre-
tenses to maturity. I never stopped laughing till I realized that
Marta, though only a girl, was going at least as fast as I was.
Then, focusing all my powers on the physical task at hand, I
tried to gain on her, and by virtue of my longer legs (but
disadvantaged by the slick-soled loafers I was wearing), I got
almost close enough to grab her. In fact, it wasn't till I was
actually reaching out, the wild, sand-colored soles of her long
feet, one after the other, kicking up the hem of her heavy skirt,
that I realized what I was doing, that I was just about to tackle
this full-grown, long-haired beauty like some halfback at a j.v.
scrimmage; and in an instant all my stiffness returned, my
stultifying consciousness of self.

She ran on another thirty yards or so; then, sensing the
lack of pursuit, turned off the path, which by now had carried
us out of the forest, into a sort of scrubland.

Here were a lot of thorn trees, century plants, and other
prickly species meant to recreate some microenvironment or
other, probably the grasslands interior to the Gulf Coast. Sr.
Martín (as I had been allowed to call him), Marta's father, one of
the tallest, thinnest, most distinguished-looking Mexicans I
ever met, had decreed at a certain point that the grounds of Las
Casuelas would be a horticultural omnibus of Mexico, and to
this end he had imported a crew of Zapotecs to work the
acreage. Scientists from the University of Mexico, as well as
plant collectors from all over the world, stymied in their own
attempts to grow certain rare specimens, were always coming
down to Cuernavaca to confer with these humble Indian gardeners, and even now, some ten years after Sr. Martín's death,
everything was shipshape, remarkably as it had been when as a
boy, I scampered all over, completely unaware that the place
represented anything unusual in the horticultural sense.

Marta now appeared; I had lost sight of her for a minute.
She was standing next to a big century plant, one of those

dusty, exhausted-looking specimens which nevertheless have a lot of life left in them, as was proved, a moment later, when she drew my attention to the fifteen-foot flower stalk growing straight up out of its heart. I had never seen one of these ugly, thorny *agaves*, relatives of the *maguey* (from which the Mexicans get mescal, tequila, and other useful substances), actually in flower, and at first I wasn't sure that a tropical tree of some kind, one shaped more or less like a giant asparagus, hadn't taken root in the same spot. But no, as Marta now made clear by gestures (having once again intuited my thoughts exactly), the 'tree' actually belonged to the *agave*, was growing up from it. Yet the clash of shapes was so strange—the flat, prickly arms of the plant proper, as against this softly tipped maypole of a thing— that I still couldn't quite credit what I saw.

"You still don't believe? Look," and she insinuated herself among the plant arms, carefully pushing them out of the way. Soon she was far enough inside that she could grasp the pole, making the asparagus-head sway.

No fool I (or so I liked to think), no stranger to the idea of 'symbols' in books, I knew very well what every columnar object was supposed to represent. I must have blushed furiously at the sight of Marta, about whom, as I now realized, I had long been dreaming in a certain way, *actually touching the thing*. Her back was turned, and a long hank of hair had gotten caught on one of the stickers. Now, as she arched her back and stood on tiptoe, the better to get hold of that meaningful shaft, her skirt also caught, and I was treated to the sight of the back of one of her legs, from just above the knee joint down. It was a sturdy, muscular leg, which, except for being hairless, might have belonged to a slightly built man. The color was strange, more red than brown, really like a piece of oiled mahogany. I watched for about half a minute. No doubt the way she was standing, still on tiptoe, with her muscles attractively at flex, added to my bewilderment, the sense I had of being half transfixed, turned into a pillar of salt. Then she felt the tug of her captured hem, and she reached behind her to free it.

Sometime later we returned to the rain forest, where she had left her sandals, and there, on the concrete bench, we sat and kissed for about an hour.

✻

That very night, in the small suite of rooms I had been given at the northeast corner of the house (the same rooms my father used to occupy in the old days), Marta came to me. She was dressed only in a kind of nightshirt, and in the moonful dark she looked positively ghostly. Indeed, my first reaction to finding her there was a loud gasp, a furious pounding of my heart, as if she really were a ghost. She had entered by a door I hadn't known about, which came off a narrow servants' corridor and left the visitor inside a linen closet, and as she emerged from this, directly into my line of sight, I first thought that someone (or something) had come to do me harm. I had been lying on my back on the big, hard, slightly unlevel bed. Completely unable to sleep, because of the repetitive progress through my mind of a fantasy much like what was just about to happen, I came up like a jack-in-the-box when I realized that there really *was* something there (or someone). Then she laughed.

"*Cálmate, cálmate,*" she said, seeming to float, in that nightshirt, ever closer. Now she sat uncertainly on the edge of the bed.

"You don't mind?"

"Is that you?"

"If I said, 'No, it's not me, it's someone else . . .' " and she laughed again.

I wasn't a complete idiot, and with my heart still pounding (but now for a different reason), I induced her to lie down. I suppose we then engaged in more kissing. After all these years my memory of exactly what was done, and in what fashion, is vague, but what does stick in my mind is my fundamental sense of disbelief. I simply couldn't get over the fact that, just as in all the James Bond novels (of which I was then a big fan), a beautiful young woman had come to me of her own accord, willingly thrown herself into my arms. As I clambered on top of her, having pulled that nightgown, with excessive circumspection, up over her dark head, whose features I could barely make out, I was repeating to myself, "This is it. This is it. You are now actually *doing* it," not so much in exultation, as in order to convince myself that I really was. But I was, and from Marta's occasional, rather demure movements beneath me, I gathered that she was, too. We hardly made a sound, and I wouldn't be surprised to learn (if there were anyone in the world qualified to assert such a thing) that I held my breath the whole time. Certainly there was a lot more heavy breathing after the event than during or before, and I suddenly felt that, if a cigarette had been available (preferably one of 007's 'Navy Cuts'), I would have smoked it. (Up to that time I had been a fanatical nonsmoker, for athletic reasons.)

"You have such hard shoulders," Marta said. "I wish I could see you."

"The light's on your side."

"No. Impossible. No one must know I'm here."

We lay still in the dark. Presently she began humming a little tune, something very Mexican, and as if this were a magic spell, somewhere out in the night the moon rose from behind some obstruction or other (or fell clear of one), and my room, because of a big window on the eastern wall, became tolerably bright. I saw Marta (and presumably, she saw me at the same time) and my heart sank, my stomach flipped: all my disbelief returned, to think that I had just been making love to this vision, this virtual goddess, who, with her iconic features strangely lit by the silver glow, looked like nothing I (or any man, let alone a green teenager) belonged in bed with. But mercifully, this moment of illumination (if that's what it was) passed; the moon, falling back into clouds, extinguished itself, and in the comfortable, fragrant Mexican darkness, I felt almost like myself again.

Now when I think back on that strange interlude, those few days of delicious, secret trysting, all my efforts go toward calling up the background details, the convoluted context that at the time I blissfully ignored.

The Señora, for example, undoubtedly spoke to me on several occasions, may even have asked subtle and quite natural-seeming questions about my father's health, business affairs, and so on. I probably answered with a fulsomeness that said more about my joy in speaking Spanish than any real knowledge on my part, and the Señora would certainly have taken this into account, would have discounted my silly, possibly indiscreet revelations, at the same time not neglecting to mine my confession for whatever it happened to be worth. I didn't know then, and still don't, all the details of the disagreement that had brought an abrupt, hurtful end to their relationship. Probably it had a purely business aspect as well as an emotional one, and in any case I wasn't aware that there had been a rupture or, for that matter, a 'relationship' in the larger sense. My father had never said a word about the Señora to me, or about any other of his adult friends, male or female; it wasn't his style to make personal confessions to his seventeen-year-old son, but beyond that, the very fact that he'd encouraged me to vacation in Cuernavaca, after letting Sylvia come to school there, argued for things being more or less as before.

What could I possibly have told her? That he'd recently broken a bone in his hand? That in the year or two previous, I'd seen him only during school vacations, my exile to Pt. Pedro coinciding with a period of much out-of-state travel for him? That he had a new Buick, a canary-yellow convertible of enormous charm, something I'd already started angling to be given (upon graduation)? Or maybe it was the simple fact of my presence in her house, the casualness of his assumption that, as always in the past, he was perfectly welcome to send me (and Sylvia) to Las Casuelas, that we would be bunked and boarded in the accustomed style, that so offended her. It bespoke a niggling estimation of her capacity for resentment, indifference to her feelings.

How my father, whose ability to intuit the resentments and intentions of others was almost frightening, stood him in good stead through decades of furious, sometimes murderous infighting among the quickest criminal minds of his age, how he could have so misread this woman, whose every tendency and capacity he had certainly, by that time, seen demonstrated, escapes me entirely. My sister's theory, that for Gerson, women fell into a whole other category, amounting almost to a different species from men, goes only a certain way toward an explanation, and I have to conclude that he was consciously, intentionally tempting the gods, acting out of some anomalous impulse for putting himself (and us) at risk.

Certainly he had to know that the Señora, no matter what

else might be said of her, could never be described as *simpática*, as *amable*, as the sort of person of whom you take casual advantage, knowing that, when conditions require, she'll just as casually make use of you. Even I, despite my youth and my skewed perception of things, was aware of her as a mighty force, a phenomenal, far-reaching will and intelligence manipulating everything toward unspecified ends. Just sitting down to a meal with her, as I did five or six times during my stay, was an education. Her very slimness and beauty, to which I had previously been immune (in fact, she was much heavier, much less inwardly and outwardly 'honed' in the 'fifties, when I first got to know her), were like having a live demonstration of some ironic principle whose importance I had never previously guessed. That a disturbing human force could come in a pretty package—indeed, in the shape of a woman at all—was new to me, and I let my mind work only around the edges of this odd idea, too young, too callow to bear its full impact just yet.

I didn't know, of course, the full details of the business arrangement (or arrangements) then still in force between Gerson and the Señora, and when I did, a few years later, learn something of them, my understanding of her character was only slightly enlarged. I can't account for my strong, basically negative, largely fearful response to her by citing anything she actually said or did to me. She was kind, in a superficial way, pointedly gracious, and supremely able to get me to loosen my tongue, to make me feel as if my verbose Spanishizing was quite remarkable and entertaining. And yet there occurred between us the subtle transfer of an alarming bit of information completely opposite to the general tenor of happy host-guest relations. I felt her evil intent; or I should say, I felt her *capacity* for such intent. Of course, since my thoughts were almost entirely about making love to her daughter, I interpreted everything in this light, attributed suspicions and resentments to her that were probably off the mark. I immediately assumed that, had she known what was going on, she would have been op-posed to it. The idea that, in some sense, she could have planned it, that nothing could have happened in her house that she didn't know about and, in some sense, endorse, was be-yond me to formulate at the time.

WHAT I REALLY should have been paying attention to, even more than the Señora, was my sister and her odd friendship with Marcela. I had noticed that they dressed alike, wore their hair alike, and even managed to look a little alike. To the extent that I bothered to think about it at all, I put this down to the sort of thing that best friends, boys or girls, often get up to, a duplication of the self that helps for that period when the self doesn't really know what it is. That they had done this along the lines of a tomboyish model, something that suited neither of them very well, only gave me another pretext for not paying attention. Marta (to take a handy example) already seemed, in contrast, well launched upon adulthood, while they, in their sexless outfits and 'secret' silliness, seemed hopelessly childish, years away from knowing anything about the world.

At that time, all three of the girls were going to the same

school, the famous Colegio de F——, which occupied the grounds of an old convent on the southwestern edge of Cuernavaca. No longer parochial or quite so disciplinary as in the past, the Colegio still numbered among its staff many nuns as well as newly emergent sisters, and the course of study was far more rigorous than I had thought. Everyone took classes taught in English as well as Spanish, no hardship for Sylvia but conceivably a great one for the others, who were almost all Mexicans, with but a light sprinkling of daughters of diplomats stationed in Mexico City. Sylvia had been advanced a grade, possibly to account for her advantage in this respect (but now that I think of it, no, she would have been disadvantaged to an equal extent in the Spanish-language classes, so the reason was probably just her testable intelligence, or maybe her evident desire to go everywhere with Marcela, to every class, every after-school meeting, etc.). Among the girls' *maestras* were one or two who, in the political turmoil of the late 'sixties in Mexico, were to achieve a short-lived notoriety: one of these, Sister María Agnes de la Riva, of San Juan Potosí, a chemistry instructor, became a *guerrillera* of a sort and ended up in Cuba, where she may still be living for all I know, and another, whose name escapes me at the moment, is that very same teacher of Romance languages whose decapitated form is featured in one of the most lurid wire photos of the era. Having left the Colegio sometime early in '67, this young woman joined an armed band that carried out a number of bold expropriations, but a couple of years later, while holding up an office of the Banco Nacional in Guadalajara, she was caught in a crossfire and her body was pierced by so many bullets that afterward it was hardly a body anymore. This was my sister's French teacher.

Not everyone at the Colegio was a left-wing firebrand in nun's habit, and I'm sure that many girls who studied there at that time came away with nothing more remarkable than a sturdy command of English. For those who were susceptible, however, a certain kind of political influencing was available, as can be judged by the astonishing percentage of graduates who went on to play notable roles in the university strikes and other turbulent events of the years immediately to come. Of these, Marcela was probably the best-known, but I remember my sister Sylvia ticking off on the fingers of both hands (and then going back to the first hand, ticking well into the second again, a look of disbelief growing on her face) the names of schoolmates who had gotten into trouble, gone to jail, been beaten up, had to go underground for a while, or even disappeared entirely as a result of their political activities. If Sylvia's accounting is to be trusted, probably as many as one out of fifteen of her classmates turned out bad, an amazing record not to be equaled, I should think, in the entire history of prep-school education in the Americas.

I visited the school only once. I had thought to surprise Marta one afternoon when her classes ended, my aim being to take her for a ride in my rent-a-car, but as soon as I entered the grounds I felt uneasy, the palpable peace, seriousness, and high moral tone of the place serving to backlight starkly the real nature of my intentions. Several groups of young girls, all dressed in the school uniform (dark knee socks, pleated green skirt, green blazer, black string tie), seated in casual circles around an instructress, who in most cases wore that 'out-in-the-world' habit just then being adopted, were arranged on the lawns. I find it almost incredible, now, to remember how little attention was paid me as I ambled along, the girls all being so intent on their lessons, on the Socratic give-and-take within their little groups, that they could really have cared less that a boy had invaded their sanctum.

I had thought to time my arrival for the end of classes, and I had hit it about right. However, on Thursdays, and this was a Thursday, a special program of 'tutorials' got under way, where all the girls who were inclined to participate sat around for an extra hour discussing religious, cultural, and political topics chosen by popular submission. I still remember the topic for that day: "Political Import of the *Corrido*." *Corridos* are the folk songs that the Mexicans have always made up in times of trouble, for example, during the Revolution, when "La Llorona" and "La Cucaracha," to name probably the two best-known, were written. In a couple of the groups, naturally, dark-haired girls in uniform or their instructresses, whose scrubbed faces seemed to be advertising their complete lack of makeup, were strumming guitars, but in the vast majority this topic had not been taken for an excuse to have a singalong, and the girls were arguing and analyzing with what seemed, to me, remarkable passion and earnestness. I think my first take was that someone important had died. Only the previous November, when news of Jack Kennedy's assassination reached my school, had I seen comparable seriousness among my own schoolmates; and even then, in the atmosphere of that unimaginable event, my fellow sons of California had soon reverted to their characteristic crude sarcasm, aiming pretend guns at their heads, then flopping down on the desktop, their tongues lolling out.

Nor was I able to imagine any of my classmates, or myself, voluntarily sitting around for an extra hour at the end of the school day, talking up the Great Issues. School for them, as for me (a notoriously serious student), was the Enemy, the Principal Thief of Time, and we escaped with every precious second that could be snatched from its hideous talons. As I was standing around trying to figure out who, then, had just died in the government, a woman suddenly appeared at my side. She was stocky, brown-haired, dressed in a severe gray suit. I took her immediately for a member of the administration, someone sent to ask if I had any idea where in the world I was.

Her inquiring, Mona Lisa–ish smile was kind, though, and rather than ask straight out, or just give me the bum's rush, she stood with hands clasped behind her back, head tilted slightly to one side. The obvious thing was just to ask for Marta, extract her from her group, and be gone, but for some reason this seemed pathetically transparent, so I instead identified myself as Sylvia's brother.

I was surprised by her reaction. A certain falling of the face—even I, having no reason to expect it, and not really caring about the esteem, or lack thereof, in which my sister was held, couldn't fail to notice. Was there also, so instantaneous as to be almost imperceptible, an appraising look thrown my way (as when the innocent, straight-arrow brother of the ax murderess appears in court, and the jury, with a collective gasp, shrinks back, not so sure that evil isn't something 'in the blood')?

"*Ven,*" she said simply, setting off on a flagstoned path that took us round the main building, past other, lesser structures in which more of the tutorials were under way. I kept looking, surreptitiously, for Marta. It seemed funny that I hadn't seen her out on the lawn, and not Marcela or Sylvia, either; maybe she, as I would have, had gone home the second her last class was over, and I began to anticipate the collapse of my careful plans for the rest of the afternoon (I had aimed to take her to a local lake, secluded enough so that our lack of bathing suits—a foolish oversight on my part, but then I couldn't think of everything—needn't keep us from getting wet).

Ah, but here was the other twin, Marcela. She was kneeling on a grassy slope, in a posture like that of the White Rock girl, with six or seven twelve-year-olds gathered round. They were disputating with an air of gravity that didn't belie what I can describe only as unashamed, unadulterated worshipfulness (on the part of the younger girls; Marcela's part was to smile upon them benignly, the goddess whose every word, every inflection goes straight to the heart of her adoring charges, and who knows it). I think I stopped, briefly, as the matron led me past this spot; my impulse was to wink and wave hello, yet in the end I didn't, arrested as I was by the quality of worship, which confirmed for me something I had always half known about Marcela. Was she a teacher, then; were the sisters, her own instructors, making use of her 'leadership' qualities, employing her to reach some of the younger girls, those who, for whatever reasons, were left unmoved by the normal course of study? Nowhere else had I seen a schoolgirl, someone still in the green uniform, playing the tutor's role. Nor, now that I bothered to notice, had there been quite this air of conspiracy, of a secret club or cabal happily sunk in its own intense, meaningful deliberations around any of the other groups, which had seemed more detached (I now fancied), more coolly seminarish.

Just then, Marcela caught sight of me. Not to disturb the ongoing discourse, she didn't wave, didn't call out; just briefly lifted one eyebrow.

I had let the matron get ahead of me. She had continued down the flagstones, and at the bottom of the slope, in front of a row of thatch-roofed classrooms, she patiently awaited me. As I hurried down, I had the feeling of going out of bounds, of leaving the grounds proper; these little classrooms were unlike any of the other buildings we'd passed, being more recently constructed, out of less-enduring materials. Here, sitting alone in one of the tiny rooms, at a rickety desk, was my sister. The matron ushered me in.

I sat down at another desk. The matron shut the door, which added to my feeling of having come to visit a friend in jail. Sylvia had been writing, and now she returned to this task, not wasting so much as a second look on me.

I read the blackboard. There were just a few words, in a language completely unknown to me (Nahuatl, the predominant pre-Cortesian language of the central plateau). I lit a cigarette. This was only the second or third smoke I'd had in my whole life—I'd just bought the pack, at a *tabaquería* in downtown Cuernavaca—but even this got no immediate rise from my sister.

"What're you doing here?" she finally asked, unpleasantly.

"Not looking for you, that's for sure."

A minute later, waving a hand in front of her face and coughing: "Boys with pimples shouldn't smoke."

"You look absurd in that outfit," I countered. "I didn't know it was a Catholic school. At St. Anne's in Westwood at least they get to wear red plaid skirts, and they don't have to wear ties. Stupid."

"It's not a Catholic school. There's no religious instruction, strictly speaking. Now please shut up or go away, I have to do my homework."

I became quiet, though it annoyed me to be doing anything that accorded with her wishes. I don't know why I didn't just ask where Marta was (she had left sometime before, to go to the dentist). Maybe I was still afraid of the matron, felt that I ought to put in fifteen minutes with my sister, for appearance's sake, or, just as likely, since Sylvia was clearly displeased to have me there, maybe I thought to disconcert her, vex her by hanging around. I can't recapture, now, how it used to affect me to be with her. I know only that the essence of my feeling was boredom, irritated, hair-tearing boredom, but our relations have so improved in the last few years, our friendship has flowered so nicely, to our common surprise, that I really have a hard time remembering that earlier condition. Like any seventeen-year-old, I considered time spent with my younger sister to be wasted, to be as good as murdered; the remarkable thing was that she, by many indications, felt much the same about me, and this unaccountable, disconcerting attitude of hers, to the extent that I condescended to notice it, was probably all that I found interesting.

I had been about to say something snide about Marcela, about her and her band of slavish worshipers. I hadn't liked that casual, self-important lift of a single eyebrow, but just as the first words, in English, were forming on my lips, something caused me to translate my thoughts into Spanish, and the insult I intended came out as a bland, benign observation about how Marcela had appeared, on the green hillside, dressed all in green and surrounded by those younger girls, who were like-wise all in green. I remember that my sister's head came up suddenly; probably it was my uncustomary tone, the neu-trality of it, or maybe the fact that, for the first time in our lives, I was addressing her in the language that we had always re-served for our respective Mexican friends, for those long-ago, precious days of fooling around with the spidery twins. Not to be outdone, she immediately responded in a musical, noble-sounding Spanish considerably more fluent than my own:

"Marcela looks beautiful in green, in brown, in all colors of the earth. Yet the source of her beauty is within, is indepen-dent of the manifest qualities of the visible world. Her strength is the real hue of her beauty, truly."

"No," I responded after an astonished moment, "I think Marta's the better-looking one. Her prettiness has a quality of kindness, or sweetness."

"Marta is a wonderful, lovely girl. Yes. I think of her as a dear sister, too. But Marcela is already a woman. She senses more about life than Marta ever will, or than I will. We shouldn't compare them, because they're as different as"—looking round the room; failing, on account of its starkness, to find material for a more arresting simile—"as light and dark."

"But which is light," I wondered, with a good-natured chuckle completely different from my normal, guarded snick-ering, "and which dark? And don't forget we're talking about identical twins here. Aren't they by definition precisely the same, identical personalities in interchangeable bodies?"

"That's what most people think," Sylvia said. "That's what I used to. But these two have shown me that that's com-plete bunk."

She went on to explain that Marcela (presumably on the side of 'light') was the top girl in her class, the best athlete in the school, and, because of her gift for seeing beyond herself, overleaping her own narrow self-interest, an inspiration to the rest of the girls (most of them, anyway). She was tremendously well-read, progressive in the political sense, and already well launched on the path to a medical degree (she wanted to help others, poor people mostly). Marta, on the other hand—but 'dark' overstated the case, I felt; 'exceedingly different' would have been more like it—was at or near the bottom of her class, always in danger of flunking half her subjects, and likely to be expelled (a fate she had been saved from, this past year, only by Marcela's brilliant counterexample, in combination with the Señora's pull with the administration). Marta had no thoughts but of boys, clothes, and herself. Sylvia had talked to her, as had Marcela, 'hundreds' of times, but to no avail.

My own sister, I gathered further, was also considered a good student (though not quite on Marcela's level). She, too, had already decided on a career in medicine: after two more years at the Colegio she would return to the States for her premed and med-school education, to be followed by a residency in tropical medicine "either at U.C.–San Francisco, or possibly the María Somoza Research Institute in Managua, Nicaragua." The long-range goal was to found a clinic in some impoverished corner of Central America. She would specialize in intestinal parasites, Marcela in surgical procedures.

I was just as surprised, hearing her recite these specific, firmly held intentions, as if some total stranger had come up to me on the street and told me something similar. I was surprised, in the first place, because there had been no inkling, previously, of a scientific bent on her part, and in the second, it astonished me that she would actually say something of this sort to me, unself-consciously spill the beans on herself. As I've already explained, we weren't the kind of siblings who routinely share inmost secrets and hopes, and this particular variety of admission, being like the ingenuous, laughable claim of some little kid ('When I grow up, I want to be a fireman.' 'I want to be a ballerina'), was just the type of thing that, under normal conditions, I would have immediately sneered at. But because the admission was made in Spanish, not English, in our language of childish innocence, I was somehow disarmed.

I remember that we talked about where she should go to college (I favored Radcliffe, she Stanford); then not to be outdone, I confessed to a plan—previously unmade, even unsuspected in myself—to follow a prelaw course when I got to Berkeley that fall. She wondered facetiously whether this indicated a desire to turn out "just like 'dad.' Will you be his little boy in every respect then, hmmm?" We went on in this unaccustomed, artificial, but intriguing mode for another few minutes. Certainly, it was the most substantial conversation we had had in years, and I had just gotten around to asking what she was doing 'in jail' (that is, stuck away in this cell-like room, while the rest of the girls gathered in their lawn groups), and she, with a cheery laugh, had begun by admitting that "yes, in some sense I am seen as a leper, or an outlaw, or something," when there came a knock at the door.

Before I could reach over and open up, Marcela barged in. From a funny, momentary look in her eye, I sensed that she had half expected to catch us in a compromising position, up to monkey business of some sort. Without a word Sylvia rose from her desk; gathering her books into a green canvas bag, turning away from me abruptly, she hurried out after Marcela, who had already exited.

I WAS FORCED to undergo tortures in the next few days of a kind completely new to me, the tortures of the ignored, of the madly jealous. My sister slipped from the forefront of my mind once again. Marta, beginning with that afternoon of her dentist appointment (which turned out to be a ruse—I think), made herself unavailable to me. Worse, on Saturday morning, after I'd looked for her all over the house and grounds, she showed up with one of the handsomest boys I'd ever seen, a 'friend' from Mexico City who had arrived the night before and danced with her into the wee hours at a little club in downtown Cuernavaca. I couldn't believe she'd do this to me—was it something I'd said, some failure, some inadequacy on my part?—and followed them around, speechless with hurt, till a sudden awakening of shame (at my whipped-puppyish behavior) caused me to stalk off.

I wandered through the horticultural map of Mexico again, ending up at our concrete bench. Here, just a few days before, we had exchanged our first grown-up kisses (there had been a few when we were little, innocent, half-reluctant embraces and rapid-fire lip pressings—I recalled them now, adding to my feeling of desolation). The rank, decay-fragrant greenery of the little glen, which had seemed romantic and suggestive the other day, now mocked me with its sameness. Nothing availed—this is what I felt; in the cruel, entropic universe of human emotions, no material force, no purely physical element or cue, had anything to say about whether or not your heart got broken. The banana trees, with their incongruous loads of green, upward-hanging fruit, and the half dozen garnet-headed, emerald-bellied hummingbirds, which on that other day had seemed to be the vibrant allies of my excitement, now simply grew and flitted. I was forlorn, bewildered. On top of my feeling of romantic hurt (unprecedented in my experience, at least in this extreme form), the thought that I had acted like a fool, had made myself pathetically vulnerable, deepened my torture, and with a groan such as a dying man makes when, in a final flash of insight, he sees that his entire life has been a waste, a fraud perpetrated mainly upon himself, I lay down flat on the bench.

It was only about four feet long; since I was lying on my back, with my head all the way up at one end, I had to have my knees bent up at the other (the heels of my shoes catching the edge). I had been staring up at the canopy of palm fronds and flowering vines, with here and there a glimpse of unclouded sky, when a sound a lot like the groan I had just made, but a parody version, caused me to sight through the V of my upraised thighs. I saw a face; it was the face I'd been hoping to see, Marta's, but the glimpse it allowed me of itself was so brief that I was unnerved. I got off the bench. I began walking stealthily toward that end of the clearing, which was almost impenetrable with tulip trees and vines and the plant called elephant's ears.

However, I was determined not to go thundering through the undergrowth again, the way we had that other day; too much of a grown-up (and painful) nature had occurred since then, so I called out in a peremptory voice, "All right, you can come out now. Time to stop playing games."

I heard her delicious, musical laugh after a couple of seconds. Then she repeated in exactly my tone, and with an excellent approximation of my accent in English: " 'All right. Time to stop playing. Come out now.' "

I wasn't amused. I think that if I had had my hands on her at that moment, I might have strangled her; as it was, there was a sickly smile on my face, and the feeling I had was that odd mixture of swooning helplessness, relief, and sexual excitement that the jealous one feels in the presence of his imagined betrayer.

"All right. Then don't come out."

After a couple of minutes, I heard a stirring in the bushes. I got ready to face her. I lit a cigarette, to appear nonchalant, but then the wall of foliage never parted.

Another laugh, from behind me. "It's not Marta, silly. It's the other one. I'm over here."

Somehow, she had sneaked halfway around the clearing, making no sound. Now she sat on the concrete bench with her legs crossed. As I peered at her, looking rather stupid I imagine, she gestured impatiently for me to approach.

"Come on. I won't bite."

I sat down next to her. I think that I had never felt, till that moment, the full force of amazement appropriate to this uncanny mimicry, this superb duplication of one living form by another; maybe because I had so much wanted her to be Marta, I wasn't quite willing to give up on that supposition as yet, and this affected my perception of her, but it seemed to me there was no good reason *not* to take this one for the one I wanted (aside from the short haircut, which, after all, she might have just had, for the fun of fooling me). When we were little, I had used to think that I could tell them apart by their eyes, one of them (Marcela, I think) having slightly protuberant eyes, which gave her a searching, more wide-awake expression. Now, though, I could see that this had been a mistake, just the way I explained to myself the different impressions they always made on me. Marcela's eyes were exactly as large, exactly as Asiatically slanted as her sister's, and at this moment, possibly because she was trying to seem to be my friend, they had precisely that devilish, alluring glint I often saw in Marta's.

"Why're you here in the woods? Why not playing tennis?"

"I hate tennis."

"Roberto"—the name of Marta's friend—"is a Junior Davis-Cupper. They've gone to the club to play some sets."

"Yes, I know. How nice."

"I don't like tennis either." She pronounced it 'eyether,' in the British way. "I still like to ride, though. But I don't go so much as I did when we were little, when we had the ponies. Do you remember the ponies?"

"Yes, I remember. Yours was called Mike. Marta's was called General Huerta."

"Right!"

"General Huerta would turn back on you when you were in the saddle and nip your ankle. You always knew he would do it, but you couldn't stop it."

"Exactly. You remember so well."

I had been looking at her legs. Under the stiff, then unfashionable denim, they were exactly the same as Marta's, the same legs that, at that moment, were carrying her back and forth across some tennis court, that had 'intertwined' with mine only a few nights before. From the legs I thought to the rest of her, picturing her, sensing her, with an embarrassing clarity, and I think this slightly shameful presumption of mine communicated itself, for Marcela suddenly looked at me in a mock-reproachful, half-encouraging way. It was just the look that Marta would have given me. But there was a difference of intent, or should I say, an extra layer of meaning; where Marta would have been half in earnest, her sister was earnest only about her attempt to make fun, to parody, as exactly as possible, a precocious fifteen-year-old's crude seductiveness. In this little bit of mockery I thought I could read much about her attitude toward her twin.

"Marta isn't very nice. She's left you here all alone, and . . . I think you like her. Your feelings are hurt, yes?"

My instinct was to deny this, to pretend indifference; instead, I hung my head.

"I think you like her," Marcela continued, "and, seeing her with Roberto, you believe she can't like you too, because a friend wouldn't act this way toward someone she also liked. But you're mistaken! She likes you *very* much. I shouldn't tell you this, but for years she's been planning your reunion, trying to think what to do, what clothes to wear. When we learned some weeks ago that you'd be coming, I can't tell you what this did to her! She's been crazy! I think she went off with Roberto just for relief. The great thing has happened, the unbelievable event, and now she needs to breathe. Roberto is nothing, just a sort of friend. She feels toward him like a brother. I mean—a sister toward a brother."

"A brother?" I exclaimed. "I thought *I* was the brother, the one she always thought of that way."

Marcela looked at me as if suddenly doubting her estimation of me. Was I really, after all, an idiot? "Please, when did she say that you were a brother? Since the age of five she's been thinking of you as a husband, nothing else."

I laughed. I felt so relieved, so tremendously buoyed by what she said, that I could have kissed her, would have laughed at anything. The hummingbirds (of which there were three visible to us at that moment) suddenly took on their prior significance, that of talismans of ardor, of romance-sweet-as-nectar. Even the bananas, which had recently become mere fruit, recovered something of their conventional symbolic value.

It occurred to me at that moment that Marcela 'knew everything,' that all our precautions (meeting in the middle of the night, using the secret corridor, etc.) had counted for nothing with her. But then twins, I thought, especially identicals, had a special telepathy, a secret channel of communication, and the fact that Marta had 'done it' would have been as obvious to her sister as if she had come down to breakfast one morning with two noses on her face. I somehow couldn't conceive of Marta actually telling her, though, putting it in so many words. She was a great keeper of secrets, was my Marta; but more to the point, the twins didn't like each other very much, had little to do with each other these days. To a considerable extent, Sylvia had replaced Marta as the 'twin' (or so it seemed to me), as the boon companion, the living reflection; maybe this had been the cause of their falling-out, or, to think again, maybe Marcela's close approach to Sylvia was the consequence of some prior development, some separation process begun long before.

I was thinking, though, not of Sylvia's role, but of nothing in particular, when I made some offhand remark about the school (the Colegio). Marcela immediately tensed up. The change in her demeanor was so marked that at first I thought she was making fun, becoming 'wary, distant Marcela' in the same spirit as her earlier impersonation of 'playful, flirtatious Marta.' Giving every impression of choosing her words with utmost care, she said, "I don't. Know. What you could mean."

I had merely remarked that their school seemed 'strange,' that the atmosphere on that afternoon had been unusual. "No," she said. "You are mistaken. We at Colegio de F—— find it perfectly suitable, natural, if you will. I think, instead, that the fault is in you, in your expectations."

"In me?"

"Yes. You thought you would find something else—some ordinary school, one of the usual type. A school like the one you go to yourself. A sort of prison. When the school, instead, has a correct philosophy, this infects all the teachers; they, in turn, pass this infection—umm, some other word—to the children, and in such a place something wonderful happens. All of those students who, before, hated to study, now cannot get enough. They fight to do the best they can. Yes, yes," she added, seeing how I took this. "I know it's hard to believe. But true."

I was highly skeptical; what was this 'correct philosophy' she spoke of, this salubrious 'infection' they were blithely passing back and forth?

"Yes," I said, "I sensed a certain . . . how shall I say, enthusiasm? A great earnestness. But on the other hand, what about my sister? What about poor Sylvia? They had her stuck away in a little shack, all by her lonesome. It seemed to me that they were treating her like an outcast."

Marcela wondered: "An outcast? But . . . how do you mean?"

"Just that. They treated her like a criminal. An undesirable. I think the word she actually used was 'a leper.' "

"She . . . said this? Your sister actually said this?"

"Yes. That was the very word."

After a considerable pause, during which Marcela's eyes looked somber, as if they were 'inwardly burning,' she laughed. It was an oddly false, mirthless sound, and for some reason it made me regret what I'd said. Maybe Sylvia had not intended that it be repeated, even to Marcela. But now, in a reassuring tone she explained:

"No. Not an outcast. But . . . there is a problem, yes. You see, your sister is too courageous. Too bold. The things she feels in her heart, she doesn't understand that, in some situations, we must hide. Even at a school like ours, some things need to be kept quiet. But she won't accept this.

"On that Thursday, the problem was . . ." But now she really laughed; the very idea of this (whatever it was) was too embarrassing, impossible to describe. "On Thursday, which is our study-group day, she was to lead a group. I was to lead another. This is a privilege, a kind of award, for doing well in your tests. Anyway, one of our *maestras* announced the topic: 'Folk Songs of Mexico.' Very good. But, as it happens, Sylvia has thought of this a lot. She has many ideas on the topic. For some reason she wants *me* to hear her ideas. We are best friends, and usually we take the same classes. She doesn't want to express her ideas in a group that doesn't include me. She refuses to lead a separate group.

"The *maestra* says: No. For once you'll do as told. Go lead your group. But . . . she won't. The result was as you saw. They stuck her in the *cabaña*."

Marcela winked; this Sylvia (her look seemed to imply), she's something else, yes? I found myself smiling back.

"But then," I wondered, "she *was* an outcast. I mean, they did it as a punishment. Stuck her off like that."

"Yes, I guess so. Yes. For this one time. But understand me: she is *not* a leper. Of all of us, she is their favorite. The best student. Top in all the classes."

"Sylvia? But that's funny. She said *you* were the best, the top student by far."

Marcela smiled; shook her head. The truth was something else, I gathered; but Sylvia, in her deep loyalty, would say only complimentary, exaggerated things about her dearest friend.

This odd conversation, in the banana glen, soon petered out. My mind was on Marta, on her imminent return from the tennis club (she did come back, and fairly soon, and without the handsome, Davis-Cupping Roberto). As it happened, this was my last communication of any length with Marcela for a long time—for twenty years, to be precise.

I HAD LOST Marta again, seen her disappear into the garden. It was three or four days later, the afternoon of my scheduled departure, and we had argued about something I can't remember now. The game was for me to finish my packing, then come after her, search her out, but for some reason I didn't want to play; I remember that I took my time, carried my bag to the car, talked for fifteen minutes or so to Isidro, one of the grounds-men, a short, dark Zapotec, who only two nights before had given me my first puffs of *mota*, a potent sample from Solón, his native village. Only then, with a studied casualness that, in my vanity, I sincerely hoped was being observed (from the house, from the trees, from everywhere at once), only then did I amble after Marta.

We had spent the last two nights together; once again I was riding high, head in the clouds over this incredible good fortune, this wonderful thing that had happened to me. Marta loved me, and while I still couldn't quite explain to myself why she should find me attractive, why, against all the dictates of her upbringing, she would willingly commit these intimate sins, I had decided that the only sensible course was that which implied a certain sophistication, familiarity with the ways of women, romance in all its amusing aspects.

Accordingly, I had strongly hinted, when Marta asked sweetly, shyly, if she was my 'first,' that she wasn't. I was a man; men were more experienced; that was all. We continued to get together only in my rooms. As before, she was adamant about keeping the lights off, and this added, I think, importantly to my impulse to pretend, some of the expressions and attitudes I felt compelled to affect being possible only given an absence of illumination. Had we been able to stage our love-making in the open air, or even in some darkened room that wasn't part of Las Casuelas, of the Señora's domain, I feel sure I would have been more direct.

I don't believe in mystical influences, in spooks that inhabit particular corners, so that whenever you pass, the hair on your neck rises, and you find yourself thinking things not consistent with your prior train of thought; or maybe I should say, I don't believe very *strictly* in all of that, yet I still think the cast of my involvement with Marta was significantly affected by the rooms we were in. Here, in this very same suite, as I may have mentioned, my father always used to stay when he came to visit, and through that very same 'servants' corridor' the Señora, not many years before Marta, would have passed, her breath anxiously held, heart pounding in her bosom. I don't think Marta knew, then or at any later time, about this odd coincidence. I certainly wasn't aware, and at that time probably only Marcela had pieced some of it together, Marcela, the more suspicious, the more cunning of the two, being even then her mother's deadly enemy (in her own mind), the self-appointed familial avenger. Even so—even though Marta and I were, as far as I know, completely unaware—we were subtly influenced, I believe, by what had happened before, by mystic residues inhering in the very walls, the very bed.

Exactly what *did* happen there can't be known, of course, beyond the level of a general surmise. Marcela is the one who, a few years later, put together what to her seemed a plausible scenario, for the purpose of convincing Sylvia once and for all that our father was a beast, an unspeakable monster who must hereafter be shunned. The substance of her theory was that in those rooms, during one of his early visits, Gerson seduced the Señora, and thereafter all of his 'business trips' to Mexico were for the purpose of further debauching his best friend's wife. Yet with a man on the order of my father, the sexual motive could never be the whole thing, and in the course of time, having gotten the Señora pretty much under his power, he revealed his other, more compelling purpose.

On August 4, 1954, during a three-day visit that I also made, Sr. Martín, previously in the best of health, suddenly blanched at the dinner table, complained of pains in his right side, and went off to bed. The pains subsided somewhat; but just before midnight, after having overruled his wife's suggestion that they call a doctor, his face once again went completely white, he clutched his side, and with the words *"Madre santís—,"* uttered in a piercing whisper, he died. The family doctor, summoned too late, ascribed death to a coronary occlusion. It was revealed at that time that Sr. Martín had sought treatment recently for back pain; tests taken some weeks before had been inconclusive.

Marcela believed—said she believed, anyway—that her father had been poisoned. My father was the ostensible poisoner. Her mother probably had something to do with it, too: *parahumara*, a root extract that does, indeed, kill in a peculiar way, through a sort of twofold attack on the liver, was something she would have known about, having been raised in Jalisco, where the plant it comes from is ubiquitous.

❉

I'm still not certain, all these years later, that there isn't some truth in what I've just called Marcela's scenario, though the idea of my father poisoning anyone is completely absurd, needs to be immediately ruled out. The relevant considerations are only: what did he stand to gain from such an act (and did he in fact gain at all); and, was this the sort of thing he was prone to, had a taste for? Taking the questions one at a time, the answer to the first has to be nothing (and no). He didn't want the Señora for a wife; it can't be said that he stood to 'gain' her (and all her properties) once Sr. Martín was dead, since he never married her, and in fact, their business and personal relationship survived the death by only about six years. Moreover, poisoning and palace intrigue were things he would have abhorred, precisely the type of 'execution' of policy he was famous for staying many levels above (or below, or to the side of). As likely that he, himself, would have emptied poison into somebody's wineglass, as that he would have ever pressed his own pants. He preferred to manipulate people from a thousand miles distant, from behind a mesmerizing veil of confusion and secrecy. In fact, I think one can say about him that in any matter of importance, his capacity for action was exactly proportional to his confidence in his hiddenness, his invisibility.

He would have hurt the Señor (if it had ever been his intention to do so) by other means, by some plausible, unspectacular business reversal; by some imperceptible shift in economic conditions, something impossible to understand, at the time, as having been man-caused. Then, as the years passed, this shift, or whatever it was, would have snowballed in importance, till ruin of an apparently natural and inevitable sort resulted. That was his modus operandi (as some fearful admirers of his professional behavior have since told me), but of course, this method was never applied to his friends, among whom Sr. Martín was prominently numbered. No, he liked this man, this amusing, cultured companion. I think that in some ways, the profound Mexican-ness of Sr. Martín and his family functioned much for my father as it would, later, for my sister and me, as a pretext for relaxation, for temporary suspension of those aggressive habits adopted out of necessity and constantly in force back in the home culture. Down in Cuernavaca, in the endless afternoon of Las Casuelas, he could breathe, he could be less like himself. He was, if you will, in the wrong mood for murdering anyone; for doing any sort of injury to a benevolent host.

Nevertheless, I can conceive—which is different, of course, from saying "I know"—of a sequence of events whereby the poor, unsuspecting Señor ends up dead, and my father's contribution to this outcome is substantial. I imagine a 'texture of relationship' between Sra. Marcela and my father, the adulterous lovers, that allows evil thoughts to exist, that encourages them; two peculiar natures reacting upon one another, drawing forth subtle personal poisons, predilections otherwise never to be known. The Señora hates her husband; never mind her reasons, she would just be happier living without him, and in time, having come to trust in Gerson's discretion, she makes some ambiguous, highly tentative remark to this effect. Gerson does not bridle; he does not shrink back. Maybe she expected some sort of disapproving display, something tinged with moral concern, but this is conspicuously absent, and he considers her proposal as if she had suggested something on the order of taking a horseback ride.

"You would have a great responsibility," he allows.

What does this mean (she wonders)? Responsibility of a moral, a legal kind?

"Think: who controls your time? How much freedom do you have now? How important is this to you?"

"I don't understand."

"Martín only seems free. He has time to play around only because he makes a mess of his business. If you were in his position I think you'd be unable to operate like that, and you'd hate it."

She is flabbergasted. In the first place: he understands immediately her main thrust, that the control of the wealth she would inherit in the event of her husband's death is her real concern, no breath needs to be wasted on such imbecilities as 'gaining her freedom' so that they can be married instead. (She had still—even knowing him as well as she does—half expected to have to put things in these terms, at first.) Second place: he knows this about her, that she could never operate as Martín has. Part of her revulsion against him is precisely on the grounds of his ineffectuality and lack of imagination, combined with an inexplicable stubbornness when it comes to ceding her formal control.

"No, you don't understand me," she says—partly because he does, so well. "I would not hate it. I would enjoy it. I would thrive under that weight of responsibility."

"You think you would."

"I *know* it. I know myself, that I—" But she needs to say no more. He understands her; from his expression, she knows that he believes her.

Later, in Martín's company, she observes him, and his complete naturalness impresses her, a naturalness (and a warmth, a genuine affection toward the man whose death he has just been discussing) growing as it were from a clear conscience, with not the tiniest particle of playacting or self-conscious cunning about it. Such naturalness can mean either a certain type of personality, a psychopathic tendency, or philosophic detachment of a sort that interests her. He can love Martín like the dearest of friends, meanwhile having an intimate relation with the idea of his death. Only further observation will tell her if this affectionate naturalness is a kind of gloating (a sinister outpouring toward the victim who is already in his power, to heighten the irony he secretly savors) or whether it truly signifies that detached condition that she, for one, is having a hard time achieving.

"*Querida.* You look frightened." (Martín has turned to her. He takes her hand.)

"I? Frightened?" After a minute: "Yes. I am frightened."

"Why? What in the world? We have our friend here. His little boy is here, playing in the garden with our daughters. Probably being tortured." (Laughs.) "The world is put to rights. Everyone has his health and his prosperity."

"Yes, his health. Let's drink to our . . . health."

(They are drinking Scotch. Gerson has brought bottles of forty-eight-year-old Ballantine's with him, and the Señora, as she hoists her glass with the others, is astounded at what has just come out of her mouth. When she puts her glass down, her hand jerks as if with a spasm.)

"I don't understand." Martín speaks to her, but his words are really aimed at their guest, his male friend. "Women amaze me. They are subject to so many whims, as if their souls were delicate wires strung in the air which every breeze disturbs. A man plants his feet in the earth and shakes off his terrors. And for this reason"—now actually turning to Gerson—"we are accused of coarseness, but without this supposed 'coarseness' no one would ever overcome those superstitions and intuitions that so abundantly assail us, whose purpose is only to keep us from accomplishment!"

Gerson nods, makes assenting sounds. Sr. Martín looks around at his wife, as if to say, There, even you can't argue with that. But the utter falseness of his tone and expression strikes fear in her heart. No one has been accusing him of 'coarseness,' and this kind of outburst is so unlike him that immediately she imagines his 'delicate wire' to be picking up the strange, malign signals that she, all unwitting, must be sending.

"I am afraid," she says now, "for good reason. This after-noon I barely escaped a bad accident. I almost caused some-thing awful to happen."

Martín—again being unlike himself—raises one eyebrow and looks at her condescendingly.

"Yes," she continues, "I was in our car. About to go downtown. All the children were with me, even young Luis. I had decided on . . . let's say, to take a new route. One I've avoided in the past. But at the last minute, something tells me not to take this street, to go around. With some difficulty, I changed to my usual route. Well, at the bottom of this street, just as we emerged from the one I finally took, I was the first to come upon the scene of a horrible accident. A truck coming the other way, up the street I had avoided, hit a car and pushed it back against a wall, and the car, colliding with the wall, burst into flames. Inside the car were a woman, a man, and some children. They were trapped. As I was the first one to arrive, I tried to get to the car, but the heat and flames pushed me back. I had to stand there and watch them burn."

Martín looks up; he seems suspicious of this story. No longer condescending, but displeased on some other account, he stares piercingly at his wife.

"And you imagine that . . ."

"I don't imagine. I know."

"I returned from town at four o'clock. I saw no sign of an exploding accident."

"It was in the Avenida Ramón Hidalgo. Against the southwest wall of the Francis estate."

"And you believe that your 'feeling' kept you from going down that road, being the car that hit the truck?"

She says, "I only know that I had a strong feeling. Then, looking at the burning car, I believed that I was looking at us, something that had been intended, in some sense, for the children and me. We avoided it only by luck."

"You mean: by your famous 'intuition.' "

The Señora shrugs as if to say, Well, call it what you want, call it that if you must; I myself don't know what to call it.

Sr. Martín laughs, pours himself another drink. Pours more for Gerson. Shakes his head in amazement.

"And you, my friend"—turning to their guest—"what sense do you make of such a thing, if any?"

"I don't know what to make of it," Gerson says flatly.

"But surely, you don't concede any validity to this hocus-pocus, this nonsense of 'feelings' and premonitions, of disasters averted only through a sort of magic?"

"Oh, most definitely," Gerson explains. "I concede it a lot of validity."

Martín, with a theatrical take, conveys the surprise of one who suddenly divines that all about him are idiots.

"I concede it validity," my father goes on, "only I think I actually believe in it more than Marcela does. In her place I would have acted differently. I believe you said"—turning to face her—"you began with a feeling to take a 'new route,' the urge to go down an unaccustomed street? This is the urge I would have followed. Never argue with an impulse that comes out of the blue, that points you in a new direction, that promises change."

After a moment, "But in that case we would have been the ones . . ."

"No. Not necessarily. You, coming down the new street, are traveling at a different rate of speed, and you see the truck in time, you swerve to avoid it. By following the original urge you spend the rest of the afternoon breathing a little faster, the blood coursing through your veins a little more quickly, and some aspect of your life that has recently been troubling you, perhaps, appears to you now in a new light. You are better for what you've done.

"Incidentally, the other people don't get hurt. No one burns up. The other car had to slow when you cut in front, and though the driver curses you all the way to the bottom, later he has a drink with his brother-in-law, they agree to buy a quarter-ticket in the national lottery, and two weeks later they collect several hundreds of thousands."

Martín chuckles, glancing at his wife. Gerson, not quite smiling, nevertheless wears that expression of rocklike imperturbability that, in certain situations, can signify a facetious intention on his part.

"You seem to be advising me," says the Señora, "to act

impulsively in every case. To follow the first overpowering urge
that comes along."

"Yes. Something like that."

"Obviously then you are unacquainted with these 'feelings,' which are not so much urges as a kind of trembling in
your soul. They really have nothing to do with the ordinary
class of sensations that make you do something. That tell you to
go to Acapulco, for example, on your vacation this year."

"I would go to Acapulco only if you would be my guide,
my dear. But as for these sensations, I may not have them, but I
actually think I do, I think most men do. Only in our experience we filter things through a rational screen, or I should say,
that impulse which comes to you as a 'trembling' becomes for a
man simply a good idea, a determination to act in a certain way
because of reasonable considerations. In a man—I'm speaking
of a special kind, a certain category of man—the will is a
healthy muscle daily exercised, while in a woman, thinking
and feeling operate more on their own. Women, therefore,
decide that there is a whole category of exquisite experiences
belonging only to them. Whereas in fact, anyone of normal
intelligence is susceptible."

The Señora shakes her head. She cannot accept this. "No,
by what you say you only prove that, in an important way, you
have no conception of what I mean. . . ."

"Pardon," interjects Sr. Martín. "Pardon, but I must dis-
agree. I think, my friend, that you have overlooked certain
'exquisite sensations'—truly, of which we can have no idea—
that belong to a woman by virtue of her . . ." And his uncharacteristic smirk (a sort of unpracticed leer), coupled with a glance
at his wife's bare knees, makes his meaning clear.

(In seven years of being married to this man, never before
has she known him to make an off-color allusion, to speak of the
physicality of her or of any other woman he respects, and at
this instant she is absolutely sure he knows her true feelings,
has divined her intention.)

"No," Sra. Marcela responds, most definitely. "You don't understand because—to say only the obvious—when I am talking about these feelings, I mean reachings into the future, small victories won from time. Surely this is different from someone who plots a rational course of action leading to a successful outcome. In the one case, there is only a certain probability that he gets what he wants. It depends on skill, luck, many things. But in the other—"

"I submit to you," Gerson says, with a smile at his own portentous tone, "that in the case of a willful action rationally conceived, immediately executed, and never for a moment doubted, the probability of an unfavorable outcome is zero. But my only proof for this—and it may go further toward satisfying you, since it shows just how prone to 'odd feelings' I am too—is the sensation that accompanies this process, a sort of pinch, a squeeze in the chest, as if the future were unfolding from within, unspooling like film from an internal projector. One knows that one has created a piece of the future, absolutely. One knows, in the end, precisely because of the presence of this feeling. . . ."

The Señora, about to make some doubting rejoinder, instead exhales loudly. She subsides into her chair. Sr. Martín, nodding vigorously, makes clear his agreement, as if this were just the point that he, too, had wanted to make, had been driving at all along. Soon the conversation passes on to other subjects.

I was right on Marta's track. I had seen her ahead of me, disappearing like a deer into the tall, saw-edged grass of the savanna section, letting me have just enough of a glimpse to know which direction to take. I was determined, however, not to run after her. Already I had spent some twenty minutes picking up her trail, playing cat-and-mouse, and I was damned

if, in these last minutes before I had to drive away, I was going
to squander the comparative advantage that, with some difficulty, I had won over her.

The savanna section—which somehow achieved a feeling
of enormous spaciousness, though it claimed only a couple of
acres—abutted an artificial hill given over to the plants of
the high Sonoran desert. She had seemed to be headed right
into the desert, but I suddenly knew that she had slipped down
to the right, along one edge of a natural canyon, a *barranca*. On
the other side of this divide was our jungle section, the model
rain forest, and it was here, I was sure, that she would be
waiting for me.

I crossed the *barranca* near its head. By doing so I gained
time and distance on her, and I figured to arrive at the glen just
about when she did. If I had been willing to run, I might have
even gotten there first, but I wasn't willing, and in fact, as soon
as I had this idea I bent over and began to examine a strange
flower, one I wasn't aware of ever having seen here before. It
was red at the base of its petals, yielding to pink farther out,
and though it grew on a long, thick, upright stem, it looked
exactly like a trumpet-vine flower. I picked it. I can still remember its unexpected smell: rotten honey, with fishy and peppery
overtones. Probably it was some extremely rare, nearly extinct
species, and if one of the Zapotec gardeners, or the ghost of Sr.
Martín, had seen me at that moment, I would have been cursed
and banished from Las Casuelas forever.

Rambling along, puckering my lips as though whistling
(though I made no sound), I gradually entered the rain forest.
The jungle growth rose up around me, 'swallowed' me, by
degrees, and as soon as it was a few feet over my head I
experienced a change of mood, became much more alert. Now
I thought that I would sneak up on the glen; Marta would be
there already, inside the ring of trees, arranged in a negligently
casual posture on our bench. I imagined myself spying on her:
just as her sister had sneaked up on me the other day, played a

joke on me from behind the tulip tree, I would silently, gloatingly observe her discomfiture as I continued not to appear, as her casual certainty of how and where I would end up failed to pay off.

Actually, I don't like spying on people, and just to imagine this little trick was enough. Having reached the edge of the glen, I raised my arms to force my way through the wall of tangled branches, but at just that moment, a girlish cry from the other side gave me pause. Now it seems to me that there must have been some quality that struck me as peculiar, that made me conclude immediately that it couldn't be Marta, who had just stubbed her toe or something; this may be the case, but just as probably the suddenness, the sharpness, of that youthful cry revived my original intention (to spy), and I froze, my arms about my head, and stopped breathing.

More cries. A whole series, at about two-second intervals. I started to breathe again, and lowering one arm, I cautiously brushed away a couple of enormous leaves (truly, the size of an elephant's ears). Now I could dimly see into the glen, which was considerably brighter than where I was (within the forest wall). Marta was kneeling by the bench. Her back was toward me, and her hands were somehow thrown back over her shoulders, elbows pointing straight up in the air. This bizarre contortion of her arms—in which I believed for a good three minutes—caused me less confusion than the question of why she should be on her knees, in a position almost of supplication, at the end of the bench, as if the bench were an altar of some kind. Her head was very still. In fact, all of her was still but for her lower arms, which, still resting on her own shoulders, sometimes trembled or jerked out to the side a ways.

The cries had stopped, but now, just as a matched pair of hummingbirds, flying as if in formation, buzzed the bench and Marta, a new sound rent the stillness of the glade. There was such urgency in this half-stifled grunt that I concluded that something must be terribly wrong (she had gotten sick, come

down with cramps, or maybe dislocated both shoulders, which
explained the airborne elbows, etc.). I took a step forward,
intending to break free of the foliage. Then I stopped. My
movement in the bushes alarmed the hummingbirds, and as
one of them shot off like a tiny, bejeweled missile, my perspective on what was before me was minutely, but fundamentally,
altered. I recognized Marcela, rather than Marta, in the figure
on the ground. More puzzling still was the transformation that
her hands (still dangling back over her shoulders) had under-
gone, turning into feet. The long forearms, leading up to
trembling elbows, into lower legs. Elbows into kneecaps.

Arms into legs—but certainly, the legs of another person—which put her face, of necessity, in the vicinity of, at the
precise latitude and longitude of . . . Imagine my confusion (I,
who was only dimly, theoretically aware of this bizarre practice), confusion intensified by a near instantaneous deduction
as to the other person's identity. Sylvia was lying on her back,
along the length of the bench (much as I, that other day, had
lain before my impromptu interview with Marcela); her head,
hanging off the far end a bit, was tilted so that all I could see
was the underside of her chin. One of her hands, clenched in a
whitening fist, hung over the edge of the bench. At this moment, a sound in the bushes, ninety degrees around the glen
from my position, caused the one remaining hummingbird,
which had continued to hover, to flit off in search of its companion. Marcela, possibly feeling this minute disturbance of the air
(or having heard my sounds in the trees), pulled her face from
my sister's crotch, looked right, then left, giving me her avid,
hyperattentive profile for several seconds.

I remember the eagerness, the pathetic urgency (for so it
seemed) of my sister's hand, which, reaching for her lover's
head, pulled it roughly down by the hair. The hummingbirds,
returning after an instant, hovered once again over the bench,
as if drawn there by some mysterious emanation or energy.

I RETURNED TO southern California. I went back to my school (where only a few weeks remained of my senior year), eagerly anticipating the fall, when I would be off to college.

My father made me a present of his Buick convertible. When I drove up to Berkeley, it was in this powerful, lemon-yellow vehicle. I drove it for the next few years—always with a feeling of pleasure, of identification with my father and gratitude toward him.

At that time (early to mid-'sixties), he was divesting himself of various overseas business interests (among them the properties he had part owned in Mexico), extricating himself from certain long-standing professional arrangements, and in general undergoing a sort of cosmetic sea-change, whereby the notorious 'King Kike' of the early 'fifties and late 'forties—who is said to have 'invented' Las Vegas (in reality, all he did was to

73

devise methods to bring dirty money into the light, to cleanse filthy lucre and make it available for aboveground investment), who, it is said, intervened directly and effectively in the presidential campaign of 1952, knocking out that Democratic contender (Kefauver?) who displeased certain of his colleagues—became a respected member of the Hollywood establishment, counselor to major corporations and sitter on various charitable boards. Now pushing sixty—though he looked fifteen years younger, as, at twenty-five, he had already looked a distinguished, prematurely silver-haired forty—he began to think of himself in a new way, and no sooner had this conception appeared in his mind than, by the magic of his prodigious intentionality, it became the truth about him.

Now the people I sometimes met through him were different, gave off a different buzz. There were some celebrities, but most were other lawyers, corporate personalities having their existence inside business institutions that they partly controlled. They came to my father for a number of reasons. By this late date, his understanding of labor law and of the multiform interpenetrations that labor organizations and businesses might work out to their mutual benefit was formidable, and probably no other individual in the West was as likely to be able to see a solution, and to put it into effect, in a certain kind of situation as he was. Some might say this was because he continued to function as unofficial agent for certain unions, that anyone anticipating trouble with a particular organization knew immediately to come to Gerson Sanders, whose line to the leadership was direct. This may have been true, but whereas in the early years (1939 to '58, roughly) it was true by virtue of edict from above, semiformal arrangement among the two or three men who controlled those unions, after about 1958 it happened because he really could work out ingenious solutions, he saw things more clearly than anyone else. His methods were unusual, and he always brought satisfaction to his employers.

He retained his old connections, but now his relationship with those who, in the early days, had 'owned' him in a certain sense was different, more like that of a former vassal, a onetime protégé released, with great reluctance, into the wide world. That he would always continue to act with the interests of his former protectors in mind was understood, and he would only have been released, I think, if it was generally conceded that anything different was unimaginable. The ties of understanding, the mutuality of interests and sympathies were so deep by now that no one could think of a situation where something had to be feared from him. In this regard, I suppose I should mention his famous 'discretion.' In a career spanning more than fifty years, he was often called to testify in front of congressional committees, federal task forces, grand juries, and the like, but each appearance only added to his reputation, and not only was he, himself, never indicted for a crime, but those whose affairs he was asked to reveal often benefited from the imperfect information he spread. It has been said that every task force looking into organized crime in the western states after the war ended up having to talk to him, but all suffered irreparable damage to the extent they acted on what he, testifying under oath, revealed as the documentable truth. I have no way of evaluating the accuracy of this claim, the justice of this high praise. Most of his testimony is sealed, or lost, and even if I could get my hands on it I wouldn't know what it meant. According to Sid Feldman, a lifelong friend and golfing partner of my father, Gerson's genius consisted in the subtlety of his delivery, the special spin he imparted to bits of promising disinformation, ingestion of which caused certain death to investigations somewhere down the line.

I, myself, know firsthand about a related talent: his so-called photographic memory. He could read pages of the most impenetrable lawyerly prose, afterward summarizing it succinctly while retaining a near exact impression of every important paragraph. Other people are born with this gift, but

Gerson had taught himself; I know because, at age fifteen or so, I was the beneficiary of attempts on his part to pass the secret on, and I was astonished to find that what I'd always assumed was a God-given talent was, in fact, a curious, cockamamie method, something he probably got by writing away to a matchbook-cover academy sometime in his youth. This method, which I completely failed to master, required one to 'free up' one's mind while looking at, say, a passage in a book; the very shape of the words on the page would, in one's 'open' state, assume a memorable personality, and thereafter one could access the text by recalling this impression. Gerson used to say that printed paragraphs, or whole pages, looked like 'a fat man' to him, or 'like a guy with a broken arm, and it's in an awkward cast,' but for the life of me, I couldn't generate ideas of this kind, and I only pretended to know what he was getting at.

On other occasions, I remember hearing him call up entire conversations that people had had in his presence; quoting as from a transcript, he would prove conclusively that Smith, rather than Jones, had been the first to mention this or that, which meant that Jones was mendacious in his assertion of a prior claim. Certain prospective employers of my father—those needing a precise, exhaustive record of their transactions, yet having a sensible fear of committing anything to paper—valued him enormously for this gift.

I hesitate to say, however, as others have, that the basic style of sub rosa deal-making in this century owes more to him than to anyone, since statements on that order, being impossible to evaluate, approach emptiness. If my father had never existed, probably the same general evolutionary course would have been followed, although the specific individuals who, in the end, came out on top might have been different. All he did, it seems to me, was to regularize, rationalize, apply sensible management techniques; he did this, however, with a special alertness to security matters, the need to evade ever more probing scrutiny from police agencies, and from the Internal Revenue, remaining ever uppermost in his mind. While others of his generation were doing similar 'pioneer work,' acting always to further the interpenetration of legal and illegal business—which I, for one, see as the principal innovation of that era—he was acting thus but in a style a little more thoughtful, always a bit more consistent within itself. If the world of crime was to be, henceforth, indivisible from that of legitimate business, then adjustments had to be made, accommodations to the norms of the invaded world. This simple idea—enormously elaborated, in ways I don't pretend to understand completely—undoubtedly was the whole of his system.

My sister, after my final sight of her in the banana glen, remained unknown to me for almost two years; scheduling problems combined with mutual mistrust to keep us apart.

Actually, I had a lot of interest, a hundred questions I wanted to ask her; I had been genuinely shocked by what I saw, since—to put it mildly—this wasn't what I'd expected was going on between her and her friend. Now I wonder if I wasn't being intentionally obtuse; many of the 'signs' had been there, they were passionately attached to each other, had always been so, and it seems to me that anyone (and especially someone like me, always prone to this kind of thinking, always half suspicious of a 'dirty secret' between overly close friends) would have guessed. But for whatever reasons, I walked into this particular revelation unawares. Marta, by the way, once said something to me that made me think the whole thing had been a setup. By way of explaining the evident disaffection, bordering on outright hatred, between herself and her twin, she tried to recall the last time Marcela had spoken to her openly, enlisted her aid in a frank and simple way. She could think back, as she put it, only to *"tu visita curiosa,"* my strange little stay at their house, at which time, I gathered, there had been some sort of collusion.

"Do you mean—" I began; but she curtly shook her head.

We were in bed at that moment, happily hidden away at a small, clean hotel we both liked, La Banqueta Azul, on the outskirts of Guadalajara. Marta had taken the train north to meet me. It was the summer of 1968—some three months before her death.

"Are you saying," I persisted, taking hold of one of her thin wrists, half bending it behind her back, "what are you saying? What did you do that time?"

"Nothing, only . . ."

She explained that at the time, her sister and mine, 'crazy' with fearful imaginings about the purpose of my visit, had tried to enlist her help in an attempt to fool me. They believed that I had been sent by my father, who, having received some communication from their school, wanted me to investigate reports of their 'misbehavior.' This misbehavior wasn't sexual, I gathered, so much as political; even then Marcela was a member of various illegal organizations, one of them the youth arm of an outlawed Mexican party, and in particular, acting at the instigation of one of their *maestras*, she had organized a cell among her peers, a supersecret little group dedicated to 'violent upheaval.'

In order to pull the wool over my eyes, Marta was assigned to 'divert' me, to flirt with me and see that I had a lot on my mind; but never would she have gone along with this plan, she said, unless it coincided with her own intention (that is, a romantic feeling for me, going back to our days of romping five-and six-year-olds). Alone among their friends, she had resisted Marcela's influence; maybe because they were twins, she was only mildly susceptible to the other's *viveza* (by which she meant, I think, 'charisma,' or maybe just 'energy'), and in fact it annoyed her that Marcela, who usually paid her no attention, had this time condescended to ask for help.

"So, I flirted. I even did *more* than flirt," she said, with an air of honest surprise at her own misconduct. "And you said nothing to your father. Thus, they could go on."

I assured her that I had come to their house with no ulterior purpose, sent on no sort of 'mission' by Gerson, who only wanted me to have a vacation. Marta, by her expression, showed that she thought this was rather disingenuous—certainly we were intimate enough now to confess such things to one another.

"No, I'm telling the truth. And I guarantee you my father wouldn't have cared about her belonging to some silly girls' club. On the other hand, if he had heard what they were doing"—and by my tone, she understood that I was now referring to 'that'—"he'd probably have done something. Brought her home."

"Yes, and you were seen talking to Srta. Braun, their enemy, the one member of the administration who took a big interest in them. Srta. Braun had said many hard things to Sylvia. Not about the club, but about . . . the other."

(We always referred to it this way—allusively, euphemistically—on account of Marta's natural delicacy. Furthermore, my Spanish, which was adequate to most demands made on it, was impoverished in certain respects, and I was incapable of adopting that attitude of crude raillery which came to me naturally in English.)

"This Srta. Braun . . ." I said, looking mildly puzzled.

"Yes, you remember. She of the interview that you had, on that afternoon when, so you say, you came only to 'look for me,' 'take me to the lake.' But we knew very well what you talked about. Marcela expected that on that very day you would announce that Sylvia had to go back, and in that case she was to disappear with a third friend of theirs, someone you don't know, and go to the capital. Here they had an apartment where she could hide."

I had to laugh; the idea of this 'conspiracy' going on behind my back was too much. Marta understood my point of

view, but she continued to look serious as, with evident difficulty, she added:

"One feature of their plan—never say to anyone, it can't
be known I told you—in the event you behaved as expected,
they would take you, with the help of other members of their
society. You would be kept in some other rooms that they
had—a kind of prisoner—while Marcela notified your father.
If he would agree that Sylvia could stay in Mexico, you would
be released. If not, a bad consequence was to follow. I don't
know exactly what."

"Let's see: one by one they cut off my fingers, mail them
back to L.A.? Or maybe just do away with me entirely, dump
my body by the side of the road?"

Still looking quite serious: "As I said, I don't know."

I took this for what it seemed to be worth—nothing—and
only wondered that Marta was playing tricks on me again,
inventing crazy tales for no purpose. In the old days, both
Marcela and she used to invent outrageous untruths about each
other—that Marta had ridden her pony in the national eques-
trian trials, won a silver medal; that Marcela had a fatal blood
disease, probably wouldn't last out the year—delighting in the
confusion that these well-constructed, well-delivered fictions
added to the ordinary confusion of dealing with twins.

"If I was to be kidnapped," I now wondered, "what part
was Sylvia to play? When they locked me up or cut off my
body parts, she would just go along, say okay to anything?"

This gave Marta pause; I imagined her straining for a
plausible note, some grounds on which Sylvia—who had always had a kind of offhand interest in my well-being—would
have seen me sacrificed.

"I don't think you understand. Between them there is
something almost too strong. When Marcela has an idea for
her, your sister has to go along. She is *happiest* when she does,
when she takes these orders."

"I see. Sort of the old master-slave thing, hmmm?"

"No. Because the other—Sylvia—can be the master if she comes up with an idea. They often speak of these ideas, 'superior' ideas, that are of a kind that has to be immediately respected. Everything must give way in front of such an idea. Everyone must acknowledge them. I know, because I never acknowledge fast enough. I've proved over and over my stupidity, always dragging behind, never quite seeing how 'superior' everything is."

"Tell me," I suddenly interposed, "whose bright idea— whose *superior* idea—was it to lead me into the woods that day? Who devised that interesting little display for me?"

Marta—for an instant not sure to what I referred—suddenly blushed. Her face, throat, and even the tops of her round, small-nippled breasts, just visible above a pulled-up sheet, became infused with new color. I was used to seeing her in varying states of encoloration, but the light in our little hotel room, on that particular afternoon, must have been unusually pure, because it seemed to me that I had never before seen such a thing, so gorgeous and moving a transformation.

"Crazy. You are *crazy*," she said accusingly.

"Crazy? Well . . . maybe so. But it seemed to me that it had all been arranged. There was a feeling of walking out onto a stage set, of a play already in progress. Know what I mean?"

"No. I don't know. I don't even know what you saw that day—what you *think* you saw."

This was, I suppose, true; that is, because of our euphemistic way of speaking, I had never specifically described what I encountered in the glen. Maybe I said I saw our sisters 'kissing,' something like that, leaving the rest to Marta's imagination. Now, though, by an association of ideas, it occurred to me that she probably *did* know, may even have seen for herself. Having led me to the glen, where she knew Marcela and Sylvia would be trysting, she, herself, would also have had to hide in the bushes. Then, of course, she would have been positioned to see more or less what I did. But this idea excited me—the thought that Marta, the 'innocent' one, had been witness to the same bizarre, abnormal act (for so I considered it at that time, as something that I, for one, could never imagine being party to) was strangely stirring.

Marta, not blushing anymore, looked at me in something like alarm. I must have had an odd expression on my face. I reached out to touch her arm—then, touched her breast instead.

"Your skin. It's very hot."

She winced. Not from any roughness on my part; her 'natural delicacy,' her instinctive modesty in all things spoken, had a counterpart in physical behavior, and by taking hold of her this way, unceremoniously grabbing on, I had as much as insulted her. All our lovemaking, even at this late date (some five years after our first nights together), was conducted in the dark, in a sort of metaphoric darkness that consisted of a less than full consciousness of what we were up to.

"Yes," I repeated. "Very hot."

I kept touching her. As I recall, we sat like this for quite some time. A purpose was forming up in me, a sort of 'plan,' and I think that Marta had a feeling for it, too. Now I touched her other breast. The look on my face—a weak, self-conscious smirk—began to interest me, as if I were observing it from outside, from her point of view; what did it mean, and why was it so frozen (and so ridiculous)? I examined her large, lovely breasts as if they were things entirely unfamiliar to me. The one closer to me, the right one, was a little bigger and had its nipple in a slightly different location. I made as if to kiss it. Marta immediately drew back; she was sitting up, against some pillows wedged against the headboard of the bed, but now, by an apparently inadvertent twisting of her torso, she brought her other breast, the slightly smaller one, right against my mouth.

I stared; I examined. I had the feeling of never having seen this object before, this particular anatomical feature; it loomed large and strange in my vision, sometimes going out of focus. I lost my ordinary sense of proportion and imagined that I was very small, that I was oppressed by it; lying on my back, spread-eagled (for so I imagined myself to be), I was in danger of being engulfed, suffocated. Suddenly pulling back—to restore my ordinary perspective—I glanced up at Marta, who, with an expression almost as odd as my own, had been looking down at me. Instantly she looked away; her head flopped against the pillows, and this jogged my memory, caused my 'plan' to take even clearer shape.

Gathering up her pillows, I made a mound down the center of the mattress. She scooted away from me; she had pulled a sheet up around her body, and she watched me doubtfully, once or twice slowly shaking her head. Now, however, with a few final pats at the mound, I wordlessly bade her lie down on it. She shook her head definitely, as I had expected she would, so I grabbed her by the wrist. Just the slightest increase of pressure let her know that I was 'commanding' her, that I had assumed control. This made all the difference, somehow, and with a chastened, almost submissive expression, she let me force her onto the bed.

At first she lay on her belly. By now I had taken up position at the foot of the bed, and the sight of her softly glowing, red-brown legs, leading up to her glorious, heart-shaped behind, so yielding and yet so 'perky,' was inspiring to me, a powerful incitement to further experimentation. Marta seemed utterly unprotected in that position, an effect heightened by the way she now pressed her legs together, her upturned feet alternately covering one another. I took hold of one of her ankles. By a subtle pressure, I got her to roll over onto her side. Then, continuing the pressure, onto her back.

I hardly looked at her. Like a solemn priest who, intent on his mystic rite, blocks out all distractions, I concentrated on her uninteresting knees, her elbows, the rumpled bed sheets. Meanwhile, I was pushing her farther up the mound. Her arms were crossed protectively over her breasts. When I got her far enough up, her head tilted back, and to get a slightly more pronounced angle, just the right position, I put a rolled-up towel under her neck. There, that was perfect: I could hardly see her face, just the underside of her jaw. Her long, slender throat, outwardly bowed like that of some defenseless gazelle, suddenly arrested my attention, and I felt a powerful urge to kiss it, to nuzzle it along its length. However, I knew that this would be death to my 'purpose,' so I tore my eyes away.

"Now I'm going to . . . do what *they* did," I said in a strange, half-strangled voice. "I'm going to do what you never saw—what you *say* you never saw."

By now, I had crouched down at the end of the bed. I remained in this position—head bowed, on bended knee—for about a minute. When, with breathless trepidation, I finally lifted my eyes, I saw that Marta had remained as before (that is, flat on her back, with her arms across her chest). But just at this moment, one of her arms dropped to the side, revealing one breast. At the same instant her feet, which had been pressed together before, fell apart, making a space between her legs. I sighted up this long, sinuous crevasse. The shine of her shins, the bumps of little knees, swell of round thighs, and there, jutting out like some proud headland, that pitchy-black home-site of womanhood, which I coveted. I say 'coveted,' although my actual feeling at the moment wasn't one of desire, more like curiosity, frank wonder at the way she appeared to me. Because of my position at her feet, she had been turned into an odd territory of hills, high escarpments, and the like, and I had a childish urge to call someone over—preferably Marta herself, who would have appreciated this effect—someone with whom to share this intriguing vista. Once again I had the sense of having become very small. Not so dizzying as before, this reduction in size brought with it also a feeling of reduced responsibility, as if, being little, I could only be held to account to a corresponding extent for whatever I might do. What I wanted to do—felt *compelled* to do, almost—was to travel up, to venture homeward. Reach that pretty headland.

I began by kissing her feet. But now Marta made a sound; as I recall, it was the first from her in many minutes, part of the 'protocol' we had established requiring absolute silence on her part. It was not a word she spoke, and yet it was a sound eloquent with meanings, a moan or groan from the very heart, from the 'depths of her being.' I stopped my kissing.

Marta, though I'd stopped, went right on groaning, and now she began to shake her head (I couldn't see her face, it was tilted away). As she shook her head, her body rocked gently on the pillows, and though my first thought was that she had been taken sick, had gotten a bellyache or something, the gentle movement from side to side captivated me, and I once again applied myself to her lower legs. More groaning. Was this the sound that a woman makes as, approaching that famous 'crisis' that I had heard so much about (but which, I regret to say, had played no part previously in our lovemaking), she begins to undergo internal transformations so momentous as to be painful? I thought that it was. Reaching her knees, I pushed on, up to her thighs. It became necessary for me now to pull her a little toward me on the mound, meanwhile lifting behind both knees, forcing them into the air. This brought me face to face with my 'objective,' put me pretty much in the position I'd seen our sisters assume that day. As if to underline the parallel further, I now carefully placed Marta's feet on either of my shoulders, despite the awkwardness of this maneuver. As I did so, she stopped her groaning; in fact, stopped breathing altogether.

It was now deathly quiet in our little room. Marta's body had become hypertense. I moved forward to kiss her—to kiss her 'there.' I remember thinking how strange this all seemed; keeping my eyes open to the very last, again I entered a 'foreign world,' a bizarre topography of dark shapes, fuzzy shadows, and so forth, but just as my lips, beginning to pucker, were about to make contact, Marta jolted us off the mound.

There was a tremendous, pent-up power in those legs of hers, those muscular, tennis-playing thighs; with a desperate convulsion of all her lower body, she flung us to one side, but, due to the scissoring action of her legs, I was actually caught, pulled up onto the bed with her, made to deliver that kiss that she so much seemed to dread. She cried out: not a sound of joy, certainly, but not a sound I could identify in any other way, either. Because of my position (held between her legs, with my ears clapped shut) I heard this sound less distinctly than I might, but even so it was quite loud. I tried to disengage. I had done the great thing, had kissed her in 'that place'; why, I thought, again, why repeat what had once been accomplished? But Marta seemed to think that there was a point to it. Ignoring the twistings of my head, my polite attempts to pry her thighs apart, she put a hand on my neck, gently pulled me upward. I submitted. I had remembered, just in time, something else from that day of our sisters in the glen: the purposeful, avid look on Marcela's face, the wholehearted way that she threw herself into her task. As best I could, I duplicated this appearance, simulated that dutiful attitude. After a while, I even began to take a sort of satisfaction in my performance, in the accuracy of my 'impersonation.'

Marta, still pulling me up, gradually began to relax. Those hard, indomitable thighs, which had seemed about to snap my neck a minute ago, lessened their captivating pressure by degrees, and as if from all their previous exertions, they now began to shiver and shake. I was unexpectedly filled, at just this moment, with a tender emotion, an impulse to cradle her in my arms, to offer her comfort in her distress. I would have stopped what I was doing, taken hold of her, but at my first movement away she grabbed me roughly by the hair.

Some moments later—just as I, in the midst of my dutiful performance, was beginning to get a little bored—a small rumbling occurred inside her. This signaled an unexpected change in attitude. Now those ministrations which had seemed to please her, which she had even demanded of me, became unbearable, and she pushed me away. I sat up on the edge of the bed.

I wanted to ask what was wrong. I was vaguely disappointed, but from the way she rolled away (and a minute later, covered her head with a pillow) I guessed that she didn't want to talk. I went off to the bathroom. When I returned, she was asleep, or pretending to be, with the sheets pulled up and that pillow still hiding her face.

I bit my nails. I lit a cigarette. I would have gotten in bed with her, but her absolute stillness told me to leave, to get lost. I went out on the veranda. La Banqueta Azul, our charming little hotel, looked out onto busy, fumy streets on two sides, but on one of the other sides (the fourth faced a derelict courtyard), the view was of a quiet, disused lane, down which donkeys were more likely to be heard passing than cars. At just this moment, in fact, not even a donkey, but just an old woman, with a fringed scarf on her head, was walking by. This old woman, clad entirely in unostentatious black, caught sight of me as she went past, and, with a wry tilt of her head, she tendered me a greeting that connoted some sort of 'special recognition' (by then, both Marta and I were well-known in the neighborhood, from having stayed at La Banqueta a half-dozen times). I nodded back to her. It seemed miraculous to me, for some reason, that I had happened to step out on the veranda just as she was passing, not a second sooner or later. As the stocky, hooded figure of this woman might, therefore, contain some special significance for me, I examined her minutely, did not take my eyes away for an instant as she proceeded on her way. One of her legs was slightly swollen, and from her right hand hung an empty woven grocery bag. Her other hand, showing below the cuff of a smooth, black sleeve, was square and mannish, the hand, I felt, of a dockworker, or of a harvester of field crops.

Now it seems to me so clear, so painfully evident what her

significance was—the freight of meaning which she, all unwitting, bore in her funereal figure and garb. If only I had been aware, surely I would have called out, have arrested her symbolical progress down that alley of memory.

I went back in the hotel room. Marta was now genuinely asleep. She slept right on through till ten the next morning, when we had to dash to the train station to get her on the express for Mexico City. (We felt it was essential that she get home by five P.M., before the scheduled return of the Señora, who had herself been gone from Las Casuelas for a week or so.) In the rush at the station, I hardly got to say good-bye to her, let alone to bid her a proper, emotional farewell. Had I known that this was the last time I would see her, that she would be taken from me in a mere eighty-five days, I would have behaved differently, I'm sure, would have expressed to her all those sentiments which, never spoken, have echoed in my ears for so long, have become a sort of litany of my ill-fated, all-important childish love.

I HAD GONE off to college. I think I expected to be a good boy and to study hard and play varsity basketball by my sophomore year, if not sooner, but everything went awry; by the winter of that first year I was on academic probation, had lost my basketball-playing eligibility, and subsided into a style of 'badness' that was shocking to me, though a pleasure to invent on a day-to-day basis.

All my friends were other athletes, and they began to draw back from me in horror; they couldn't understand why I would want to do this to myself. I couldn't understand, either, though the swift evolution from good boy to bad was exhilarating, and I had the feeling that I was on to something important, the first unfoldings of my adult destiny.

Not that I was so daring. By contemporary standards my fall was laughably tame, just a cautious tipping off a low pedes-

89

tal. Had I been without pretensions to rectitude, probably no one would have noticed; as it was, only those who, before, had suffered from my high opinion of myself took note of what was going on, and if they also took some satisfaction from it, I don't really blame them.

My sister, whom I hadn't seen in two years, unexpectedly came to Berkeley for a visit. This was in the spring of 1966. She had graduated from the Colegio a year early, at the age of sixteen and a half, but rather than enroll at Stanford at the earliest opportunity had lived for a while in East L.A. Not once in that mysterious year when she lived by who knew what means, in who knew what company, had she contacted my father or me. She was much changed. I remember thinking that I had seen this girl before, that I would remember her name if only she gave me a chance; the faded blue jeans, wrinkled work shirt, wire-rimmed glasses, crudely cropped, mid-length hair (badly in need of a wash) all added up to a certain 'look' that was then often to be encountered on the streets of political Berkeley.

"Come in," I said, in the tone I would have used with any semi-stranger.

She slipped in the door. At that time, I lived in an apartment on the top floor, rear of an old, redwood-shingled house, a veritable warren of similar flats. The landlord, who had lived in the house himself as a boy, had put up a lot of dividing walls, and now twenty or thirty students lived in a space that could have comfortably housed six. Luckily I lived in the most private unit, in what had once been the attic; a splintered, creaky staircase led right up to my door, in the back of the house, and visitors came at all hours of the day or night, their arrival often announced by frightened shouts as the staircase swung out from the building, or as segments of banister came off in their hands.

There had been no shouts, though, as Sylvia came up, and I was mildly annoyed that I had been so absorbed in whatever I was doing that I hadn't heard the creaking of the stairs. I relied on these sounds as a kind of early warning system; as a result, there was now on my kitchen table a felonious quantity of seeded, crudely dried Mexican marijuana. I had been in Sinaloa only the week before, to buy as much as I could stuff in the trunk and under the seats of my father's Buick. In those days border crossings were a simple matter, a question mainly of smiling at the right moment, maybe of offering a bottle of whiskey to the right individual, and my big worry on that trip, as on several others, had been to stay awake at the wheel (it was eleven hundred miles in either direction). Turning to the kitchen table, with a sweeping gesture meant to invite examination of what could not now be hidden in any case, I suddenly realized that this was my sister, not some semi-anonymous 'prospective buyer.' I had been rather taken with her, had already formed the impression that she was 'quite a beauty' under those wire-rimmed glasses, and my tone, therefore, may have been slightly tinged with disappointment as I said:

"Why, it's you. It's Sylvia, right? My own little sister."

My little sister, now just an inch or so short of six feet, with the rangy build of a Scandinavian high jumper, looked at me rather coolly, seemingly not so sure that she shouldn't turn right around and head back out. Her silence and expression added up to an accusation, somehow, and I racked my brain to think of some dereliction of brotherly duty of which I'd recently been guilty, something to explain this probing, baleful examination that went on for a good thirty seconds. Finally she sat. Her long, supple wrists extended two or three inches below the cuffs of her shirt, and I couldn't help noticing that she wasn't wearing a brassiere—these were the days when that custom was just being adopted, when middle-class girls were first starting to liberate their chests.

"I was in the neighborhood. I thought I'd drop by."

"Good. I'm glad you did. Here, have a seat. I mean . . ."

—and I cleared away some of the pot from the tabletop.

Following some further exchange of pleasantries, we subsided into an unpleasant silence. I was still unnerved by that look she'd given me, and though she'd now begun to smile vaguely, as if to signal her willingness to have a 'good visit,' somehow I believed more in that first moment, when I had actually not recognized my own flesh and blood, and when she had seemed the bearer of some dreadful news relating to my essential character. I was also embarrassed to have been caught out like this; though with everyone else I was nonchalant, even proud, to be taken for a drug dealer, an 'outlaw,' one who lived by his wits and in daring contravention of the ordinary rules, with my sister I became aware of a new significance, a different meaning to the whole arrangement.

"I like your hair."

"Oh." I laughed. "Needs cutting, doesn't it?"

"No, it looks good. Sort of romantic. Byronic."

"And just where," I said, to change the subject, "have you been? I haven't heard from you in two years."

"I've been around. Living in L.A. With some friends from school. We rented a house. It was right under the freeway, in Belvedere Park."

"Let's see: you take the Santa Monica. Then the Santa Ana, then—"

"The Pomona."

"Right. Make that twenty-five, maybe thirty-five minutes from his house. No more."

"No more."

"Yet I keep getting complaints that he doesn't hear from you. He's worried. He even wrote letters to Mexico, to your crazy school. They said—"

"They wouldn't know, and they wouldn't tell him if they did know. But let's not talk about him. He's a dead subject, as far as I'm concerned. I won't be seeing him ever again. I'm trying to forget about him . . . forget all of it."

What was this 'all of it'? Presumably, her monstrous, unspeakable childhood; those years of grinding deprivation, threadbare outfits and thin potato gruel. I myself had not been averse to seeking in the unusual arrangements of our childhood grounds for resentment, for imagining myself deprived or otherwise interestingly warped; other than the slow, embarrassing decline of our mother—which, undoubtedly, had a strong influence on both of us—there had been considerable, but not overwhelming, material abundance, consistent parental concern (from our father, mainly), interesting trips to Mexico, fun summer camps, piano lessons, etc. By any reasonable standard, we had never suffered or lacked for anything. As to the more complex, possibly more pertinent question of psychological influence, I couldn't help remembering the kick my father had always seemed to get out of her (and she out of him); there had never been anything like favoritism shown to me (because I was the boy), and as I may have mentioned, she had always seemed less interested in our mother, less concerned for her welfare than I was.

I'm not going to say that she wasn't more seriously—I almost wrote, 'more profoundly'—affected by his being crooked, by the subtle skewing of our family's moral atmosphere, than I. Maybe she took such a thing more to heart, although, from my current perspective, it seems that I've spent my entire adult life doing nothing but work out this element in my questionable background. I may be wrong, but I think at this point she was actually not so well informed about him; it was the famous 'dossier' that Marcela had been compiling, a sturdily anticapitalist account of his investments in Mexico (along with the Señora, who was the main object of her daughter's venomous investigations), that was her main source of information, and I think she had decided that she hated him not because he was a crook, but because he had actually once dared to own property. (Only in the next couple of years—when she was blossoming as a student radical, to end up stepping far beyond the bounds of legality herself—did she learn who her father really was, I would say.)

"I was wondering . . ." she began; but then shook her head.

"Yes?"

She took her time, seeming to summon her courage, and finally said with a show of only now being candid, "I have to confess something—well, it's about this," and she nodded at the triple-beam balance sitting on my kitchen table. Stacked behind it were three bricked kilos wrapped in white plastic, one of them cracked wide open, to reveal the low-grade pot inside.

"I have to say that . . . well, I know all about you. What you've been doing. Marta must be telling Marcela, who tells me. I know about your trips down there, and all that."

"So? I'm not hiding anything. As you can see."

Still, I was taken aback. Marta—whom I generally managed to see whenever I went south—had been sworn to darkest secrecy, and I really wouldn't have thought, until that minute, that anyone could have gotten anything out of her.

"I know where you go. How much it costs down there . . . and then up here. The profits that you've been making. I even know which car you drive. It's the old man's yellow convertible, right?"

"So? What's this got to do with anything?"

"Nothing. I'm just telling you. I guess . . . that you should be more careful. That's all. That's all I wanted to say."

There was more; I could tell. I waited for her to continue, but instead she started talking about Marcela, about the political 'struggles' she was currently involved in. I was immediately bored to the point of sleepiness; political discussion, political earnestness, has always had this effect on me, and I perked up only when she mentioned the recent falling-out between Marcela and her mother, a development of the last year, of which I'd already heard something from Marta.

It had all begun, she said, when the Señora suddenly declared that Marcela—but not Marta—would be going to Switzerland the next year, to continue her studies at an institute run by the nuns who had once run the Colegio. Marcela of course had refused; she had already applied to universities in the States, been accepted, and was leaning toward the University of Texas, where she could study all the science she wanted and still be within hailing distance of Mexico. But the Señora insisted; Marcela, on the very day when she was supposed to board a plane for Europe, disappeared (to come live with Sylvia in L.A., I gathered). To this date, she had had no further contact with her mother.

The real reason for their falling-out, however, was something else, Sylvia now insisted; beginning two years before, a series of articles had appeared in ¡Cria!, a Mexican newsmagazine of the left, detailing various land-development schemes involving the Señora. That she should play a big part in the development for tourism of lands on the Caribbean coast, lands previously owned by the indigenous Indians, was a surprise to no one; nor was it surprising that officials high up in the government of López Mateos, even López himself (as some believed), were aiding the Señora by condemning vast tracts and summarily relocating the Indians to barren wastelands in the deserts of Chihuahua state. What was surprising to everyone, and had made the Señora almost a figure of fun in certain circles, was the incredible detail of the conversations she was reported to have had with various cabinet secretaries, bank directors, and so forth. The Señora, who was known for a certain intensity of manner, was so exactly captured in these vignettes that it was widely believed they could have been written only by someone present at the actual meetings. Since the Señora couldn't reasonably be suspected of testifying against herself, suspicion had fallen on this or that official (actually, on three of them acting together). Some observers believed that, in this way, the government was trying to 'cast out' the troublesome and ambitious Señora just as López Mateos, who had been president since '58, was about to yield the reins of power to Díaz Ordáz.

Here was the funny part (Sylvia added); the Señora, who kept good records of all her important meetings, somehow had got it in her head that Marcela had looked at her notebooks, which were stored in a locked case in her room at Las Casuelas. But in the notebooks, there was nothing like a straightforward or transcriptional record, just weird markings in a hieroglyphic script that the Señora had made up herself. She suspected that Marcela had cracked her 'code,' and then, for ignoble personal reasons, had turned around and sold her findings to the writer from *¡Cria!* The Señora was quite aware of her daughter's fierce dislike of her on ideological grounds, but she insisted that their disagreement had to do mainly with 'other things.' Unlike Marta, who was respectful and clearly the favorite these days, Marcela was an ungrateful and unnatural child who would 'stop at nothing' to bring about her mother's downfall.

"So," I mused, "did she? Did she actually do it?"

"Do what? Look at those notebooks?"

"Yes. Stab her mother in the back."

"That's not it at all. That's not the important issue here. The important thing is: can someone get away with a thing like this, outright steal Indian lands, take these people who have lived there for thousands of years, who love their land, consider it holy, and condemn them to death in a dusty desert where they'll all get tuberculosis? That's what this is about."

I nodded, patronizingly perhaps, and said, "Yes, but did she do it? Did she really?"

"I don't know."

I think Sylvia really didn't know; though she was Marcela's closest friend, she knew little about the actual dynamics of Marcela's relationship with her mother, about that curious attachment which has ended up being so important—and so disastrous—to us all. Probably she thought that filial loyalty would, in the end, have prevented Marcela from doing what her outraged sense of justice demanded, and she may even have been a little disappointed in her on this account.

Anyway, assuming that Marcela did, for whatever reason, steal her mother's notebooks; assuming, further, that she then sold them to some enemy of the Señora, someone who wanted to embarrass her and her colleagues, we are still, I think, short of proving that harm has really been done, that the Señora actually regrets this development. If she could have determined, a few steps back, what would happen, she might not have kept any records at all; but since she did, and since they somehow came to light, is it necessarily true that she has been dealt a grievous blow? Assume that at this parlous juncture—the time when administrations change is always difficult, always dangerous in Mexico—it behooves her to appear less formidable than she is in fact. Maybe her purposes are better served by seeming to be assailed from the left (and in the next couple of years, as more details from the 'dossier' surface, she will continue to be assailed, to seem to come dangerously under attack). In that case, has Marcela's betrayal really been a stab in the back? Or is it not, in fact, something like the opposite, a helpful gesture, almost a useful boost?

My sister and I—blissfully unaware of any of these possibilities—soon dropped the subject of our Mexican friends.

"I need money," she said straightforwardly, getting on to the real reason for her visit. "Lots of it. I need—just for starters—$14,500. In cash."

I nodded; indeed, that was a lot of money. I was a big dealer, though, and talk of this kind didn't faze me. At any rate, I hoped my sister had gathered this much about me, that she was suitably impressed. I answered—rather ingenuously, it now occurs to me—"How're you going to get it then? Going to rob a bank, maybe?"

She quickly enumerated the various categories of expense she anticipated for the coming fiscal year. Her little group had to pay rent on several houses, and then there were transportation costs, food, legal expenses, and so on. What seemed most remarkable to me was her plan to pay for college herself: the idea of taking anything from Gerson was so repugnant to her that she was undertaking to come up with the necessary $4,000 on her own.

"You must be kidding," I exclaimed, dismissing such an idea out of hand. "He *expects* to have to pay for things like that. He'll be pissed if he doesn't get to."

"Well," she said, "he'll just have to be pissed then, won't he? I'd rather cut my own throat than take another penny from him. I told you, I'm through with him. He doesn't exist for me anymore."

I smiled at that; I wondered how long she'd be able to maintain this stance, and I also wondered where she thought she could come up with such an amount of money. She explained at this point the principal project of her little group: they were going to be 'importing' into the States a number of political fugitives, people who, she said, were being 'mercilessly hounded' by their own governments. (I took it she referred to some young Mexicans, probably friends of Marcela's, who, in the way of aspiring revolutionaries everywhere, imagined that the authorities had taken trepidatious notice of them.) Sylvia's organization would escort them across the border, house them, feed them, and furnish them with new paper. This project alone was going to cost in the neighborhood of twenty or thirty grand.

"And that's why," she concluded, with a momentary drop of her eyes—the only sign of a failure of self-possession during this entire interview—"I've come to you. Why I have to put the finger on you. I have to come up with a lot of the money, you see. Everybody has a specific responsibility, with a specific project, and this is mine. I can't promise I'll ever pay you back, either. I'll try, of course, but things don't look so good for the next few years. Maybe when I get out of school, when I go to medical school, I'll be able to come up with some federal loans. Anyhow—I'll try."

That was considerate of her—to try, to say that she would

try. I remember that I had just finished rolling a big number, and now I lit it casually, took a healthy, luxuriating puff. I offered her some, but she declined. Some of that look of cool, baleful estimation of me, of disapproval too fundamental to put into words, had returned to her features, and it was this, I think, that now confirmed me in my intention. If she had asked, humbly, for a loan of a few hundred dollars, something to tide her over the summer; or if she had asked for help with her tuition (I thought her idea of shunning our father ridiculous, but I was willing to grant her this eccentricity, this bit of callow rebellion), I might have decided otherwise, but there was something so superior in her manner that I relished the idea of saying no.

"Say that I did make you this loan," I began, wanting to string her along. "What's my guarantee that you'd use it as you say, to get these fugitives over the border? How do I know you won't turn around and blow it on a Hawaiian vacation, for instance?"

She was puzzled by this tack; how could anyone doubt her sincerity, the intentions of a sworn revolutionary? Since I was stupid enough to say such a thing, she reiterated the intentions of her group, how they planned to bring various 'illegals' into the U.S., and now she actually mentioned a name—Alfredo Nuñez.

I immediately exclaimed: "But that Nuñez—he's a killer! He's the one who assassinated the mayor of Nuevo Grandosa, isn't he? They've been hunting him all over Mexico. You're not helping people like that, are you?"

I could see that she was a bit abashed, afraid that she had gone perhaps too far. She wasn't supposed to mention names, of course, and in years to come never would, but having let the cat out of the bag, she couldn't resist the opportunity to correct my thinking.

"Nuñez is . . . never mind all that you've heard. Never mind what they show you on their grisly TV shows, in their sordid magazine pieces composed in the bedrooms of PRI fat-cats. The truth is completely different. Whether or not some-one who they claim is the mayor of Nuevo Grandosa was assassinated, Nuñez is absolutely innocent, was two thousand miles away—as I happen to know personally—at the time of this so-called 'revolutionary outrage.' Besides, we owe him many favors. He's been like a father to certain of us. A great help in many ways."

I let this pass; I wasn't all that interested in Nuñez, or in her relationship to him; I preferred to return to the subject of her loan. Already anticipating how bitterly disappointed she would be, how upset by my cruel, casual crushing of her socially useful hopes, I said,

"But really. About this money. The truth is, I just don't have it. I did have money a while ago, but a friend of mine, someone I work with down in Mexico, got in some trouble. It cost me a bundle to get him out. I'm sorry, but that's the way it is. Otherwise I'd probably help."

She was taken aback. I could see her trying to puzzle this out, figure out what this might mean. She probably knew I was lying. As I recall, I made my confession with a facetiously straight face, so that my real feelings—that I would never, not in a million years, give her a damned penny—would be clear. Looking me straight in the eye she said:

"I didn't hear about any friends. I thought you always worked alone down there. If you've had trouble of that kind, I'm sorry. That's too bad. But really—even so, you're going to have to come up with this money. Let's just say that if you don't, you'll get in even more trouble of that kind. You, your-self, will take a fall. Understand me?"

I'm not sure that I did. For a moment I must have stared at her peaceably, exhaling clouds of marijuana smoke.

"Unless we get what we ask," she repeated, "we'll be making some phone calls. We'll ruin your little 'operation' here. It's simple enough to do: all you have to do is call the police. I don't want you to think, just because I'm your sister, that I won't do what I say. These plans are more important than you are."

"Oh, are they? Are they really more important?"

"Yes."

She was looking at me strangely—almost in a sort of alarm. I had leaned far back in my chair, and now, placing my hands against the edge of the table, I pushed it forward, effectively pinning her in her seat. As my own chair clattered to the floor, I rose up above her; I must have been looking at her so intently, so fearsomely, that she was afraid to take her eyes away.

"Get . . . up," I said. "Get up. And then get out of that chair. And—get out of my house."

But she was already getting up. With a haste that it pleased me to witness, she backed away, hurried to the door. Then, as I made as if to lunge at her, she turned and fled down the back stairs of my apartment.

I WISH I COULD report that this was the last I heard of the matter, that my sister never again tried to shake me down, that I magnanimously forgave her; or even that my response to this and other attempts was so frighteningly firm that they gave up, and Sylvia and her friends had to make it in the cold fiscal world without my help. The truth, though, is that I caved in; a few more communications from my sister, which struck a more ingratiating note, plus some minor physical harassment—too embarrassing to describe, since I took it so seriously—and one day I was handing her a manila envelope containing $7,000 in cash.

"I won't count it," she said. "At least, not now."

"That's good of you. Very trusting."

"But . . . when can we expect the rest?"

I glared at her. I was getting a lot of practice staring

balefully; she had managed to cast me in the role of the spluttering, helpless father (or older brother) who disapproves categorically, but finds himself so far over the barrel that all he can do is fume, give out with the occasional dirty look.

"It's like I said. This is it. There is no more. You've extorted $7,000 from your own brother. You'll have to be satisfied with that. I'm not giving you any more. I'm through."

She shook her head slowly, sighing; when would I learn, when would I get it through my thick skull?

"All right. Okay for now." She took the envelope, jammed it in her ragged woven bag. "I'll tell them . . . something. I'll make up some kind of story. You'll be safe for a while. But really, you're going to have to get with the program. You're going to have to accept this as part of your operation, so to speak."

We were sitting in the 'Cab' at that moment—the Café Caribbean, a relentlessly dingy coffeehouse on the south side of the Berkeley campus. All around us were the people, or rather, the types, that were destined to populate the countercultural dramas of the coming years. There were aging bohemians who had pounded bongos, smoked tea, and grooved to bad poetry all through the 'fifties, to end up now with surprisingly slack, dull faces; pretty college girls; college boys not so different from myself, in dark glasses; old black hipsters, outlandishly dressed, plunking African thumb pianos. Some avant-garde types, wearing bell-bottomed trousers and beads, looked to be making minor drug transactions; I knew a couple of them, and I didn't wave. Then, sitting unpleasantly close to our table, two U.C. assistant professors were loudly, flamboyantly arguing a point in Marcusian socio-aesthetics, their leather-patched elbows, owlish spectacles, and bushed-out hair sufficient to identify them as members of the faculty of Arts and Letters. I actually knew one of them by name, if not personally: he had flunked me in 'Introduction to the Novel' only a few months before (returning my only paper, a section from the unpunctu-

ated novel I'd been writing since age fourteen, with the terse
notation, "Unacceptable—and truly bad").

I fixed this professor type with a look of perfect disdain.
When, in the course of his extroverted disputations, he happened to glance my way, he was startled (I could tell) by my
look of causeless animosity, and a moment later, dropping his
argument in mid-sentence, he exited the Cab.

I had become aware, over the last year or so, of a power I
was coming to possess, an ability to work my will sometimes
simply by looking a certain way. The face that had been, in my
boyhood, girlishly pretty and sweet, had metamorphosed in the
direction of ultra-manly threatfulness, had become a mug it
would have pleased a Turkish assassin to wear. My long, 'wolf-
ish' jaw, and my slablike cheeks, with their deep vertical inden-
tations, required shaving morning and night (and even so,
always had an unearthly, bluish tint). My prominent, deeply
cleft chin, an inheritance from my father, had a strange effect on
certain people (mostly older women), causing them to stare, to
smile nervously, and sometimes to approach me, to confess that
a favorite uncle had had one "just like that." Notwithstanding
the attractiveness—or remarkable ugliness—of this feature, the
rest of my face tended to arrange itself in expressions of the most
unpleasant, off-putting kind. I was only twenty, and I had a
horror of being overlooked; that someone might think I was a
patsy, a pushover (which I surely was) disturbed me badly, and I
expended much energy just occupying space in a frightening
way, trying to give off emanations of murderous intent.

In this, I suppose, I was assisted by my great size. I had
grown to be even taller than my father—who, at six-foot-six,
was virtually a giant, a monster for a Jew of his generation.
Ever since giving up basketball, too, I had put on a lot of
weight; I wore it well, even if it was all flab, and for the first
time in my life felt that my physical displacement roughly
corresponded to my sense of my own importance.

My sister, with a prolonged glance at someone at a nearby
table, gathered up her bag and got ready to leave.

"Someone you know?" I wondered, archly. "A member of a rival sect? Or is it one of your own comrades, sent to see that everything goes according to schedule?"

The man she had been looking at—middle-aged, thin of face, gray of head—suddenly hauled himself out of his chair and limped to the bathroom. He was wearing one of those orthopedic shoes, on his left foot I believe, the sole and heel a good four inches thick.

"I don't know who he is," Sylvia claimed. "He just keeps showing up."

Putting on an expression of false concern, I said, "You mean, he seems to be following you? Shadowing your every step?"

"Yes. Sort of."

"But . . . that's unforgivable. I won't allow it. You want I should break his other leg, sort of even him up?"

She looked at me in disgust. But then, she surprised me by saying, "I wouldn't mind it, really. He's starting to get on my nerves. He spooks me."

"Well, we can't have that, can we. Big brother will take care of everything."

At that moment, the fellow came back from the bathroom (or wherever he had gone). As he hobbled to his lonely table, on which sat a tiny espresso cup and a pack of Pall Malls, I had my first look at him full-face. I immediately ruled out having a 'word' with him: not that I had been serious about protecting my sister's honor, but the harrowing sadness of his face, and in particular of his melting brown eyes, made me feel like a fool for even contemplating such a thing. His long, bony nose had been broken at the bridge, giving it a swerve such as I had never seen on a nose before; and now that I was staring at him frankly, I noticed a series of horrid scars, all on the left side of his face, the worst being from a cut going through both his upper and lower lips.

"Who," I whispered to my sister, "*is* that guy? And what in God's name happened to him?"

It was the essence of his sadness—I understood immediately—that his face had been ruined, that what had once
been a refined, probably rather beautiful visage had been put
through the meat grinder, and now he must wear his misfortune forever. The nose that took a most ludicrous leftward
swerve had once been classically imposing, and the ruined
mouth, with its perpetual suggestion of a sneer on one side, had
once been movie-star unusual (wide, downwardly curving,
intriguingly 'sensual'). I suddenly realized that the man,
though he appeared to be gazing blankly off into space, was
acutely aware of my scrutiny of him. I was not exactly powerless to look away, but at the same time, I somehow felt obliged
to go on staring, to survey his facial wreckage until I 'comprehended' it.

"Don't stare," Sylvia advised me. She was sitting with her
back to him. "He feels bad enough as it is, you know."

"How do you know how he feels?"

On this note she once again gathered up her bag—containing my seven thousand—and headed for the door. The
stranger glanced up as she passed. A few seconds later, with a
kind of crippled grace, he followed her out.

I soon forgot all about this incident. In my perambula-
tions about the town of Berkeley, I never saw the man again,
and my sister either didn't mention him, or she spoke of him
dismissively, as of a problem already solved. That September
she enrolled at Stanford; though required by the university to
live on campus, in a supervised freshmen's dormitory, she
continued to spend a lot of time in Berkeley, and it came as an
unwelcome surprise when, one night, she brought me along to
a party being thrown by some of her 'friends.'

I suppose the occasion was the safe arrival of Alfredo
Nuñez in California, and I was duly introduced to the great

man. As far as I know, I had never expressed any desire to be introduced to him, or to any of the others, and I remember making a special effort to act displeased, to indicate to all present how utterly beneath interest they (and the whole occasion) were. Nuñez was then in his early fifties, a potbellied little fellow with the mien of an out-of-work accountant. According to everything I had heard or read, he had most definitely killed the mayor of Nuevo Grandosa, and it bothered me that my sister should be so blinded by ideology or misplaced loyalty as to deny this incontrovertible fact. (About the guilt or innocence of Nuñez, or the willingness of government-connected organs of information in Mexico to generate the most astounding fabrications, I no longer feel quite so qualified to judge—but never mind.) As soon as my sister came into the room, Nuñez, who had been perched timidly on the forward edge of his chair, jumped up to embrace her. There was something excessive, I felt, about the way he clung to her thereafter, sometimes merely beaming at her, like a doting father, at other times, despite the presence of other people, giving in to an urge to nuzzle, to paw her in a not quite fatherly way.

"Comrades," my sister said at one point in the evening, in Spanish, "we who consider ourselves fortunate, deeply honored, to have you with us tonight, ask only that you relax as you would in your own homes. The potent struggle that you have launched—that we, your North American allies, desire only to serve in some small capacity or other—will surely succeed as long as there are" etc. etc.

Looking around the room—not so much to see who was there, as in hopes of encountering some other roving eye, some kindred spirit with whom to share this opportunity for ironic distancing—I was surprised, truly startled, to see the man from the café, the one with the ruined face. He was standing by himself in a distant corner, and at first, since I really couldn't make sense of his being there, I tried to convince myself that he was someone else. The room was by now full of young people, members of Sylvia's 'collective' as well as assorted others (Pan-therish blacks, mannish-looking females, anti-Vietnam war-riors, working-class heroes, etc.), and the stranger, by his age and his elegant attire, stood out from the rest. He was wearing an old-fashioned, beautifully tailored English shooting jacket, of a large brown-and-white houndstooth check, with a silk scarf at the throat; what really distinguished him, though, surrounded him almost with a visible aura, was his posture of profound suffering, that unfathomable sadness I had noticed before.

Elbowing the couple nearest me, I started toward his corner. I had the vague intention of asking, in my capacity as older brother, what in the world he thought he was up to, following my sister around, but my real purpose (not con-sciously understood) was just to get closer, to try to fathom, by the simple device of standing within it, that aura of deep unhappiness which for some reason intrigued me. However, it was at this moment that Sylvia introduced me to Nuñez. The apologetic little Mexican, with the limpest handshake I had ever felt, immediately began to tell me about a recent car trip he'd taken, a jolting ride over dirt roads through the deserts of northern Mexico. It seemed that his *riñónes* had been affected, and he was hoping—if Sylvia could only arrange it, as she had arranged so much else so beautifully—to get prompt medical attention, as there was a history of kidney trouble in his family.

"If only you would take your kidneys," I replied, "and sauté them with onions in a mild sauce of *chiles poblanos* and ground coriander, you would bring relief to those thousands of friends of the late mayor, who curse you for your cowardice and stupidity."

Blinking his eyes rapidly—whether from the effort of understanding English, or in surprise at my tone, I couldn't tell—he turned sharply toward my sister, as if to hear a transla-tion. She mumbled something, and a moment later, grabbing me by the sleeve, he laughed companionably.

"No, no," he reassured me. "I am *not* indestructible. I am *not* some ghost, some mere force, something that appears wherever it wants, whenever it wants. No, my friend, I am only what I seem: a man of flesh and blood. One subject to the ills and restrictions of that condition, of course."

I nodded, but as I turned to go, for some reason he tightened his grip on my arm. Out of the corner of my eye I saw the stranger—who, I knew, had been watching us surreptitiously—ease into the crowd and begin to make his way toward the door. In sudden anger at Nuñez, who was keeping me from my object, I tore his hand away roughly. Sylvia blanched, and I actually thought for a moment that she would burst into tears; her feelings for Nuñez were so highly developed—feelings of a sincere respect, of a misplaced daughterly devotion—that my show of bad manners took on the proportions of a hideous crime, and only quick thinking saved me.

"Pardon," I explained hurriedly, "I'm so sorry. You see . . . I have a wound. A chronic affliction. When I was little, we were in a bad car wreck—both my sister and I—and the bone in my upper arm was shattered. It's all metal now. Or almost all. When someone touches me—right here, in this certain spot—an instinct takes over. I snarl. I lash out like an old, arthritic dog."

Nuñez had to wait for Sylvia to translate this, too; as she was describing the steel pin in my shoulder (and imagining the pleasure of inserting one through my head), I felt a creepy twitch in my *other* arm, the one he hadn't touched. But here was the stranger: he had slid up silently, to position himself uncommonly close, unnervingly close to me. I remember thinking that his mangled nose, which was the first thing I saw, had almost been in contact with my shirt sleeve; my first thought was that he had been sniffing, that he wanted to identify me, not just by sight, but by this more conclusive means.

"Well, well. Look who's here. The Lurking Presence," I said nervously.

I immediately regretted these words; shrinking back, with a controlled, balletic movement (which fixed forever in my mind the idea that he was a 'sensitive plant,' a delicate quantity not to be subjected to the full force of my personality), he averted his face and, with a pathetic hobble, prepared to go off. I stuck out my clumsy paw and groped for his, which seemed to take him by surprise.

"Wait. Wait, I have to talk to you. I've been wanting to ever since I saw you in the café. You remember; I was sitting there with Sylvia, and when she went out you did, too. I'm her brother. I'm Louis, Louis Sanders."

He nodded morosely. "I know very well who you are."

Sylvia had gone off with Nuñez by now. The stranger cast about for her, seemed upset to have lost sight of her, if only for a moment.

"You know," I said not unkindly, "you really should stop bothering her. It's not polite."

"I beg your pardon. 'Bother' her? Am I 'bothering' her? I'm not aware of bothering anyone. If you think my attentions are a bother to her, then I suggest that you speak to her. Immediately."

"All right, I will."

Soon Sylvia reappeared. She must have gone to the kitchen, because she was hauling a jug of cheap wine, plus a platter of crackers, and Nuñez, rather in the manner of a blind man, was trailing behind her, his arm stuck out and his hand attached to the back of her neck. As she deposited the bottle on a card table, this hand slid down her back, to linger fondly—an instant too long—on the curve of her firm, youthfully pert behind.

"Some people," the stranger hissed through clenched teeth, "have no right to exist. Have you ever noticed? Certain slime deserves only to be effaced, fully eradicated. I wonder that no one has done the world this service in the case of our friend over there."

"Oh," I said, as he nodded toward Nuñez so that there could be no mistaking the object of his feelings, "I don't think he's that bad. He's just her 'friend.' She admires his integrity, while he appreciates her . . . intelligence. Besides, in a couple of weeks he'll be gone. Then you can have her all to yourself again."

Just now, Sylvia caught sight of us. She dropped her eyes immediately; I think it was seeing us together, me speaking to this curious character who, only weeks before, she had half wanted to be saved from, that caused her embarrassment. The stranger at that moment stood up quite tall, came to attention like a soldier about to march into battle. With a summoning of inner resources which I found remarkable, he proceeded to stare daggers at her across the room, and Sylvia, as if physically affected by this, slowly turned her back to us.

But an instant later—with a sudden droop of her rectilinear shoulders—she approached. The stranger watched her every step of the way, scarcely disguising his feeling of triumph (to have won her to us, separated her from the 'enemy'). Now she stood before us in a posture that can be described only as humble, beseechingly contrite. I hardly recognized her, and I must say it annoyed me a little to see her like this, used as I was, in our recent dealings, to an attitude of cool hauteur, of scarcely disguised disdain.

"Can I get you . . . a cracker? A glass of wine, or something?"

"Yes," the stranger sneered, after an accusatory pause. "You might very well have brought me a cracker. But I'm not hungry now."

Another pause. Eyes to the floor (hers, and finally mine as well). "I assume you've been introduced? This is my brother, Louis."

The stranger smiled bleakly. "There could be no doubt whose brother he is. The resemblance to a certain individual of my lamented acquaintance is remarkable. I must assume that the inheritance extends into the moral sphere, as well."

I was taken aback. Looking curiously at my sister, I found her eyes still glued to her shoes, and she had begun to rub her right wrist in a peculiar way, almost as if trying to strangle it.

"So . . . you know my father? How interesting. Are you an old golf partner of his? A law client, something like that?"

"Let's just say—I remember him very well. From a long, long time ago."

Clearly, this terse declaration had a lot of meaning for both of them. Sylvia bowed her head further, almost bringing it onto her chest, while the stranger's mouth, the side with all the scars, began to tremble. Every second or so he seemed to be grinning at me, then his lips would relax, once again forming themselves into a sort of sad leer.

"You'll have to tell me more," I persisted. "How long ago? And in what connection, exactly?"

"In a"—prolonged twitch—"very painful, very damaging connection. But perhaps you could get him to tell you about it. Why don't you ask him sometime? Ask him: whatever became of . . . Franklin Howard?"

I stared at him for a long moment. "That's you? You're Franklin Howard?"

He nodded. "You've heard of me, then?"

"Why, of course. My mother spoke of you often."

"Ah," he said, with icy dryness. "How gratifying."

I CHATTED WITH 'Franklin Howard' for a few more minutes—trying to decide if he could really be who he said he was—and then, making polite excuses, caught a ride back to Berkeley.

My mother had mentioned a Franklin Howard a long time before, in connection with her brief film career, but I was fairly sure that this couldn't be he, that the man she had known by that name was already long dead. While under contract to Republic Studios in 1937 and '38, she appeared in sixteen episodes of a Bud Austin Western serial, and Franklin Howard, at that time also employed by Republic, wrote most of the episodes and also directed them. From what I had gathered, they became close friends, and she ever after spoke of 'Mr. Howard' with a certain wistful respect, as one does of someone too fine, too pure for this sordid, cruelly deflating world.

Republic in those years was a seedy, second-rate operation, not quite as low as some others (Chesterfield, Monogram,
Bluebird Studios, etc.), but deserving in most respects of its
popular cognomen of 'Repulsive Productions.' A stable of offhanded, gleefully cynical hacks (most notable among them:
Nathanael West) wrote terrible scripts at a phenomenal rate,
and every week saw the release of two, sometimes more, pieces
of raw filmic garbage, shorts and serial episodes but also full-
length 'features' on sensational topics. Howard, who had origi-
nally been a New York stage actor, had a hand (I later learned)
in a hefty chunk of Republic's entire screen production for the
period 1931–44. His credits take up four inches of a two-inch-
wide column in the *Dictionary of Film Biography* (Arbor House,
1973), which also flatly states that he died in Phoenix, Arizona,
in 1957.

I didn't go and look him up immediately after meeting
him at Sylvia's party, but instead made a mental note to ask my
father about him (as 'Howard' himself had suggested). I had
always been curious about those early days, anyhow, about the
precise mechanics of my mother's rise in the film biz; from an
unknown with no theatrical training and nothing to recom-
mend her other than her face, she became in quick order a
featured player at Republic, RKO, Fox, Warner Bros., and
finally RKO one last time (for only a few weeks, however).
Always she worked on relatively good terms (except at Republic, where she claimed to have been paid $55 a week), and
always she moved on well before the term of her contract was
up, to some yet more attractive situation.

My intuition was that my father had helped her 'get
along.' Her first appearance in a film produced by a major
(RKO's *Diamond Eyes,* with Richard Dix and Ann Shirley) was
roughly coincident with the beginning of their affair, and the
high point of her career (in my opinion), her charming portrayal
of the love-struck pathologist in *Two Weeks to Live,* looks like a
plum dangled in front of her (or casually, backhandedly

dumped in her lap) on the occasion of her agreeing to marry
him. Certainly Gerson would have done whatever he could for
her; he had no reason not to want to further her career (up to a
point), and yet he was so secretive, so subtle and guarded in his
professional behavior, that I doubt that ever a word was spoken
between them on the subject. And my mother would have
understood this, I think, would have instantly grasped the
necessity of making no crude, direct requests for help. In these
years of relative sobriety, she herself—if I'm not entirely mistaken about her—was rather sensitive, uncommonly 'awake' to
the moods and peculiarities of others; nor was she yet so disillu-
sioned as to think that she wasn't forging ahead largely under
her own power.

But to return to Mr. Howard (who would have much to
say about all of this). Following the night of the party, I returned to my usual haunts and activities, but then in January
(of 1967), not having seen my sister in about two months, I
received a note from her. It requested me to join her and "F.H."
for dinner, a few days hence, at an address on the Stanford
campus, the meal to be followed by a showing of films at an
auditorium nearby. I would have made unexcited-sounding
excuses, but this note of hers—and how absurd, to be mailing
notes to her own brother, when he lived only forty miles
away—was scribbled on the back of a dittoed announcement
that intrigued me. Franklin Howard ("actor, scenarist, director,
secretary of the Bord Film Archive in Hemet, Cal.") was pre-
senting, it said, a program of forgotten films of the 'thirties and
'forties (mostly comedies of the genus *Screwball*, with heavy
reliance on the work of Sturges and Hawks). Two films—not
'movies,' of course—were going to be shown each Tuesday
throughout the semester, after which Mr. Howard would make
brief critical or film-historical comments.

This was the first confirmation I had had—that I was ever
to have—that someone other than Howard himself believed he
was who he said he was. Presumably someone in the Depart-

ment of Comparative Literature, the sponsoring body of the program, had bothered to check him out, nor were his lectures (I went to two or three in the next few months) so inept that one had reason to doubt him. Clearly he had seen thousands of old movies, and he spoke of filmland and of the 'great personalities' of the old days with an intensity that, in itself, tended to convince. Anyway, having transported myself to Palo Alto on the appointed evening, I found my sister, as if cast in a bad old movie of her own, diligently setting the table in a leafy cottage on the Stanford grounds. She was wearing an apron, it astonished me to see, and as I came up the flagstoned, periwinkle-bordered walk, I caught a glimpse of Howard through an opened window, contentedly smoking a pipe as he mused in a leather-covered armchair.

He seemed to be going through some notes; but as soon as I tapped at the kitchen door (the cottage was shaped like an L, with the kitchen catty-cornered to the den), he jumped up, simultaneously emitting a sort of bellow of welcome, and hurried to the front door. Like an old comrade greeting a long-lost chum, he opened his arms to me. I feel sure I would have had to embrace him, except that some pages of his notes, which he had brought to the door, scattered down just then.

"You don't know how happy this makes me," he said, as I knelt before him, picking them up. "We're so gratified that you could come see us. Never mind"—as I picked up the last, hen-scratched sheet—"I know the whole damned thing by heart, anyhow."

His talk was all of the absurdity of his position, the stupidity of the Stanford students he had met so far; if he had known with what overwhelming, benumbing consideration he, as a visiting professor, was going to be treated, he would have long ago declared himself an 'authority' and sought such appointments at colleges all over the country.

"But she's very happy here," he assured me, "very content. You should ask her yourself. Go on . . . or perhaps, wait till dinner. She's so busy cooking right now. But she's settled down to work—I mean, her schoolwork—with a vengeance. She's an intelligent girl, really." (He sounded surprised—I disliked him for this.) "This summer, if all goes well, we'll be traveling in Europe. Stanford has a campus in Grenoble, and she'll be taking twelve units of French. I'm to give some 'seminars' there, it appears."

I drank sherry with him, and about half an hour later dinner was announced. My sister, as I've said, was wearing an apron, but there the resemblance to June Allyson ended. I had never seen her looking so poorly, and only my customary reserve in her presence (and hers in mine) kept me from asking outright what was wrong. She had lost about fifteen pounds, I guessed, and a sort of dimness had come to infuse her lovely features, giving them an out-of-focus quality that weirdly added to her attractiveness. Howard, smoking nonstop (first the pipe, then Pall Malls), entertained us with chirpy, ill-natured observations about the 'academic types' he had met so far. A couple of young associate professors wanted to establish a permanent department of film, he said, with Howard as acting chairman; besides the fact that powerful figures in the Stanford administration would never agree to such a thing, he himself had doubts about the 'teachability' of a genuine film aesthetic, etc.

"You're not eating," Sylvia interrupted him. "You haven't touched your chicken."

"Oh? Haven't I?" He looked archly down at his plate, on which sat a juicy piece of baked breast. "I guess I'm just a bad boy, aren't I. My only excuse is that I ate only four hours ago. At the faculty club."

"But you have to eat," she insisted.

"I know. I know that." He winked at me broadly.

On the way over to Broyle Hall (where the movies were to be shown) he linked arms with me. Sylvia walked a pace behind, still in a minor snit because he hadn't, in the end, touched any of his supper, and because he had categorically refused to be driven across campus. It was a fairly long walk, and I gathered that his leg had recently been bothering him. (He was soon to have the hip joint replaced; this was on top of six or seven prior operations, which had never really succeeded in restoring full function or relieving his almost constant discomfort.) He was too proud to be "carted around like a cripple," he said; if necessary, he would crawl to the hall on his hands and knees.

"They broke it," he mused, tapping his left thigh. "Yes, they surely did break it. Then they put me in the back of an old Willys pickup. Drove me out somewhere in the desert. I was comatose for several days, since they hadn't bothered to set the break, and when I awoke, I was in a hospital in a city I'd never heard of before—Feldspar, Arizona. A pretty nurse was taking my temperature rectally. Her name was . . . Felíz."

Sylvia—still a pace behind us—suddenly grabbed my free hand. Howard didn't notice, and when I half turned toward her, to ask what she wanted, the strength of her grip told me not to, to go on as before.

"Yes," he continued to muse, "Felíz. I believe it means 'happy' in Spanish, am I right? But she was very kind. Truly compassionate. In the afternoons the temperature sometimes soared up into the hundreds—both mine, and that of the surrounding air—but we were fairly comfortable, as I remember, almost cool in that small adobe structure built on sand. Eventually the infection in my leg was controlled, but only then did I realize the extent of my injuries. My . . . face. What they had done to my face. Broken my nose, of course, but then someone had also taken the trouble to rub dirt—or more probably, some specific chemical—into deep cuts that had been made all over one side. At that time it wasn't easy to find a good surgeon—let alone a good plastic surgeon—within five hundred miles of a town like Feldspar, and Felíz, as I recall, did most of the treatments herself. The cuts wouldn't heal, but as she was of that country, she asked her aunt to go out into the desert, to some magic spot they knew about. Here it was possible to gather medicinal herbs for making into poultices. Eventually the cuts, which had swelled into suppurating welts, began to dry out, but the scars they left behind . . . they're rather unsightly, wouldn't you say?"

We had reached the other side of the campus by now. This was a region of libraries, classroom buildings, milling students, and so on—and now he let go of my arm. Sylvia, still behind us, continued to squeeze my free hand. The strength of her grip was a sign of her distress (I realized), of intense emotional disturbance upon hearing the details of his catastrophe (for the first time?).

"But the funny thing"—Howard laughed merrily—"after I was all better, more or less healed, I somehow got it in my head that that girl, Felíz, might have a special feeling for me. I returned to California. Wound up my affairs here. When I got back out to Arizona, I was surprised to learn that she had moved, had gone to Phoenix, in fact, where she was working in a modern-type hospital. Here I accosted her one evening on her way home from work. I smiled and handed her a bouquet of flowers, but, strange to say, she pretended not to know me. I couldn't even get her to admit that she had ever been in 'Feldspar,' wherever that was, and she quite frankly told me that if I imagined that I was someone she might want to know, I hadn't looked in a mirror lately. . . .

"Later, I found a job there. In Phoenix. Some years passed . . . a lot of years. I'm not really sure what happened during that period, to tell you the truth. I simply existed."

❊

During the break in the program that night—*Sullivan's Travels* and *Maid's Night Out* were the offerings, the latter featuring an astonishingly youthful Joan Fontaine—my sister said:

"He's never talked about any of this. Never, before to-night. I think he has a special feeling for you; that's the only way I can explain it. He's been obsessed with getting you to come down here, so that he could see you under more 'conge-nial circumstances,' as he put it."

I smiled, somewhat puzzled by it all. "That's very flatter-ing, I'm sure. But why does he think I want to know? I'm sorry about his leg, of course. That's terrible, and I hate what hap-pened to his face. But why tell me, of all people?"

"Because . . ." But immediately, she fell silent. We were sitting in the back of the theater, almost in the last row; the house was about two-thirds full now, and I could dimly see Howard, arms braced against the lectern, chatting with a group of frizzy-haired students up front. My sister's elegant hands, ghostly in the semidark, flexed up and down on her knees in a sort of milking motion. I remembered this habit from her childhood, when it had always signaled inner turmoil of some kind—I almost said something comforting, to draw her out.

"Because . . ." she repeated, "because . . ."

The houselights suddenly went black. Like the good little film students all around us, we automatically sat back, directed our attention to the screen down front. *Maid's Night Out* began to roll, and about five minutes into it, someone came clumping up the aisle past our position. I couldn't actually see who it was, but the irregular rhythm of his steps made me take him for Howard. Allan Lane, an actor I'd never seen before, is the son of a self-made millionaire who, to prove that the younger gener-ation lacks 'mettle,' dares his son to work for as long as a month at some menial job. Lane becomes a milkman, and when he meets Joan Fontaine he takes her for a simple worker just like himself (for a housemaid, in fact). Lane thereafter endeavors to hide his upper-class origins from Fontaine, while she—just as 'high-born' as he, in truth—gradually falls in with the charade.

It was a funny movie, and I came to consider it a good choice (for that program, for Howard's semester-long argument

about the 'nature of American cinema'). The attribution of
honesty, simplicity, and other positive values to the working
class; the corresponding identification of the upper class in
terms of sloth, overrefinement; meanwhile, the reservation to
the leads of all the glamour of secret wealth, of 'good breeding'
humbly concealed—all this marked it as essentially 'thirties,
quintessentially American, and profoundly hypocritical. I forget exactly what Howard had to say about it, though, because
just before he delivered his commentary, there occurred an
incident that confused me, that caused me to sit through his
little speech with ears that didn't hear. Just behind our heads
was the projection room, and when the final reel was about to
roll I heard voices raised inside of it. The screen down front
went briefly dark, and then, instead of a seamless segue into the
last part of *Maid's*, there played a cinematic incident not anticipated by any of the previous action.

Someone with a rough resemblance to Allan Lane was
standing by a curtain. His hair was wavier, lighter-colored than
Lane's, and as he turned to give the camera his full profile (à la
John Barrymore, the chin contemptuously lifted), all impression of resemblance disappeared. He wore kid gloves, the kind
with perforations on the fingers. His perfect face—not really
like Barrymore's, much less masculine, with a porcelain fine-
ness having little to do with the actual size of his features—
exerted, briefly, a strange fascination, cast an unpleasant spell.

I had seen faces like this before, but never in real life. Not
that movies are real life, but such a face belonged on a medal-
lion, an ancient Etruscan frieze or something of the kind. The
feeling I had was of seeing someone long dead, with a concentrated, malevolent inner power—seeing him unhappily, unfortunately brought back to life. This feeling, an instant later, was
deepened when a second character entered the scene. She was
small, slender, with inky, tightly curled hair. Her clothes were
rich, elaborate. However, there was something inappropriate
about her outfit, as if she were a street urchin gotten up to look

like a banker's wife. With every gesture she made, she evinced
her slavish attachment to the man with the perfect face, who,
meanwhile, had sat down casually on the edge of a bed. He,
with an attitude not even of disdain (which would have been at
least human), allowed her to kneel in front of him, still dressed
in her gorgeous, shiny fur coat (probably mink—maybe bea-
ver), and remove one of his half-boots.

Some members of the audience—sophisticated cinéastes
all—made snide sounds at this, to signal their advanced acquaintance with 'foot fetishism,' other odd practices. Up to this
point, though, there had been a remarkable lack of noise, even
though the last part of *Maid's Night Out* had clearly been misplaced. The male character—whose dark, necromantic power
held us all spellbound—now began to remove his clothes.
When he took off his starched shirt, keeping his pants on, a jolt
went through the audience, a measurable electric thrill; my
sister, sitting beside me, began to milk her knees again, and a
perfect hush settled over the gathering. The young woman,
who had by now removed both his boots, demurely averted her
eyes—it was as if she were afraid to look directly upon his flesh,
and yet the camera—the ally, as always, of our voyeurism—
zoomed in for a close-up.

We saw his bare chest. Just a chest; the frame cut off his
head and arms, turning him into a mere torso, a male Venus de
Milo. Only after this shot had been superseded by another (of
the girl, tears oozing from closed eyes) did I register the complete absence of nipples, which, when I'd been seeing the shot,
had seemed perfectly natural, exactly as such a man's chest
ought to have appeared. Now the young woman—daring once
again to look at him—implored him silently, begged him to
respond to her somehow. Not really answering—since gods, or
statues, never really do respond to us, they only sometimes
choose a course of action which, perchance, accords with our
mundane wishes—he languidly unbuttoned his fly.

Behind our heads, an argument broke out; the house

projectionist—a Stanford employee, no doubt—was loudly complaining about this questionable reel he was being forced to run. The screen down front went completely black again. Two minutes later, *Maid's Night Out* resumed, sound and image a little out of synch; and we traveled with it to its saccharine, altogether ordinary and predictable conclusion.

ONLY AFTER *Maid's Night Out* was finally over, Joan Fontaine, with her patented look of myopic perplexity, having confessed her true identity (that of marriageable rich girl), did I wake up from my trance. In a flash I understood that the handsome demigod was Franklin Howard: the physical ruin who, at this moment, was lurching toward the lectern down front, though he bore that glowing icon no resemblance, was unmistakably he, just as the girl, the tearful banker's daughter, was someone even more familiar. I remember being amazed, not so much at this 'coincidence,' as at my own tardy recognition of the truth. It had taken me a good twenty minutes to become conscious of something I must have known, on an unconscious level, from the first shot.

My sister, with a pained, almost frightened look, sat rigidly beside me, staring out into empty auditorium space. Tak-

ing my cue from her I furrowed my brow and looked for a while
on the portentous side of things, but then this seemed ridiculous, and I tried to listen to Howard's speech.

I was unable to concentrate, though, and soon got up and
wandered outside. It was a temperate night, and as I smoked a
cigarette I reflected on his possible motives for showing us that
snippet, whether he wanted to shock us, or impress us, or
simply allude to a whole area of experience which, were we to
court him and coax him diligently enough, he might further
reveal. But I wasn't really interested in my mother's dark secrets. I was largely immune to her by then, had walled off the
memory of her, the very thought of her, pretty effectively, and I
couldn't imagine ever changing my mind, wanting to know
more about her. If she had appeared in a hundred productions
of dubious value and taste—if she had been, indeed, a 'thirties-
style porn star, as this snippet seemed to suggest—I didn't
really care, because I couldn't see how it related to me.

My sister came out after a while, and we sat on the steps of
the building. Here was an opportunity for me, as older sibling,
to put things in perspective, by making some sarcastic comment about it all, expressing a well-tempered skepticism, but
her mood of gloom was just too strong. Anything I said would
have been taken amiss, as an insult to her, or to Howard, or
possibly to the memory of our dear departed parent.

"They were lovers," she finally said, in a tone of dramatic,
adolescent gravity; "it started when she was really young,
probably only fourteen. He came to Hollywood first, then she
followed him. She didn't even want to be in the movies. But she
had to do something, and he got her work. Then when he was
out of town once she happened to meet Gerson. She didn't like
him, she just wanted to make Franklin jealous. But Frank
wouldn't get jealous—he *never* gets jealous—so on an impulse
she married Gerson.

"They came from the same town, you know. Hemet.
Remember her talking about Hemet, 'the godforsaken hamlet

of Hemet'? Well—that's where it was. They practically grew
up together. They were 'kissing cousins,' he says—I don't
really know what he means by that. Maybe that they really
were related . . . anyhow, they were very close. They depended
on each other for everything. He got her her first jobs, and
later, when she'd be on a big picture, she'd always get him
brought in, in some capacity or other. He was an assistant
director, scriptwriter, soundman. Always working at something, improving his 'understanding,' as he puts it. Finally
they had him directing low-budget features. But it was such a
waste, when you think of how far he could have gone—I mean,
as an actor. With that face.

"Gerson knew all about him. They were even friends, sort
of. They played tennis together, went to parties, once they even
went to Mexico together—all three of them. But you know
how Gerson can be so charming. Such a good listener, the man
of 'immense influence' who's ten mental steps ahead, even
though he doesn't say a damned word . . . well, that's how he
was with Frank. Paternal, but cold. Maybe he's pulling strings
for you, or maybe wrapping a cord around your throat. Frank
and Mother had stopped being intimate by then, but there was
still warmth, a friendship. Then when she had you she stopped
working, but when I was two, she wanted to come back, and of
course she got in touch with Frank. He immediately put her in
a movie he'd written, which was just about to start shooting.

"I've read the script—it's called *The Palace of Smiles*. It
would've made a great movie, but . . . Gerson said he didn't like
it. Said it was 'boring.' It's anything but boring: sexy, and
daring, far ahead of its time, but not 'boring.' This was 1950,
'51. They weren't making movies about real life then, about
how people fall in love, helplessly, but sometimes they won't go
far enough, because they have hangups, inhibitions. They
know how to love one another, but they just can't make themselves do it, you see. It's a tragedy, in a sense. Gerson didn't flat
out say 'no,' but he was opposed to it. But Mother wanted to
work, so she went ahead.

"In the third week of shooting, the producer got sick. He was a hundred percent behind the project, but now they had to replace him, and the guy who took over was a jerk. He wanted changes in the story . . . so Frank rewrote the script. Then they had trouble with one of the actors, who'd been in all the footage they'd already shot. He went off on a bender, and Frank had to track him down. Then, when it was almost done, the studio announced that they were shelving it. For 'financial reasons.' Frank was crushed, about ready to give up, but Mother sent him to see someone she knew at another studio. This guy read the script, saw how great it was, and he started negotiating to acquire the rights. But then—he had an accident."

After a moment, I cleared my throat. I had smoked another cigarette, lighting the second from the first, and standing above her (she was sitting on the steps of the building), I must have given the impression of hanging on her every word. Just then some people came out; Howard's lecture must just have ended. I was grateful for this interruption, as it allowed me to compose myself, and I said with a certain nonchalance:

"But who had an accident—the new producer?"

"No. No, I'm talking about Franklin—his big accident. The one that left him . . . crippled. Terribly disfigured."

"But wait—we know who caused that, don't we? We know who had to be behind that, as he's behind so much else that's wrong in the world . . . your father, of course. Your terrible father. The evil genius. Isn't that what you think?"

A horde of students came spilling down the steps at just that moment. To avoid being trampled, my sister moved over to one side, while I, not responding quite so quickly, was unceremoniously pushed to the other. I kept an eye on her, and a moment later I fought my way to her side.

"Well? Do you think so? Is that really what you believe?"

"I . . . yes. Of course I do. How could I not? Don't you?"

"Well . . . but it's absurd. Just on the face of it, he'd never do something like that. Someone like him"—I jerked my head back toward the lecture hall—"how could you even think, how could he ever, in all his wildest dreams, pose any kind of threat? A pathetic little loser. Someone not even worth stepping on. If Gerson even noticed his existence—which I seriously doubt—he immediately took him for a screwball, a weird one, an 'actor'. . . ."

Unaffected by my dismissive (yet also vehement) tone, she scanned the crowd. She was looking for Howard, whose imminent reappearance was of infinitely greater significance, it appeared, than anything I might have to say on this subject.

"And by the way," I suddenly found myself adding, "you're not fucking him, are you? Not actually fucking him? Getting in bed with him? Because that would be . . . just too obscene. Too sick for words."

She paused. "Oh, would it? Is that what it would be—'obscene'? And who do you think you are, talking to me that way?"

"Well, I'm your brother. That's who I am. I'm your brother. And—"

But just at that moment, a loud *boom* interrupted us. Howard, supported at the elbow by an apple-cheeked coed, had suddenly appeared at the door of Broyle Hall; and the door, swinging back sharply, had been made to slam resoundingly against the wall of the building. All of us gathered on the steps looked up, as if in response to some priestly summons, the beat of a primordial tom-tom. Then Howard, with a mad gleam in his eye, looked down upon us, searched our faces until, to his seemingly devilish delight, he lit upon my sister's. And she, with a gay smile, bounded up the steps, ran to greet him, her legs full of a springy eagerness.

FRANKLIN HOWARD WAS to disappear from our lives a few months later—the mode of his disappearance, I should say, being the most important thing about him, or about our contact with him—and I find it hard to remember the details of our few subsequent meetings. What I do remember very well is reading *The Palace of Smiles*, his silly, slimy, perverted movie scenario, which my sister took it upon herself to send me; full of camera-movement arcana, and detailed descriptions of the fabrics and furniture to be used in various scenes, it gave me a headache just to look at it; and it convinced me—if I hadn't been convinced already—that the guy belonged on a funny farm somewhere.

"Picture this," I remember saying to my father—on my way back from Mexico that spring, I had stopped off at his house, wanting to refresh myself—"a minor actor, a hack director at some third-rate studio, comes 'this' close to getting them to make a movie about sexual enslavement. Yeah, really. The whole thing takes place inside a creepy mansion whose windows and doors are nailed shut. The walls are covered with mirrors, so that each frame, each image in each frame, is reflected ten times, and the hero spends the whole movie walking around in a pair of woolen diapers, with his hands manacled behind him. The girl—his 'love interest'—is a fairly normal person at the start, who only wants to do right by her boyfriend. He brings her up to the mansion, nails her in with him, and then he explains to her that from now on she's to humiliate him any way she can, beat him, curse him, make him lick her shoes, etc.

"Not able to get behind this, the girlfriend spends the first half of the movie crying. The guy, on the other hand, can't stop smiling, he's so pleased with the situation, and you constantly see his stupid face reflected in all those mirrors. Finally, when you want to wring his neck yourself, the girl accidentally spills hot coffee on his bare thigh. He falls on the floor—writhing in pain/pleasure—and the girl, of course, has an 'illumination' just then, sees how maybe this cruelty business ain't so bad."

My father had gotten up from his chair; there was a wet bar in his library, a cunning little cabinet that folded out, and I assumed, as his back was toward me, that he was fixing himself a Calso water. (He never drank before six in the evening, and he had recently given up smoking.) But no, he wasn't getting himself a seltzer water, I found: climbing onto the mobile library ladder—which, as a child, I had often longed to play on, but had rarely dared—he pulled down a dusty volume from one of the higher shelves.

"Have you read this? Here—it's pretty good."

It was a copy of *Call It Sleep*, by Henry Roth. As it happened, I had acquired a copy of it—though I hadn't yet looked into it—only a few weeks before. "Yeah, it's pretty good," I allowed. "A little slow, but you can get into it. Say, what is this here—a first edition? A signed copy? Jeez, you're getting a whole collection of Jewish memorabilia, aren't you? Rare books, all that kind of stuff."

He smiled—but very faintly. In the last eighteen months, he had pressed on me a number of unusual books, novels such as *The Rise of David Levinsky, Yoshe Kalb,* and *Salvation (The Psalm-Jew),* plus scholarly works offering an introduction to the Talmud, an explication of the 'Divine Throne and Chariot' imagery of the Cabala, and histories of Hasidism and the Shabbataian heresy, no less. I had deflected these as well as a number of other offerings, pleading lack of time and inclination, but I was secretly pleased that he should care enough to try to Judify me (my previous religious training having consisted of four weeks of Sunday school when I was about ten).

Folding himself casually into an armchair—that high, uncomfortable, pea-green wing-back, which I had often clambered upon as a child—he proceeded to fall into a brown study, his eyes fixed on a spot just to the right of my knees. He looked absolutely smashing, I thought—trim, broad-shouldered, smoothly tanned. For a man of sixty-four or sixty-five, he was so powerfully present that an estimated life span of a hundred twenty seemed about right, not unrealistic at all. I remember particularly on that afternoon admiring his white buckskin oxfords, which no one not fully conscious of his surroundings, of the figure he cut within them, would ever have attempted. The white of these shoes was comically pure, I remember, and it played subtly to the off-white of his trousers (of some duck or sailcloth material), of his linen jacket, and of his full head of straight, high-mounting hair.

"So . . ." I said eventually. "Are you . . . interested?"

"Hmm?"

"In this movie. In this stupid movie I was telling you about."

He made a vague 'go ahead' gesture. I was a little miffed, having expected to get more of a rise out of him, but I contin-

ued, that is, I related the rest of Howard's scenario. (The theme
of incarceration with an innocent female, who tends, but also
tortures, now suddenly showed itself forth in sharp relief in my
mind; it recalled the roughly similar story of Howard's days, or
weeks, in the Arizona desert, cared for by the faithless Felíz.
He had established a kind of simulation of these conditions
with my sister, I suddenly realized, in that cottage he had on
the Stanford campus; and I wondered whether, in his putative
relations with my mother, he had likewise locked himself away,
sequestered himself for a period of time.)

". . . and finally breaks free," I concluded, having told the
whole sick story. "This is her ultimate betrayal, you see: that
she won't kill him, that, knowing he only wants to die at her
hands, she goes 'normal' on him at the end."

"Really, it makes you want to puke, doesn't it?"

My father said nothing. As I spoke, he had removed the
dust jacket from *Call It Sleep,* and now he examined the volume
with care, as if suspicious of some flaw in its construction. I
waited about five minutes. In that space of time, a remarkable
change in my state of mind occurred, and I became somewhat
ashamed of myself; trying to fool him, to trick him into an
unusual revelation of his feelings, of his history with Franklin
Howard and my mother, I had succeeded only in embarrassing
myself (it now seemed to me), and as he slowly raised his eyes
to my face, I was mortified to see that he had anticipated even
this final modulation, this ultimate failure of will on my part.

"So," he said rather blandly. "You saw this thing—this
movie. What about it? Did it upset you? Did it bruise your
tender sensibilities, my boy?"

After a moment I spluttered: "No. No, not at all. I only
mean that . . . well . . . I didn't really see it. It's never been
released, actually. They got most of it in the can, they say, but
then the studio backed off. They wouldn't let them finish it."

He nodded, very slowly. He had put *Call It Sleep* down on
the table beside his chair, and now he rested his hand upon it.

Time seemed to come to a halt; another period of deep, pernicious silence, which I survived only by staring at the floor, ensued, and I began to writhe inside. Finally daring to look in his vicinity, I glanced at the alcove behind his head, where a new canvas—a Nathan Oliveira, I believe—had recently been hung. This stark, El Greco–ish nude, pale green but for a purple crotch, struck me as one of the most forbidding, ugliest objects I'd ever seen.

"No," I now added weakly, "I didn't see it. Nobody's ever really seen it. The studio suppressed it. A friend of Sylvia's—a guy she met at Stanford—gave her the script to read. He's an older man, actually, a teacher. He claims to have written it himself, but . . . I don't know. It's hard to tell. But they've become quite close, she and this man. She sort of takes care of him now—lives in the same house with him, and all."

Despite myself, I peered at my father surreptitiously. I badly wanted to see what effect this would have, this last revelation. If my father had, indeed, been the cause of Franklin Howard's manifold agonies—if he knew him at all, in fact—then he could be expected to betray himself in some way at this point. But Gerson had anticipated my curiosity; the look he returned me was flat, impenetrable, massively unforthcoming. If a rock face, a mountainous wall of granite, can be said to have an expression, then this was that look, with only his self-possessed breathing, and the occasional blink of an eye, giving evidence of a living presence.

"So . . . how is she, anyway? This sister of yours."

"Oh—she's fine. Really good, in fact."

Gerson scowled. He rarely asked about her anymore, and always with a show of sour amusement, as if her defection from him were a sort of bad joke. To say that he had been 'hurt' by her behavior—by her decision never to think of him again, to act as if she 'no longer had a father'—would be, not so much an overstatement, as an inappropriate usage, I feel, a rank misnomer. While I didn't doubt that he was capable of being 'hurt,' in all honesty I must report that I had never seen the evidence of such a thing myself.

If something had ever happened to her—if she had been injured in a car wreck, crippled, or killed—I'm sure he would have been 'devastated,' that life ever after would have been much bleaker for him. He cared, I feel it safe to say, and as events were to show, he was interested in all her comings and goings, kept tabs on her as best he could. However, there was a total absence of any outward signs of such caring. In any upsetting or unwelcome situation, he was able to respond only with extreme objectivity, with efficient and cold-blooded dispatch; emotional expressions of how he felt at such times were either wholly lacking, or so oblique as to defy perception.

"Ray had a look at your car," he now remarked. "He says it's riding kind of low—must be a problem with the shocks, or something."

I was taken aback. His handsome, powerful Buick—now badly dented, with several tears in the ragtop—was sitting at that moment in his driveway, burdened down with a hundred kilos of Mexican pot. As usual, I had driven it south of the border, met my supplier, paid him part of what I owed him (but only part—he sometimes carried me for months at a time), then taken on a big shipment with no more trouble than if I were loading up with *serapes* and *huaraches* to sell at a flea market back in California. Only because other 'importers' I knew were extra-cautious had I hollowed out the door compartments, as well as an area inside either rear quarter-panel, and it was here I stored all my 'weight' (as we called it in those days). But really, I felt that I could have driven across with the marijuana sitting beside me in the front seat, in big burlap sacks labeled MOTA, so lax was the scrutiny I was usually accorded at the border.

"I love that car," I now confessed with sincere, substantial feeling. "It has a great spirit, great drive. All you have to do is change the oil every few months. Then, just let it go."

"But you should take better care of it. It hurts me to see it looking like that. All the dirt, the bald tires and everything."

"I know," I said, remorsefully. "A car like that should be pampered, never revved above four thousand. It's just that I keep having to go south all the time. You know—I like to visit my Marta. But I've been thinking. Maybe I should get something else, an old truck or something. Then I could keep the Buick just for special occasions."

"Well, whatever you do, be sure to tell me about it. Then I can put the other one on the insurance, too."

What was that insinuating look—was there a twinkle of complicity in his eye? I so much wanted to tell him, or at least, to hint to him broadly, that we were 'brothers under the skin,' like two peas in a pod; he had his 'business,' I had my own, and the world beyond the law was a home to us both. So often, in the course of my illegal dealings, I had found myself in situations that to me seemed full of the glamour of criminal existence, and my first thought was always: 'I wish that *he* could see me now, that he could be here with me, to see how well I'm behaving.' Someone would have carried a gun into a meeting with me, a big, greasy revolver dating from the days of Pancho Villa, and I would think: 'So *this* is what it feels like—you sit on one side of a table, and on the other, Death protrudes from the belt of a guy you hardly know, an ugly, unpleasant fellow with a cold sore on his nose. And you calmly take a sip of your beer, and . . . you smile.'

"Dad," I now wondered, "why did you stop going down to Mexico? I thought you always had such good times down there. Whenever I go south, I feel like the whole world's opening up, like I can do anything I want. Any damned thing, and it's sure to come out okay."

He coughed softly into his broad hand. "Is that how you feel about it? Really?"

"Yes. I know—it must sound crazy. But I love it down there. Mexico's like another world for me. Things work so differently there, and for some reason I fit in. I've got the right temperament, or something."

"Well—good for you. I'm glad to hear it. That's very

nice." I waited for him to speak further to this important issue—it was of great concern to me at the time—but he had suddenly become mountainous again, impenetrable.

"Well," I continued anyhow, "it's like I've finally found my home. It's like I've stumbled on the right 'role' for me, the right 'impersonation.' Everything feels like it's full of possibilities. And the people—they really like me. We just understand each other instinctively."

"Good. That must be a very good feeling, indeed."

I was about to tell him more, to describe to him some of the friends I'd recently made—all my contacts in the 'trade'—when he stood up.

"Listen, Louis—I'm sorry, but I can't talk now. I just remembered something. A phone call I have to make. It's real important. I'll see you at supper, okay?"

"Okay, Dad. And—thanks. Thanks for everything."

He nodded, then quickly went out of the room.

WE NEVER DID resume that intriguing conversation. I never reported any other details of my 'other life' to my father, nor did he ask, and in the years that followed (years in which I kept busy traveling to Mexico, developing my little business down there) I never once, as I recall, suspected that there was anything amiss, anything unusual in my situation. However, I found myself remembering our conversation—recalling it most vividly, word for word—on an afternoon a few years later. I had just been put in a holding cell, a verminous little cage, out back of state police headquarters in Culiacán, in the Mexican state of Sinaloa. Along with about forty other low-level players, I had been rounded up in a police sweep, and I remember feeling intensely irritated (I had never been arrested before).

"This is just the ordinary," I remember thinking to myself, "it's just that in the past, I've always escaped this kind of bullshit. And the way everybody keeps looking at me—like I was responsible for all of us being caught. Hell, I don't even know most of these guys; but they all look like they think they know me."

I felt a new, intense sort of discomfort. In the past I had always been happy to tower over everybody, to be known as *el gigante*, the gringo *enorme*, but now I could see the advantage in being able to cringe, to gather yourself low to the ground. Every time the state police guards or officials came to the window, they would look in at me—inevitably at me—and then mutter sneeringly among themselves. I was somehow the reviled, highly vulnerable center of this unhappy event.

"And I remember that day," I thought further, "with the old man. Telling him how great Mexico was. How I came 'alive' down here, could do no wrong. Well, I suppose fate is always waiting to slap you down—fate has a long memory."

"*Sí, verdad,*" said the man next to me. "*Es la fortuna, claro.*"

"Pardon?"

"You said, 'Fate does this.' Fate is a fucking bitch, man."

"I said that?"

"You don't know what you been saying. You been mumbling all over."

I was sure I hadn't been mumbling. Anyway, I took this man's comments as an overture, an offer of comradeship; I was grateful for any sign that I wasn't universally hated, so I followed him when he retired to a nearby corner, and we smoked a cigarette. He said his name was Chuy and he came from Ronda, a nearby farm town. On his uncle's considerable acreage he had been accustomed in the past to grow marijuana and opium poppies. The beauty of his situation was that his uncle's wife's nephew worked for the state police, so he always heard in advance when something like the current anti-drug campaign was to be launched.

"But this ain't no *estado* fuckup, man. This is something worse. *Lots* worse."

"Why? They look like the state *narcóticos* to me."

"No. If they was, I would've heard, right? And look—look at that *cabrón*."

Another man was peering in the window—someone we hadn't seen before. He was wearing a seersucker suit and little black sunglasses, and he had a mustache that went all the way across his face, almost from ear to ear. He took off his sunglasses and flicked the cigarette he'd been smoking in through the window bars. Someone picked it up and nodded gratefully.

"I never seen him before. Uh-oh. I never seen that one before."

This new official scanned the crowd, taking no especial note of me. I was half hunkered down in the corner, with Chuy in front of me; I felt much better in this position, partially protected. When the man in seersucker went away, Chuy shook his head vehemently and asked if I had ever been inside 'La Perla,' the infamous federal prison, which was about forty miles north of Culiacán.

"No. I've never been there. I've only seen it from the outside."

"It's a hole, man. It's . . . like hell. *Como el infierno*, understand? You don't come out of there with an asshole that still belongs to you unless you got bigger balls than I think you do. You got any money? Lots and lots of money?"

I don't know why, but I tended to trust this man Chuy. I immediately assumed that he knew 'the ropes' better than I, even though I'd been trafficking in and out of Mexico for almost seven years by then. I had never been arrested. I'd never spent time in any sort of jail, yet I had absorbed a certain amount of fairly reliable information, I felt, upon which I was inclined to base my strategy at this point.

If ever arrested (I had decided long ago), I would simply contact a certain friend on the outside, who would make the necessary payments based on his assessment of the situation. If it was necessary to hire a lawyer, then by all means hire the one with the most pull; if not—if direct payments to the arresting agency would suffice—then take that route. I had several friends, in fact, who were capable of handling such arrangements.

If all else failed—if I actually ended up having to do some time—I planned to survive in jail in the most comfortable fashion possible. In most Mexican jails—all those I'd heard of—one was more or less responsible for one's own sustenance; the prison authorities offered little in the way of food, bedding, clothing, medical services, and so on, and the inmates thus were thrown back on their own resources. Those who lacked money, or who had few contacts inside or outside the institution, could reasonably be expected to perish in short order; while those who, being better connected, were capable of living well found that no one offered any serious impediments to their enjoyment.

"No," I now responded cautiously to Chuy; "I don't have much money. Why? What's that got to do with you?"

"Nothing, man. Only—it's too bad. What they going to do to you, and what they going to do to me too, I think. We just got some bad *chingando en el culo* by this fucking fate, man, that they pick us up right now. 'Cause it's a bad time right now. We going straight to La Perla. That guy with those *mostachos como este*, growing out of his nose like that, he's not even a *federale*. He's a fucking DEA, man."

('DEA'—at that time I had never heard this term, this peculiar acronym. However, I correctly assumed it referred to some arm of the laughable American campaign to interdict the flow of drugs. There had been Operation Intercept, which had recently failed miserably, and now there was something going on called Operation Cooperation, whereby the gringos, in their rabid anti-drug fervor, gave the agreeable Mexicans helicopters and guns and expected them to stamp out the problem themselves.)

"DEA?" I said curiously. "You really think he's DEA?

Well . . . I don't care. He could be CIA for all I care. All I want is two minutes alone on the telephone. Then I'm out of here, baby."

Chuy shook his head. "You still don't understand. This is a whole new game, man. The gringos sent down their own agents this time—*they're* the ones in charge. They give us some airplanes, all that shit, but they get to run the show for a while. The first thing they doing is to put everybody down in La Perla. But it's not like the old La Perla—you can't buy your way out, you can't buy nothing, man. They put everybody in a fucking cage, with a mad-dog killer. And—catch this—you gotta wear their stupid prison clothes. Just like in some fucking joint up in the States."

"But . . . they can't do that," I protested, truly annoyed now.

"No? Well—they doin' it. Believe me, they doin' it."

I was badly shaken. This was the first really disturbing development, much worse than my arrest. Like others in my line of business I had a negative image of American prisons; it was a matter of faith among us that to do time up north was tantamount to a sentence of death, that one emerged, if at all, permanently crushed in body and spirit.

If La Perla was being transformed—even only temporarily—into a North American–style lockup, then I wanted no part of this situation. I looked around our little cage of a room (which contained forty or fifty sweating, disgruntled, and pugnacious men) as if expecting to find a door marked EXIT.

By the middle of that night, most of us had been put on flatbed trucks and driven north, into the desert. I had never worn chains before, and I forced myself to pay attention to the way the collars hugged (or rather, crushed) my anklebones, feeling sure that this detail would serve well in the memoir I would write someday about my prison experiences. Chuy still stayed close to me. When we drove beyond the turnoff for La Perla, he shook his head—now even he didn't know what was going on.

Sometime during the night, the man next to me on the chain, an old guy with dentures, unceremoniously ground his fist into my crotch. I pushed him away, and someone else immediately leaped in to defend him. We wrestled clumsily, the truck bed tilting and shuddering as we drove over dirt roads. Feeling a bite of cool, intimate nighttime air on my throat, I held the little runt at bay with one hand, meanwhile stretching my neck up at the sky; the feeling of a 'bite' became a stinging sensation, and I indignantly realized that I had been cut with something, probably a piece of glass or a penknife. Chuy rushed in at that moment; he was two or three men behind me on the line, and he swarmed over my enemy with furious energy, to a great clanking of chains. When he was done the man lay still at my feet. I must have passed out at that point; when I awoke, the sky had begun to lighten, with streaks of gorgeous lavender showing over the peaks of the Sierra Madre Occidental. Chuy was gone, and so was the man who had lain at my feet. The rest of our truckload of detainees lay around in crumpled postures of painful, half-frozen sleep.

We drove a little farther. There was hardly any talk, and the mood was sullen (rather than confused, or fearful). Finally, a little before noon, we stopped in a valley full of treelike chollas. The heat was intense, but even more disturbing was the stark light, that unmediated, high-mountain brilliance that makes you feel almost cold inside. I kept looking around for somewhere to hide, some sheltering object to put my head under, but there was nothing—we were still caged on the back of that truck.

The men tried squatting down, putting their heads between their legs, or pulling their shirts over themselves. Then at a later stage, everybody simply relaxed and shut his eyes and let the sun grill him as it would. We hadn't had anything to eat or drink for over twenty-four hours. Sometimes we could hear the guards, up ahead in the cab, laughing and popping the caps off beer bottles, and I happened to be looking forward when a well-picked-over carcass of greasy chicken went flying out a window. I didn't yet think I was going to die, but my indignation had given way to a simple desire to make it to sundown, just to have this terrible weight of light and heat lifted off my burning back. I could see that the others were also going a little crazy; some had begun to wander around like zombies, dragging their chains ghoulishly, while others were crowding into the southwest corner of the truck, where a tiny patch of shade, thrown down by the truck's siding, was beginning to lengthen.

At around four o'clock, a man with big, hyperthyroid eyes approached me. I hadn't noticed him before. He was fairly tall, and his skin was red like a boiled lobster. (Certain Indians of the north-central region have this kind of complexion, and it often goes along with eye problems and kinky, dust-colored hair.) This fellow smiled at me ingratiatingly, held out his hands, and mumbled something, and not being quick to draw back, I soon found that both my hands had been gripped by his, which were incredibly large, rough, clawlike. Then—with hallucinatory slowness—two other men materialized out of the pack, and while one fumbled to get something out of his pocket, the other poked me repeatedly high up my back. I struggled to get free, but the lobster-man had me by the wrists, and now the other guy had found what he sought in his pocket. I twisted to get away, managing to deflect or evade several of his halfhearted, feckless thrusts, but all the while the other guy, with greater industry, kept poking me in the back with what felt like a sharpened nail.

The crowd, meanwhile, parted around us. Chains clanked gloomily, and faces presented us with expressions of bored desolation. If I had asked anyone to help me, or if I had fallen to the floor, thrashing madly in my attempts to get away,

I would have been finished off quickly, I'm sure; instead, I held my ground, only now and then wincing when a blow struck home. Someone blundered into us—he had tripped over his chain (it seemed), and lunging forward, he fell against the red-faced man. The latter's grip was temporarily broken, and I turned slightly to my right, evading thereby a desperate thrust by one of my attackers. The one I had not yet seen, the one behind me, was simultaneously pressed up against me by a surging, tidelike movement of the whole crowd; his freedom to strike me as he wanted was compromised, and for half a minute or so I was safe.

Back and forth, surging and retreating . . . I can't account for what happened then. The whole group of us seemed to be organized in a common enterprise, but the nature of this effort was deeply ambiguous, so that I would be untouched for a while, but then, as if the crowd had had second thoughts, my enemies would return to their bloody work. I couldn't understand what was happening to me. Was I being killed? And if not, then why not back off, why not let me go? Even my attackers seemed half of a mind to abandon their murderous task: the one with the bugged eyes, who had regained his grip on my wrists, kept looking at me imploringly, as if expecting me to say something reassuring. I didn't know what he wanted to hear, so I kept quiet; I must have been infected by the general mood, the sun-dazed, weak-willed ambivalence that had descended on us all.

Shots rang out—I didn't really hear them, or believe them. I had begun to subside toward the floor, yet I thought this was preordained, exactly what was needed for my protection. I had been poked twenty or thirty times in the back. The front of my shirt was a bloody mess, but I was less and less anxious as time went on; I figured that if I had not been done in yet, then there was less of a chance, the longer I managed to survive. Assuming that my injuries weren't cumulative (I quickly assumed this), I could be killed only if there were a 'conscious' decision on the part of everyone on the back of the truck at that moment, a general agreement to do me in. But each moment that passed offered proof that there could never be such an agreement.

Everyone was pushed both ways, torn by conflicting impulses; the forces of good and evil, of light and dark, were warring within us, and each was so profoundly divided that the forging of a general consensus was unthinkable. As this thought occurred to me, I was filled with a delicious feeling of lightness, of impending physical and spiritual release. The lobster-man was pushed on top of me; I hardly cared, and if I could have spoken, I would have welcomed him. Meanwhile someone was reaching around his throat from behind, clumsily trying to throttle him. In order to deal with this, the lobster-man had to let go of my right hand; coincidentally, a straight razor he was holding, which he had been slowly working open, fell against my chest. Pressed between my body and his, the razor looked dangerous, as if it might give someone a bad cut; I reached out, but then, before I could fold it, my arm was rudely jostled.

The blade flew up. The lobster-man let out a moist yell, which, blending with the sound of more gunfire, didn't surprise me. Twenty bodies collapsed on top of me at that point, and my shoulder hit the floor of the truck.

WHEN I WOKE UP, I was in the backseat of a sedan. Sitting beside me, chained to me at the wrist, was someone I didn't know (probably someone else from the truck). Up ahead, I could see a stretch of road I recognized. It was Highway 15, the main north-south route into Mexico, the one I'd driven probably a hundred times.

"Hey, he's wakin' up."

The driver looked at me in his rearview mirror. He handed back a plastic bottle of water.

"You better drink some," he advised.

"Yeah—drink some," echoed the man next to me.

I was very sore. My whole body ached, but vaguely—as if from a distance. I took the bottle, and my partner's wrist rose with my hand. I wanted to snarl, but I couldn't. I became aware of his extreme agitation—his eyes were wide open, and he kept swallowing. He had a big, pointed Adam's apple.

"Yeah, you better drink a lotta water. Take it easy. It's hot out there. Get some rest."

"Okay, okay—shut up back there," said the driver good-naturedly.

We were on a small rise. About a hundred yards below and ahead of us was the highway, cars and trucks whizzing past. As far as I could tell, we were in a sort of abandoned grassland, or wasteland. There wasn't even a donkey-track behind us, and I vaguely wondered how we had gotten here.

The driver looked like a state *narcótico*. But he spoke unaccented English, and the car smelled new and somehow American. A Mexican driver would have crapped up the front with statuettes of the Virgin, fuzzy dice hanging from the rearview, a fabric fringe along the windshield, and so on. I put my hand on the driver's shoulder.

"Excuse me, but could I get out for a second? I have to take a piss."

The man beside me, his face contorted in terror, shook his head. No, no, a thousand times no. Don't go out there, don't even think about it, he seemed to be saying.

"Sure," the driver now said cheerily. "Can do. Have a good time." He pressed a catch up front, and the lock on my door released. I swung my legs out, but I was restrained from going more than a foot away by the chain on my wrist. My backseat partner actually pulled me in the opposite direction, as if to keep me from venturing too far into the 'danger zone.' Again I felt like snarling at him.

It was late afternoon. Almost evening. Was it the same day—had I been on the back of the truck only a few hours earlier? The sun would be going down in just a few minutes. I saw a big rancho across the road—there were hundreds of acres of tomatoes, some irrigation equipment, a few fallow fields. The air smelled clean, colorful. Definitely Mexican.

I opened my fly with my left hand. But my fingers were caked with blood, and I had a momentary aversion to touching myself. Just then, I heard someone hawk and spit.

Maybe fifty yards below, down the other slope of the hill, was another sedan. It was parked close to a thorny hedge. A man was standing at the driver's door, which was half open. His position was actually much like mine, half inside the car, half out. I saw him speak into a radio microphone, and as he waited for a response, he lifted his face up to me. I recognized the man from state police headquarters—the one Chuy had said was 'DEA,' the guy with the funny mustache.

As I peed, he began to walk toward me. Getting back in the car I was aware of a numbness in my back, as if the skin around my shoulder blades had turned into a hard shell, a sort of carapace. I was breathing hard just from the effort of getting in and out. The front of my shirt was also like a shell; the dried, hardening blood created this effect, and my skin had gone partly numb, self-protectively. The man I was chained to, my seat partner, now found something funny in our situation. Each time he looked at me, he would be convulsed, but his laughter was breathless, almost silent. I decided that I hated him, wanted to kill him. All my problems were his fault somehow; if I could but get away from him, just slip out of this hateful chain, I would be much better off.

"Shut up. I'm getting sick of you," I said in Spanish. "Be silent, please."

The driver had gone away. He was talking to the other man. I could just see them out of the corner of my eye.

"They're going to kill us," now whispered my seat partner. "Going to blow us away—you just watch."

I looked directly over at our captors, who were a few yards away from the car. They were smoking, chatting harmlessly. The man with the mustaches plucked deeply at the seat of his pants.

"Maybe so, but what of it?" I replied. "They already tried

to kill me once today. Just take it like a man, whatever happens.
That's the only thing."

My partner rolled his eyes; he had stopped laughing.

"Oh. My Christ—look at that."

The lock on his door had been left open. Either it had
been sprung accidentally, or it hadn't been reset when I got
back in. The lock on my side was also open.

"So? He just forgot to lock the door, that's all."

"No. You're such a cretin. I heard you were stupid, and
now I see that it's true. They want us to make a break for it.
Then they can shoot us going away. Running off. It's like a
game for them."

I looked back at the driver. He happened to be looking our
way at that instant—smiling.

"You're dreaming," I said. "They don't care about us.
They could've killed us back at the truck. Where's the rest of the
men, anyhow?"

"Oh, you idiot. You imbecile. You stupid."

His hand moved slowly toward the door. Then it began to
shake.

"Now . . . I'm going to open this door," he declared
firmly. "Mother of God—please help me. Put wings to my feet.
Give me speed, make me bolt like a pony jumping the corral
fence. You jerk—you better run fast, don't you dare hold me
back. Pick up that huge ass of yours and haul it, or I swear, I'll
kill you myself."

He couldn't control his hand. It shook too much; he
needed his other one, the one chained to mine, to steady it. I
resisted his vicious tugs, then relented. I was somehow cowed
by him, puzzled by what he said; his whole tone of address
threw me off. Why did he resent me so? What was it that I had
done to him, or that he imagined I'd done? His hand came a bit
closer to the door handle. But then he glanced up; he seemed to
notice the empty, trackless grassland round the car for the first
time, all that distance down to the highway. I could see him

losing courage—it leaked visibly out of his eyes, out of his big, mobile Adam's apple.

"Oh shit. Dear Jesus—help me now, please. Please help me."

I watched him closely. It was fascinating—he simply could not make his hand go that extra inch. To encourage him I said:

"I'll come along—don't you worry about me. I'll even run faster than you, I bet. As soon as we get to the road, you hide behind me so the cars can't see our chain. Then I'll flag someone down. I think we're just outside Los Tecos—yeah, I think I recognize that big farm."

He shook his head. He just couldn't grab hold of the door handle, so I did it for him.

I urged him out. I felt like a father, trying to get his child to take his first halting, uncertain steps. The evening air hit us in the face. I loved its freshness, felt inspired by it. We began to stumble down the hill. My legs weren't working too well, but I was keeping up with him. He had begun to whimper when we first got out of the car, but now he was laughing, windmilling his free arm. Once he fell, pulling me down. We got to our feet, immediately started running again.

A little ways ahead was the road. There was a low fence, then the spread of pavement. If we could get across to the other side—to the southbound direction—we would have a chance, I felt. I hadn't heard anything from our captors. I couldn't spare the time to look back, but I had the sense that they weren't following—maybe we had fooled them, maybe they were only now noticing our escape. When we finally reached the fence, I offered my free hand to my friend. But when he was exactly mounted on the top of the fence, his rear end awkwardly up in the air, a shot caught him in the right buttock. He was thrown headfirst over to the other side.

"Are you all right?" I asked, rather stupidly I suppose. "Here—let me help you."

For some reason I thought that if I could get him back on this side, cover him with my body, he would be safe. I started hauling on our chain. After a second or two his left arm, and then his agonized face, came into view. His eyes were shut tightly and he was groaning. I kept pulling, trying to get him over.

"Let go. You stupid fuck—they just shot half my ass off."

I looked up the hill. One of our captors was loping down toward us, while the other remained at the car. He had mounted a tripod on the hood of it, something to shoot from. Then I saw, rather than heard, another shot. The chain jerked fiercely at my wrist, almost pulled me all the way over. I ended up hard against the fence, bent over it at the waist. My partner was lying flat on his back on the other side.

"Get up," I urged. "We've gotta get out of here, really."

He had taken a bullet in the forehead. He actually seemed to be alive for a few seconds; I could swear he blinked at me. Then the driver arrived at the fence, our other captor, and he put his hand on my neck.

N OW DID I SAY THAT?" asked the man with the mustache. "Did I say anything like that?"

It was night—probably about ten o'clock. We were in one of the sedans again, driving south on Highway 15.

"No," I said, "but it's the truth. I just wish you'd get it over with."

He chuckled. "Now . . . why would you think we want you dead? Don't you know what's been happening to you? Don't you know we've been protecting you . . . that we're your *friends*?"

I did have a strong compulsion to believe just that—I wanted badly to think they were on my side, that somebody was. But the mustache-man was so dreadfully insincere. He always seemed to be mocking me, as if he were trying on the role of weird, sadistic cop, the kind who likes to encourage you to hope (just so that, when you do finally get it in the neck, he can have an extra laugh at your expense).

"That guy wanted to kill you back there," he said archly. "When we picked you up from the truck, we just needed somebody to chain you to in the backseat, but while you were conked out he offered us 300,000 pesos to leave him alone with you for a minute. The first thing he would've done was spill your guts on that road. You got a lot of enemies, fat boy."

We were nearing La Perla. I recognized the towns, and I knew that we would be at the gates in about fifteen minutes. I had changed my mind about wanting to go to a Mexican jail: if La Perla was under American control for the time being, I preferred to go there, thinking my chances of survival might be better. My belief in the relative benevolence of Mexican incarceration had been shaken. All I wanted, at that moment, was a grim, four-by-eight-foot cell, a cinder-block cage that no one else could enter.

"Listen, if you're taking me to La Perla," I said, "that's okay. I should be allowed to talk to my lawyer first, but . . . never mind."

"Oh—that's okay with you?"

The driver snickered. The mustache-man looked over at him and smirked.

"You don't mind going to La Perla?"

"No. Of course, if that's where they took all those guys from the truck . . . then maybe it's not so smart. They wanted to kill me, you know. I told you, it was like half of them wanted to, but the other half wouldn't let them. And I was caught in the middle. They couldn't seem to make up their mind."

"Don't worry about those guys. We fixed it so they won't bother you no more."

"You did?"

The mustache-man looked at me with a completely blank expression. Once again, I felt that he was 'trying out' something, using a technique on me that someone had recommended to him once. Meanwhile the driver—working on his own impersonation—took his eyes briefly off the road and glanced over at his partner, as if to reprove him for an indiscretion.

"Let's just say . . . they won't be gettin' no more suntan out in the desert, okay? You understand what I'm saying?"

"Yeah. Sure, I understand."

The radio crackled just then. All evening, they had been calling out, desperately trying to get in touch with someone, and here was the first call in. The mustache-man grabbed for the phone.

"Yeah . . . roger," he said. "Yeah . . . the stupid fish . . . I said 'fish.' Seventy. I don't care; that's it, no more. . . . No, we're about seven miles short of . . . Wha'? What you say? Wait a minute, don't you dare—"

I hadn't been able to understand this message, and the mustache-man's responses seemed to be in a sort of code. He now slammed the phone several times against the set, then screamed curses into it and with an apoplectic rip at the cord, tore it completely free. The driver responded with curses of his own; the mustache-man screamed at him, shoved him, and so that they could conduct their argument in relative safety, the driver suddenly pulled onto the shoulder of the highway.

Their anger carried them out of the car, and I watched them shoving and cuffing each other in the headlights. Off in the distance—probably a lot closer to us than seven miles—was a glow of lights that was either a truck stop set back from the highway, or part of La Perla, the outermost guard checkpoint or possibly some other facility. I had an irrational urge at that moment to flee in that direction, to seek the protection of those floodlights. Even if they represented La Perla, I would be safer there (I thought) than in the custody of these two, and I tried the chain that connected my ankle and wrist to the car door (it had been run through the armrest). In normal circumstances I might have been able to pull it free, but I was weak,

almost sick to my stomach from fear and confusion. I had the
disquieting sensation of being not at my best, of being simultaneously trapped in some sort of nightmare, from which I
could hope to awaken only if I had all my powers at my
disposal. The mustache-man and the driver had by now staggered out of the zone of the headlights. There was a ditch
alongside the road, then a huge field, completely black and
featureless. I could dimly hear them in there, wrestling and
slapping. Finally, a tremendous grunt produced momentary
silence; I rattled my chain, and a second later the mustache-
man appeared at my window.

"All right. Get out now," he said, waving a gun at me.

"I can't. I'm chained."

"Why, you stupid fucking . . ."

Instead of opening my door, or coming in through one of
the front doors, he smashed his gun against the window. The
plexiglass cracked, and he hammered it several more times and
finally made a hole big enough to stick his arm through. He
unlocked my chain, and a minute later I was walking along the
ditch with him, his gun pressed against the base of my spine.
After about twenty yards he made me cross the ditch. It was
full of muck that sucked at our shoes, and he angrily cursed the
ditch, the muck, and me, not neglecting to blame me for
making us cross at just that point. I was frantically trying to
come up with some plan for escaping; once far enough out in
the field, he would put his own plan into operation (I was sure),
and I desperately wanted to avoid being shot out here. I had an
uncommon horror of these surroundings. It wasn't so much the
idea of being shot—I told myself—as the grim foreignness of
this place, the clayey dirt that stuck to my boots, the smell of
chemical fertilizer, the chill in the moist air. Nothing at all
could be seen in the direction we were walking, and the idea of
my body being left here, for the vultures and rats to pick over,
was nauseating, caused my stomach to rebel.

"Wait a minute. I have to throw up."

"Come on. Come on," he kept saying, as I vomited repeatedly into a plowed furrow.

After a while, I got off my knees. I turned toward the mustache-man, and I was surprised to see him on the ground, half leaning against a little mound. His chin was pointing up at the sky, and his seersucker jacket had come unbuttoned, revealing a paunch with a stain in the middle of it. I waited for him to get up. When he didn't, I cautiously took a few steps away, farther into the field, but this disturbed him, and he looked in my direction. I stopped immediately; his gun hand, which had been resting in his lap, rose up.

"Wait a minute. Don't shoot me," I urged. "I have to tell you something. You see, I'm a kind of businessman—I've got a lot of money. I want to give you some of it. All of it, in fact."

His response was a kind of gargling noise. Then he threw up on the ground, just as I had done. Afterward he seemed very weak. The muzzle of his gun pointed at my chest, my waist, my feet. When it had been pointing at the ground for a few seconds, I approached him cautiously. His only response was to purse his lips in a senile sort of way, as if trying to spit out some object, a lemon seed or something of the kind. I reached down to take his gun. But his hand tightened around it, even while the rest of him remained completely immobile.

I returned to the car. Twenty yards short of it I found the driver; he was propped on his elbows and knees, his face stuck straight in the mud. I walked on by, but thinking better of it, I returned, and while rummaging through his pockets I found a ballpoint pen clenched tightly, desperately in his fist. I continued to the car. The keys weren't in the ignition, either, and I was too weak to figure out some other way to get it to start. But just then I caught sight of the lights up ahead—that island of bright lights that signaled, for me, some kind of relief, a way out of this frightening dream. I lurched forward, determined to make it there before I collapsed.

I WAS IN a hospital room. There were three other beds, all empty. It was tremendously white, overpoweringly clean—I had never seen such an antiseptic-looking room before in Mexico.

When I tried to stand up, I discovered a stiff bandage covering my entire upper back and most of my chest, running from just under my chin to below my navel. The feeling it gave me was exactly like the feeling I had had in the car—the sensation of being encased in a shell, a hard protective covering, and I found it almost impossible to move from side to side. I went over to a mirror. I was pale, weak-looking; I must have lost fifteen or twenty pounds in three days. I shuffled over to the window. There were bars implanted in the stucco, and the view was of stark, sterile-looking fields under a washed-out sky. I was on the third floor of a sizable building, and to my left was the rear wall of another, lower building, with a chain-link fence running around everything. A car came into view just then—it was driving slowly along a dirt track, just beyond the fence. It was the same kind of sedan the mustache-man had driven; for all I knew, it was the very one he had abandoned, back on the hill.

From time to time, I heard steps in the hall. I would turn that way as rapidly as possible, trying to get a glimpse through the window in the door, but always my stiff bandages prevented me from seeing anyone. Finally I heard steps approaching, and my painful effort to turn was rewarded: the door came unlocked, and three men in the uniform of the federal judicial police, grunting and swearing, entered, tugging and pushing among them a fourth figure, a man with a big bandage on his head. They had a hard time getting him over the threshold, and when they came to the first empty bed they pushed him down and clumsily tied him in with canvas straps. Then they hastily retreated.

After a few moments, I said, "I'm here—there's someone else in the room with you."

His bandage came to just below his eyes, and he responded to my words with an alarmed convulsion of his whole upper body. His head moved pathetically this way and that, and I said, "Over here. On the other side of the room. A little to your left."

As best he could, he arched his neck and oriented himself toward me.

"If you want, I'll undo your straps."

"Of course."

When I had taken them off, he rubbed his sore arms and shoulders and then, still flat on his back, reached up toward me. I placed my hand in his, and he shook it with feeling. I tried to pull away, and he said:

"You're a good fellow. Thank you. Thank you so much."

"What's the matter with your eyes?"

"Nothing . . . that is, since I was hit on the head, the less stimulation the better. That's what the doctor says. Sunlight gives me a bad headache. They take such wonderful care of you here, you see. But once you're better . . . out into the snake pit with you. Out among the cutthroats."

His name was Jaime Morgan, he said. He came from Tepic; he claimed to have been a science teacher in a high school there. A few years before, the mother of one of his students, angry because he, Jaime, had refused her advances, accused him of interfering with her fourteen-year-old son. There had been a court case, and his lawyer failed to distinguish himself. The result was an indeterminate sentence—in effect, a sentence of death, since supposed sex offenders were mercilessly mistreated in the federal prisons.

"So far I've managed to survive . . . who knows how. Just now I was battling with them because they taunted me, saying they were taking me to La Perla for treatment. I wouldn't last in La Perla for one hour. But all along, they had only been intending to bring me upstairs, to this infirmary."

I expressed surprise—I had quite naturally assumed that I was already in La Perla.

"Yes?" He laughed. "No. You are not in La Perla. You're in a little jail in Sinaloa de Leyva, a hundred miles north of La Perla. Just thank your lucky stars you're not in that shithole, that filthy cesspool. Excuse me, but I must speak frankly. All hell has broken loose there. The old system has been subverted, and something new and monstrous is taking its place."

He proceeded to give me his version of events in La Perla—in many respects, it resembled the accounts I had already had, except that my earlier informants, in emphasizing the Americans, had mistaken cause for effect. Yes, the gringos were now in control, he said, but only because a 'mighty revolution' was under way in the criminal culture. Certain changes in the way northwestern Mexico was to be divided up—an alteration in the underlying balance of illicit forces—

had created a situation that the U.S. Justice Department, in its abysmal ignorance, believed it might somehow exploit. The results of its attempts were, of course, chaotic.

"So the Americans have arrived . . . so they've arrested a few entrepreneurs, people previously untouchable. Never would this have come about without 'collusion' from above. When the air is clear, the mountain trembles. Never can we see into that realm where reality, in its primordial condition, first takes form. The 'Original Will' must always be hidden from us. . . . If we were to encounter it, experience it directly, we would be blinded. Destroyed.

"Three days ago," he continued, "a convoy set out from state police headquarters at Moluta. On the backs of some trucks were two hundred men who had been recently arrested. They were to be taken out into the desert, where a little camp had been set up. After a few days in the hot sun, without food or water, they would be released. But now . . . these two hundred men are dead.

"On one of these trucks, there was someone else. Let's just say . . . a cipher. A nonentity. The intrinsic value of this individual, this low human insect, was the same as that of the others, but someone had taken an 'interest' in him. The rumor is that he was the lover of a certain man—someone whose name is such that no one dares speak it out loud. If anyone can cause the mountains to tremble, this is that man. When he determines that the system shall change, that the orderly life of years, involving thousands and thousands of people, shall be no more, it happens, for certain. Enough for the idea merely to occur to him, to pass across his consciousness. However, he had forgotten one thing. He had forgotten about his insect.

"The one who had been so protected—now he had to swim with the others, to live or drown in the sea. Maybe he didn't understand his new vulnerability. Because when the mountain trembles, something *under* the mountain also moves, as we say. Something working against it. A force, perhaps, for good . . . or more likely, only a different sort of evil. An even more unspeakable kind. But the little insect was afraid, and in his terror he cried out, 'Save me, oh mighty protector, please, come to my aid. Don't let this scum pull me down. Don't let these bandits and pimps have their way with me.' However, it was too late. Many times, they cut him with knives.

"At the last minute—this is a happy story, after all—help arrived. Some people took him away, protected him. The forces of the underworld, you see, could not have their little victory. The Protector never forgets a friend: he may seem, from time to time, to have made a mistake, to have overlooked someone, but this is always an illusion. A snare for his enemies . . ."

For a long moment, I was completely silent. Sr. Morgan's remarkable story, to which I had at first listened only casually, had ended up ringing many bells with me, but I was eager not to seem too concerned about it, too intrigued. In a casual tone of voice I inquired:

"But—what about these others? The ones who were on the trucks, as you say—they were all killed?"

"Yes. In such a situation, it's better not to have any survivors. They were simply marched out in the desert, then shot."

"Shot? Just shot? But . . . how do you know this? You were in jail at the time. And it only happened yesterday, I think."

He smiled. "How do I know? How? But let me ask you something: can certain things ever really be hidden? If the world is to be turned upside down, can we who must walk upon it not be aware?"

"Yes, but—"

At that moment, there came a crash outside our door; a prison trustee, dressed in a white smock, had come to bring us dinner, but he had tripped at the threshold, spilling our food. Actually, only one of the dinner trays had fallen, and when he entered the room he still had the other one in his hands. After deliberating for a few seconds, he awarded it to Sr. Morgan.

As soon as he left, Morgan beckoned me to his bed. He

insisted that I eat the food. I protested this kindness, but in the
end, since I was ravenously hungry, I ate every scrap.

"Yes, it's good, hmmmn?"

"No. It's terrible—like eating dirt. Incredibly vile. Probably make me sick as a dog."

"No. It won't make you sick, I promise. The other one—
the one that he dropped—this might have made you sick. I
don't know."

As I went on stuffing myself—disregarding this gnomic
comment about the other tray—he put a comradely hand on
my shoulder. He remarked on how 'large' I was. His hand
sliding along my shoulder encountered the edge of my plaster
bandage, and he asked me how I had come to hurt myself. I
answered that it was nothing—that I had fallen off the hay
wagon around noon.

"Ah. And then they found you; and they brought you
here, to this clinic. Dr. Gómez is the man in charge. He likes to
put people in casts, I know this very well. Sometimes, just for
the fun of it, he breaks an extra bone. So that he can 'practice.' "

His hand began to rub the back of my neck, and I pulled
away. I was still eating his food, so to keep him occupied, I
asked him to tell me more about the so-called 'Protector.'

"More? You wish to know more?

"Well . . . he is enormous. Simply colossal. His influence
spreads to every city, every little town. In northern Mexico, he
is like the god who sits above, who turns upon us an amused,
indifferent attention, except when something happens to upset
him. Some say that he has hundreds of sons. Others say that he
has only one natural son—indeed, the very insect I spoke of.
This worthless, corrupted little fool, who never understood
one thing about his unique situation in life, has enjoyed all the
riches and the protection provided by his 'father,' yet without
acknowledging them. Finally, even his father grew disgusted
with him, and he arranged for his downfall.

"The truth, however, is much stranger—even more un-

fathomable. The insect and his Protector are not connected by
any natural tie, no, far from it. The insect—who, like you, is
very large, but fat, grossly misshapen—spent his early years
living on the street, where he corrupted other children and
committed unimaginable crimes. At about the age of fourteen,
he landed in jail, and here he befriended another young prisoner, the son of an important, powerful family from Morelos.
This bad son, who had conceived an undying hatred for his
own parents, had hatched an evil plan, and he recruited the
insect to carry it out for him. As soon as the insect was released,
he went straight to the family's house, in Morelos. He knew on
what day of the week the servants were off, and he also knew of
an entrance into the garden, which was otherwise surrounded
by a mighty wall.

"At the door of the house, he asked to be allowed to speak
to the father. But he was very ill—he was lying in his bedroom
upstairs, weak, utterly wasted. The mother brought the insect
up to the bedroom, and the smell in this enclosed, darkened
place was immediately familiar to him, as he had had occasion
to 'experiment' with poisons before. The father could hardly
keep his eyes open. It was clear to the insect that someone had
been administering doses of some concoction or other, and that
the father would soon be dead.

"The insect, in any case, delivered a message that the son
had sent: unless the parents went to Mexico City that very day,
to meet with an official in the prison authority, the son, who
was still locked up, would be murdered in his cell. The mother
immediately rushed off, hoping to save her boy. But the father—too weak to move—had to remain behind.

"As soon as the mother was gone, the insect smothered the
father, and then, carefully following a list given him by the son,
he went through the rooms of the mansion, gathering up all the
most valuable and portable items. The house was filled with art
treasures—those too large to be carried, he cunningly damaged
beyond repair, as per the instructions of the son. Having made

a circuit of all the downstairs rooms, he returned to the bedroom, where the corpse of the father now lay. His instructions
were to steal some pieces of jewelry here, and then—to drive
home the 'authorship' of this outrage—to destroy some articles
of clothing, plus a certain oil portrait, a famous depiction of the
family. Having gathered up all the mother's jewelry, the insect
turned to look for that portrait; but, strange to say, it was
nowhere to be seen in the room.

"The insect went to the door of the bedroom. To his
surprise, he found it locked. He immediately saw that his
situation was serious. The door was made of solid wood, and
therefore couldn't be smashed; and the lock was of a sort that
worked from the outside. But this suggested that someone else
was around, that someone else was afoot in the house. The
insect began to grow nervous. He went to the bedroom window, thinking to climb out; but he found it massively barred on
the outside. Then, as he stood there at the window, feeling
frustrated, frightened, he happened to glance over his shoulder,
and here, all of a sudden, was the oil portrait, the very one he
had been unable to find a moment ago. It was right there in
front of him—displayed in the middle of the bedroom's largest
wall.

"As the insect approached—thinking to carry out his plan
of desecration, in any case—a door opened up, a secret entrance in the wall, and here, right before him, stood a man, a
tall, handsome gentleman with silver hair. The insect cried out
in alarm. But the stranger, as if to reassure him, put a hand
gently on his shoulder. The insect fell to his knees; there was
that feeling of power, of imperturbable command, in the
stranger's touch, which caused the insect to quake down in his
very vitals. Then the stranger spoke—he asked to hear the
insect's 'true name.'

" 'I am . . . so-and-so,' the insect replied, lying instinctively. 'And I haven't done anything wrong. I came here because I heard that the old man was sick, and I wanted to help
him. But you see what's become of him.'

"The stranger nodded. 'Yes, someone has murdered my friend. And someone has been looting his house, dishonoring it. But you and I . . . we can do something about this. Working together, we can restore this place, this noble temple. Will you'—and here he quoted the insect's actual name—'will you, yourself, now turn to my side, will you dedicate yourself to this holy service?'

"Thinking to gain a momentary advantage, the insect eagerly agreed. The gray-haired man smiled, and the insect rose to his feet.

" 'Go out of this room,' the stranger ordered him. 'Find all the places where damage has been done. Replace what has been taken away. The broken things are lost. . . . Repair them if you can, only if you can. When you arrive back at this door, take off all your clothes. Then lie down flat on the floor, and touch your tongue to the threshold. Don't make a sound.'

" 'Don't make a sound . . . all right, very good,' repeated the insect, as if this made complete sense.

"The door to the room came open. The insect went out, hurried to the front of the house. But as soon as he stepped out into the garden, thinking to run away, a fierce storm blew up, with powerful winds and driving rain. Though he could have made his way through this storm, he was strangely reluctant to do so. He retreated into the house, and, as if to pass the time, he took an item out of one of his sacks, a tiny pre-Cortesian figurine, and put it back on the shelf where it had been. The sight of it there, in its proper spot, caused a turmoil in his heart; he intended to grab it back, to stuff it back in his sack, but for now—just for 'a moment'—he left it where it was.

"Then he took out some other pieces. He likewise returned these to their original display positions. Soon he had completed the restoration of an entire room. The father of the family, whom he had so casually murdered, had been, in addition to a collector of artifacts, an expert on antique Mexican silver. Several rooms were stuffed full of old, heavy sets of service, and when the insect entered this part of the house, he was appalled at the damage he had done. Almost with tears in his eyes, he now did his best to restore the form of some larger pieces. The lesser articles had been smashed almost to the condition of lumps of ore, and it gave him a peculiar discomfort—almost a physical pain—to realize that they could never be reformed.

"In other rooms there were crowns, girdles, and breastplates of gold; obsidian knives; Olmec fertility totems; Aztec robes woven of gorgeous *quetzal* feathers, and so forth. It gave the insect pause to think that a family had actually lived here—had passed its mundane hours surrounded by these fabulous pieces, which amounted to a sampling of the entire wealth of the nation, artistic, historical, and spiritual. Sometimes it seemed to him that there was even an overall 'plan'—that there was a reason, for example, why this one room, with its propagandistic woodcuts by Orozco, gave onto a parlor full of silver, which in turn led to a gallery containing hundreds of depictions of the Virgin of Guadalupe. If only he had not been so hasty— if he had but refrained from smashing this or that suggestive piece—then the 'mystery' might have revealed itself, become intelligible. As it was, he had to strain every faculty to grasp it for an instant; and then, inevitably, it fled, left him feeling forlorn, stupid.

"Soon his steps brought him back to the bedroom. As if in the fulfillment of a prophecy, the insect fell straight to the floor, abjectly prostrated himself. Without quite thinking what he was doing, he took off his clothes, and he kissed the tiles at the threshold of the room. There was a radiance coming from inside—a subtle, golden glow, perceptible no matter how tightly the insect shut his eyes. At first, he feared this strange light, which seemed to penetrate him, to warm him down in his innards; after a while, though, he turned his face toward it, and the glow caused a sensation such as he had never experienced before. Something so pleasurable, he felt, could not be dangerous, and he opened his eyes completely.

"At the end of the bed, he saw the feet of the father. The corpse had been turned over onto its belly, and these feet, alone among the objects in the room, emitted no magical light, were not in the least radiant. To one side of the bed stood a figure bathed in an especially intense golden glow—it was the stranger—and on the other side, not quite so radiant, and completely naked, was the mother, the woman who, supposedly, had run away only an hour ago, to save her son. As the insect stared, this woman began to fondle her rosy breasts, which were swollen and sweaty. It was his impression that she had just completed some physical task, which had left her not quite out of breath, but enlivened, eager for more effort. Now the stranger turned slowly in his cloud of light, and he gestured to the insect. Accordingly, the insect rose to his feet, and as he did, the naked mother began to jump up and down, to wave and jerk her bare arms and legs. There was something so startling about this behavior that the insect could hardly suppress an urge to run away; in this arrangement of personalities, with the mother to his left, the stranger to his right, and the dead father straight ahead, he felt under the influence of a malevolent force, almost a magnetic force, which was slowly drawing him in, 'claiming' him.

" 'Here,' said the stranger, in a perfectly ordinary voice. 'Put this on.'

"He offered something. The insect took it from his right hand; it was a cup, or a cusp, a hollow, fragile object shaped like half an eggshell. As he held it in his fingers, the mother approached; her touch indicated which part of his anatomy the object was supposed to fit. The insect pulled away from her; her wantonness disgusted him, but to his surprise, her brief touch had caused a change, made him swell and grow. The mother greeted this sudden alteration with more of her wild, celebratory 'dancing,' if that was what it was, and the insect, in mortified confusion, found himself doing as told, placing the object on the very tip of his manhood.

" 'Now come over here,' said the stranger matter-of-factly. 'Do as you've always done. Bring unto him . . . the light.'

" 'The . . . what?'

" 'The light. Give him the light.'

"Ahead lay the body of the father. The mother threw back a sheet, and the corpse was now completely revealed, a wasted, sinister form, deader than anything the insect had ever seen before.

" 'Bring . . . the light to him?'

" 'Yes. But do it now—do it quickly. Your fate, and his, as well, hang in the balance.'

" 'But I can't. No—no . . .'

" 'You must. Think of it as a favor you'll be doing for me—for me, myself. I will be forever in your debt for this. Believe me, I'll remember you always for this.'

" 'No, I can't. . . .'

"Some minutes having passed, the insect began to feel uncomfortable. The cusp, which fit him closely, had begun taking on the heat of his body, and as it did it began to melt. At first he had thought it was made of plaster, but now he saw it was actually composed of a fine white powder, some sort of chemical that had been pressed in a mold.

" 'It's . . . burning me!' he cried. 'Help me, please—'

" 'No. Do as you're told,' replied the stranger.

" 'But I can't. Really—it's burning me!'

"At a certain point—the pain now increasing rapidly—the radiance of the room all concentrated in his mind, and the insect collapsed on the bed. The white powder, melting with his skin, caused a pressure to mount inside him, and his only recourse was to thrash about wildly, to try to rub it off him. But here he was on the very legs of the dead man; then, as if pulled in place by an invisible hand, he was actually on top. He entered the body of the dead father. . . .

"Sometime later—maybe only a few minutes—he awoke. His thrashing had carried him onto the floor. The radiance was now gone from the room, and the simple clarity of normal appearances, after what had happened, seemed like a blessing, a miracle. The stranger was gone from the room. The hole in the wall, through which he had appeared, had somehow sealed itself up, and everything was as before. The mother, now fully clothed, was standing calmly at the head of the bed. He saw her fluff some pillows, and then she busied herself with a bottle of medicine and a glass of water. She was getting ready to take some pills, he thought.

"At first—he didn't understand. But there was someone else—someone else was sitting up in bed, propped up in those pillows. It was—the father. It was the dead father, returned to life! As the insect stared disbelievingly, the father lifted a bony hand, and his mouth came open slowly, getting ready to accept some pills. His wife placed them lovingly on his tongue, and after some slight difficulty he swallowed them.

"The insect backed away. He crawled off as quickly as he could, unable to believe what he saw, horrified in extra measure because this miracle, this weird restoration of life, had been visited upon so unlikely a subject, a dying man, in any case. When he had reached the outer rooms of the house, he saw that everything was as before—all the stolen and broken objects, everything he had taken or damaged, had been perfectly re-stored, and the house was as it had been when he arrived. He quickly found the front door. He ran out into the gardens, into the night. As he breached the stone wall surrounding the gardens, he heard voices behind him, the evil whispering of ghosts, or demons; they were urging him to stop, to come back, saying that he was 'theirs' now, that by his actions this day, he had surrendered unto them his immortal soul. . . ."

MY PURPOSE IN repeating this story, this 'parable,' in as complete a version as I can put together, is simply to try to create in the minds of any readers I may have an impression of my utter confusion at this dark moment. Inexplicable and frightening events had been assailing me for three days, and now to top it off, I had been locked in a room with a crazy man, someone whose hallucinations unaccountably drew on elements of my own personal history. I had of course immediately identified the 'mansion' with the Señora's house in Cuernavaca, and the whole mad tale of the poisoned father, the evil mother, and the mysterious stranger who popped out of walls reminded me uncomfortably of Marcela's theory of her father's demise.

I think I was already starting to put things together, though, even as I lay there, in the dark, on the bed across from Sr. Morgan. He was not just a 'science teacher,' as he claimed, but an associate of my father's; his slavish and, indeed, worshipful attitude toward the 'Great Protector,' whom he had quite possibly never met in person, reminded me of the awe I had seen demonstrated before Gerson by others, and this attribution to him of magical powers, of an influence in the world that can only be described as godlike, was not so far from my own secret fear of his widespread control. For underneath my ridiculous, inexcusable misapprehension of my whole situation, there had always been a suspicion that I operated on the sufferance of someone else; that an 'unseen hand' had been guiding my destiny all along.

How Sr. Morgan came to know so much about him—and in such compelling detail—I still can't explain. From one or two things heard here or there, he had cobbled together an entire saga, but what amazed me even more was his intense and avid interest, as if the existence of such a figure—a 'Protector'—were a life-and-death issue for him. It was as though a criminal universe not presided over by a single, omniscient boss were a terrifying concept, his fear of it to be measured by the very plenitude of his imaginings.

Why it had to be my own father, though—why he couldn't identify someone else in this way—I can't say. I wasn't quite ready to admit that there was a simple factual truth to his accounts, yet what had been happening to me recently—the incident on the truck, for example—was hard to explain without reference to some sort of 'conspiracy,' with my personal safety of such moment that other lives had been sacrificed, events ingeniously organized to result in my survival. Probably the most telling conspiratorial fact was Sr. Morgan's presence here—that of all the possible infirmary rooms in all the different prisons, this was where he had happened to pop up, and just when I was here.

How much did I really know about my father, I wondered; did I, for example, know for sure that he no longer had business interests in Mexico? And what exactly had those interests been, those vague 'holdings' that he supposedly shared with the Señora? Wasn't it possible that, while appearing to withdraw some years ago, he had in fact simply surrendered his affairs to various associates, who were even to this day acting as his agents? I had always before taken comfort in the idea that I was alone, that I was far beyond his reach out here. I had placed myself in a remote environment—if you like, had lowered myself to a certain level—that I was sure he could have no interest in. But all of a sudden, it seemed the most obvious of blatant likelihoods that he was still 'connected'—that information about my comings and goings was getting back to him. Recalling that afternoon when I was first arrested, when all my fellow detainees had seemed to resent me so, I saw things in a new light. Yes—it was indeed possible that I *was* responsible for what was happening to them. If I had been protected—if all along I had been secretly sheltered, and others, knowing this, had crowded close, to share my immunity—then my sudden arrest would have seemed a very serious development.

If my father was the head of a widespread criminal enterprise, then everything that I believed about myself, all my comfortable ideas about my 'independence,' my 'self-reliance,' had to be reevaluated. Furthermore, I would stand convicted, in that case, of precisely that degree of stupidity that people had recently been accusing me of: only a true idiot, someone blind to the most obvious of straightforward conditions, could have acted as I had.

Sometime just before dawn—as I was engaged upon these unpleasant cogitations—a hand touched my thigh. I immediately struck out with both arms, somehow managing to push him away; it was Sr. Morgan, who, assuming I was asleep, had tried to join me under the covers.

"Don't do that," I snapped. "I'm warning you—I won't stand for it."

"Wait. You don't understand me. . . ."

I saw him holding his bandaged head. The way he carefully touched the stiff, turbanlike wrap suggested a colossal headache, and I waited for him to say something about it. But no, after a minute he lifted the bandage straight off; then in the weak, silvery light, which was now spilling in through our single barred window, I saw his entire face for the first time.

I was appalled. There was something terribly wrong, highly abnormal; his eyes were enormous, protuberant like a frog's. Each one looked as big as a tennis ball. Then he turned, catching the light in a different way, and I saw that what I had taken for his eyes were, in fact, two surgical pads, one taped over either eye socket.

I remembered him saying there was nothing wrong with his eyes, that he had only suffered some sort of "head injury." The right eye, especially, looked very bad; the pad on that side was stained black, as if it had absorbed blood, which had then dried.

"Now . . . you must help me," he said. "Please. Come over here. Help me take them off. I don't think I have the strength. . . ."

Before I could answer, he moved toward my bed again. Grabbing me by the thigh—but only because he was blind, had to feel his way—he sat down uncertainly on the edge. Not giving me any choice in the matter, he placed my hands directly on his face, then right on the pads themselves. As I began to fumble with the strips of tape, he encouraged me by saying:

"Yes . . . as the light comes. Before they come. I have to guide us; if they've left me anything with which to see, that is. . . ."

The left eye wasn't so bad. It looked as if someone had just punched him up a bit; it was swollen, bruised. But the right one—even though I had, to some extent, steeled myself for this—made me gag, as it seemed to be entirely missing, simply, utterly destroyed. I suppose that all the fluids had leaked out, as the result of some terrible blow. Even now there was a further leakage, and I hastened to put the pad back on.

"No—I have to see things. Leave it alone. Please."

Trying to avoid the bandage, he turned away from me, but as soon as he faced the window he jumped to his feet. I heard a cry of pain—no, it was that, but also a sort of triumphant groan, a deeply relieved, moistly grateful sound. By the way he turned his head this way and that, as if to rub his face in the light coming through the bars, I gathered that he could still see—at any rate, still receive some sort of visual impression.

"It's all so . . . broad," he exclaimed happily. "Like a giant burning sphere inside a frame, and the frame, though sturdy, is about to burst apart. When it does goodness will rain down upon us . . . unfortunately, I can't make out all the details. The color is just red, and the feeling warm. That's all I can say."

Then we heard voices in the corridor. Sr. Morgan rushed back from the window, and with a fearful quaver in his voice he ordered me to get out of bed, to 'prepare' myself. But the voices, not even pausing at our door, passed along the hall.

"Are they gone?"

"Yes. I think so."

He came over. "Still, you have to get up . . . give me your hand." Because of my plaster chest bandage, I was clumsy in my movements, and it was actually useful to have him to lean on. Somehow my boots had disappeared. Nor could I find my pants, or my papers (they had been appropriated some days before, just before we got on the truck), or my much-torn, bloodied shirt. I was going to have to leave the infirmary—if that was what was about to happen—dressed only in my underpants and cast, supported by Sr. Morgan, who at least still had his pants on.

"All right—now listen closely. Stay by my side. Stay always next to me. If someone gets between us, come back quickly, using force if necessary. When I ask you something, answer me immediately. I can't see well, so you'll have to act as my eyes. A certain man will try to show himself to us—even I don't know who he is. But he will demonstrate certain qualities, indicate himself by various tricks. Others may try to fool us—you have to report exactly what you see. Don't become confused, and at all costs, don't be afraid to—"

They had sneaked back—our door came open suddenly, and six men rushed in. We were borne out into the hallway, thrown and pushed. Sr. Morgan, holding tenaciously to my elbow, resisted being pulled away, but someone beat him over the head with a stick, and my last sight of him, as I was pulled away, was of him falling to the floor, with one arm held pathetically in front of his eyes.

MANY PEOPLE HAVE this dream, but I was actually living it: in the middle of a crowd of strangers, in some anonymous public gathering place, you look down and find that you've forgotten to put your pants on. No one else seems to notice . . . you do your best to hide your 'shame,' and in the meantime, a test gets under way, some crucial examination that you've neglected to study for.

In the middle of the gathering place—the inner courtyard of the prison—was a monument of some kind. I dazedly made my way toward it. The prisoners moved away from me like a sea parting. There were hundreds of them—it must have been the morning call-up, the assemblage before they all went in for breakfast. Almost everyone was Mexican, and almost no one looked my way; I might have been invisible, nonexistent, but for how they parted, carefully avoided crossing my path.

Lots of them were wearing new, prison-issue denims. I noted this, remembering the stories about a new 'regime' at some of the prisons, the introduction of the baleful North American influence. When I arrived at the central monument, a fat man got up quickly, but with an appearance of nonchalance; up to the instant of my arrival, he had been sitting on a mosaic, a convex, roughly circular design sunk in the concrete, composed of oddly shaped pieces of mother-of-pearl. The way he suddenly got up—almost as if he wanted to call my attention to it—caused me to examine it closely; at first, I thought it was nothing special, but the longer I looked the more I felt its antiquity, and I finally decided it was pre-Columbian, an Indian artifact probably unearthed when they'd built the prison.

"*Siéntate*," said a voice. I turned as quickly as my bandages would allow, but saw no one. Not a single face was turned in my direction, and as if to defy this commanding, but secretive, personage, I did not sit. Then a group of men, consisting of about six of those nearest me, bolted off into the crowd. They seemed to have some important purpose, and I felt exhausted, helpless, comparing myself, in my half-naked, confused condition, to them, so sure of whatever it was that they were about. A wave of indolence, of an abject need to surrender, washed over me. But as soon as I started to sit down, a man materialized out of the crowd. He grabbed me by the elbow.

"No. Don't sit. Don't lose strength, my son."

"Who are you? Are you the one who—"

As soon as he saw I wasn't going to sit, he stepped back into the crowd. I wanted to follow, to have him lead me out of here, but I could see that he wanted to get away. Now a couple of other prisoners, one of them very small and youthful, moved into my vicinity. The other one, older and with bad skin, addressed me in bad English:

"Why don' you sit? C'mon, my fren. Put you ass here on this rock. Then we get you a doctor, everything gonna be all right."

"A doctor? I don't need doctors. I'm feeling fine now."

The small, youthful one, insinuating himself between his friend and me, looked up at me with brown, syrupy eyes. I waited for him to get out of my way, to step back, and when he didn't, I simply pushed him down. As the other one continued talking, this little one sneaked behind me, and a few seconds later I realized that he had stuck a hand up under my cast—so gently, so subtly did he accomplish this, that I hardly felt anything.

". . . gonna go *a dentro*. Be like real soon, my fren. Everybody go inside an' eat. But then you gonna be in trouble, 'cause you don' know where to go, do you. Best thing is sit down, here on this here *perla*. Let them go on in. Maybe somebody come over an' help you then."

"Did you say— Did you just call it a—" I whirled around, having to club the little one away from me again. He fell on his backside, all the while smiling at me in the most irritating way.

"Uh-oh. Here they go. They goin' in now. . . ."

The bad-skinned one was calling my attention to a movement in the crowd. In a few minutes, everyone would have slipped away from the area of the monument, pressed forward toward a distant corner, which was presumably the entrance to the mess hall. But I was more concerned with what he'd just said—that he had called the monument, the design embedded in it, a 'pearl,' which, of course (now that he mentioned it), was exactly what it resembled. But if the centerpiece of this prison yard was a pearl, then the prison itself, taking its name from this notable feature, was undoubtedly the famous La Perla. Despite Sr. Morgan's claims to the contrary—and why he would have lied about this to me, I couldn't say—I had ended up exactly where, from the start, I had most feared going.

"It's . . . La Perla," I said weakly, distractedly. "I'm actually here. . . . I'm here, in La Perla."

As the crowd continued to drift, the bad-skinned one kept advising me to sit, to take a weight off. He seemed most

adamant about my sitting precisely on that spot, right on top of
the pearl design. I instantly imagined an entire folklore of this
place: that those who were marked out for execution, the intended victims of prison-gang reprisals and vendettas, were
maneuvered toward the monument, forced to take the fatal
seat, and then—like the recipients of the deadly 'black hand' of
Mafia legend—dispatched forthwith. I had no desire to play
out this ritual, with myself in a central role, but when I tried to
back off the little one got in my way again. I tried to push him
from me, as I had done before, but somehow our legs became
entangled, and the next thing I knew I was sprawled facedown
on the rock.

"Good," said the bad-skinned one, as soon as I had
touched the design; with impressive haste, he grabbed his
friend by the shirt collar, hoisted him to his feet and back-
pedaled into the crowd. Seconds later I was surrounded by a
squad of uniformed guards; they likewise lifted me up, and
menacing the few nearby prisoners with their automatic
weapons, they led me away, toward the main building of the
prison.

NEVER MIND. You don't need to know all that," said the prison *comandante*. "Just sign thees papers."

I watched as Ray Narciso, my father's friend, scrawled his name at the end of a long, official-looking sheaf of documents. I felt as if I were being let go after a drunk-driving arrest, now seriously chastened, with a splitting headache and 'a lot of explaining to do'.

"Assholes . . . don't know how to run their own country. Whack you myself, if I had the chance . . . gonna get you for this, I mean it . . ." Ray snarled sotto voce.

Soon we were outside, and I was pushed into the backseat of a car. We drove quickly to a local airfield, where a small plane took us up into a dusty sky, which is confused in my mind with a feeling I remember, a certain greasiness all over my chest and back. Ray began to take off my bandages, but then something bothered him (it must have been my smell, that of my septic wounds), and I remember saying, "Yes, it's a filthy, greasy sky, isn't it, Ray—it kind of makes your skin crawl."

"You gonna be okay, Looey," he replied. "You wanna drink?"

"What kind of drink?"

"I don't know. We got bourbon, cognac. . . . I think you used to like Crème de menthe, right?"

"Right. Oh, Jesus. That makes me want to throw up."

"Hey—hey there—"

I think that I had been sick for a very long time—I'd just been repressing it, not letting it become symptomatic. I was to spend the next several weeks under a doctor's care, in a clinic on the road to Big Bear Lake, where my father owned some property. Ray stayed at a motel nearby, and we played a lot of chess and gin rummy in the afternoons. Once I suffered a minor relapse, because they were medicating me with a penicillin derivative that I was allergic to—I must have become unconscious, because when I woke up, it was days later and I had lost even more weight. (I've never really gained back the thirty to forty pounds I lost in the course of my Mexican adventure.) A nurse was in my room, and she smiled at me as soon as she saw my eyes open. I think that she had been about to change my pajamas, or maybe give me an alcohol bath, because I was completely naked on the bed.

"What're the windows doing . . . such fuzzy lines. Have to call home now . . . lending libraries."

"How are you?" she asked politely. "Would you like something to drink? You must be very thirsty. Can you show me your right hand, Lew-iss?"

I puzzled over right and left for a while. I finally decided that it didn't make much difference, and I used both hands to pull a sheet over my groin.

"Someone was just here," the nurse now said urgently, secretively. "He'll be very disappointed that he missed you—that you hadn't come around yet."

"I know who it was," I responded brightly. I concentrated

fiercely, and when I was sure that I had the name—Ray Narciso's, of course—I spoke it out loud.

"No," she said with wide eyes—"someone else. Someone
you know . . . even better than that."

I was flabbergasted. I remember feeling deeply confused,
and then being inwardly angry with her—and the certainty,
the purity of this anger was what really brought me around,
finally—to think that she would toy with me, would be so coy
with me, in my current pathetic, devastated condition.

"No. It couldn't be."

"Yes. It was . . . it was *he*."

How did I know whom she meant—that she was talking
about my father, that it was Gerson who had visited my room,
bringing me a number of interesting books, plus a stack of old
Playboy magazines? I guess it was just her peculiar manner, her
'sharing a mystery' expression—and for a bad moment, I
thought I was back in Mexico, that from now on, everyone I
met was going to be referring to him, thinking about him, in
that strange way that Sr. Morgan had. Suddenly I knew that
my real struggle—the final step I had to take, to recover my full
strength and sanity—was just to think about him as naturally
as possible, to refer to him as I would to anyone else, with no
inward trembling, no tacit acceptance of this awful 'respect'
that they all seemed to want to demonstrate.

"Oh, if he comes around again," I said casually, "just tell
him I'm on the toilet. Something like that. I don't want to see
him. I'm angry with him. You wouldn't believe what he's put
me through—what I've had to suffer, just on account of him."

Ray's position on the whole affair (as I soon learned) was
that a simple mistake had been made, that they had arrested me
by accident while I was on one of my Mexico vacations. Then,
things had simply gotten out of hand, and only a lucky break
happened to put him at La Perla on the day when I was brought
in (that is, brought down from the infirmary). As anyone who
read the daily papers knew, something funny was going on

between Mexico and the U.S. at this time (according to Ray), an adjustment was being made in their cooperative campaign against across-the-border drug movements. This explained all the 'feebs' and other Justice Department types he'd run into while "shagging my ass all over northwest Mexico, trying to get you released, you jerk."

"But Ray," I earnestly corrected, "you simply don't understand. You haven't been listening to me. *I* was the cause of all the trouble; when they picked me up, they disturbed a delicate system that's been operating for years, that involves thousands of people. I was the very centerpiece of it, the guy in the middle who, even though he doesn't know it, is crucial to everything, is being watched by everyone else. The important thing was just that I was Gerson's son—that my father, who controls everything down there, had let me take a fall."

"Your own . . . What, are you crazy? Let you take a fall?"

"Wait a minute, wait a minute, let me finish—he let them have me, because that was how he showed that things were going to be different now, that the whole system was changing. Everyone had better be on his toes from now on, you see. '*Cuando la sierra tembla, los insectos bailan*,' as they say down there—which just means that I was expendable. I had a certain value for him, and he cashed me in. But he didn't count on how loyal they all are to him—they're so scared, so used to doing whatever he wants, that they couldn't believe that he'd actually sacrifice his own son. So other guys got beat up instead of me; some got killed, because they were trying to protect me, and one little guy—he's probably dead by now—he got his eye poked out, his bloody fucking eyeball. . . ."

Ray refused to accept this version of events; no matter how much I argued, how clearly and rationally I explained it all, he persisted in the belief that I was confused, that my systemic infection was clouding my mental processes. Gerson no longer had any business interests in Mexico, he assured me; as long ago as 1960 or '61, he had let go of everything he once owned with the Señora, and as far as Ray knew, never once since that time had he even been south of the border. If I imagined that something 'funny' was going on there, that I had been treated differently, on account of who I was, I would do well to remember that, in the first place, I was an American; that these Mexicans liked nothing better than to trap unsuspecting North Americans, whose families then could be forced to pay handsomely to gain their release. And for another thing, I was such an unusual physical specimen—so big, so impossible not to notice—that someone must have reasoned that I'd bring more on a strictly pound-for-peso basis. It had cost Ray (who, I'm sure, was being bankrolled by my father) almost $12,000 to track me down, to grease the palms that opened the doors through which I finally walked.

"But Ray," I persisted, "don't be such a schmuck, Ray. You know very well who he is. If anybody does, you do. All those years he was protecting me, you knew what he had in mind, you were probably helping him. I just want him to know that I'm on to him now—that I'm not so stupid anymore. I understand what it means when they say 'the mountain trembles,' Ray, and I think I know who's *under* the mountain, too, the one who's been working against him, if she isn't working for him. Somebody like him will always have an enemy, Ray, because if he doesn't, if he acts unopposed, then all us insects just get blasted, we can't take the heat, you know. . . ."

With a worried look, Ray rose up from his bedside chair. "Relax, Looey. Hey—just relax. You better lie back. I'm gonna go get the nurse now. I think you got a fever . . . yeah, lie back, lie down in those pillows."

S OME YEARS PASSED . . . he traveled. . . .

The truth is, I hardly went anywhere. Instead, I retreated to my little hideaway, my run-down ranch up in the mountains. I had acquired a small property in western Trinity County, far up in northern California, and here I settled in for a spell of recuperative self-absorption, determined to lead a simple life from now on. I had a few friends in the area, hippie types in the grip of a back-to-the-land phase. Within a few months I was indistinguishable from the rest of the local recluses, a tall fellow with a scraggly beard, hollow cheeks, 'haunted' eyes, and a panel truck.

I planted marijuana—it was all I really knew how to do. I had somehow arrived at my twenty-eighth year with no useful skills, no legitimate talents or interests, nothing to serve me during my long march through life (should there be an ex-

tended, self-supporting journey ahead of me). I was in rather
bad shape financially, but even worse was what might be called
my spiritual condition: as recent events receded into memory,
as I achieved a more commonplace understanding of everything, I was rather more depressed than relieved, enervated in
some fundamental, unresolvable way. I had apparently survived my trial, but I was left feeling pointless, powerless, and
distant from everything. Feeling self-indulgent, despising myself for this late-appearing character fault (for so I took it to be),
I languished for a period of several years, never quite able to
rise above myself.

During this time, my sister was released from prison; she
immediately enrolled in nursing school, earned her certificate,
and found a legitimate job. We saw each other only once or
twice in this period—I had visited her at Lawton, the mini-
mum-security facility where she was kept, but several letters I
wrote her from Mexico went unanswered, and in general, she
seemed not to want to have very much to do with me.

Once I settled in at the 'Boneyard,' however—our name
for our Trinity County ranch—she began to come visit me on a
fairly regular basis. We had found the place together, in those
hectic days when she and her friends were first running from
the authorities, and she had a certain proprietary interest, I
feel, which she sought to protect by traveling up every few
months, arguing with me over any improvements I wanted to
make. The old farmhouse, which had been built as a summer
cabin, with batten-and-board walls, had to be winterized; and
then as the years went by, I added other rooms and outbuild-
ings, all of which additions she at first resisted. The floor of the
house (there wasn't any subfloor, or even a foundation proper)
had to be replaced after the first year, and while digging under
the house we found quantities of extremely dry, chalky bones,
which we assumed were just cattle remains. But later, a friend
of mine, who had a scientific bent, saying that the bones were
too big for cows, took some of them over to a professor he knew

at Humboldt State University, and we learned that our ranch was a sort of burial ground for a rare, nearly extinct kind of elk, *Cervus nannodes californiensis*, which had once been widespread but was now to be encountered only in zoos.

Just what such remnants were doing on our property, and in such quantities, can't be determined, although my friend says that at the time of the Spanish conquest, a number of native species suffered severe spontaneous diebacks; without even the pressure of heavy hunting, they simply gathered in remote wild places, somehow willed their collective demise, and immediately perished in great numbers, as if, having glimpsed the future, they were reluctant to share the fate of California under the white man. Whether this is true or not, I know that wherever we dug on our property we found bones. Soon we were making fences of them, grinding them up for fertilizer, and hanging them in macabre displays over all the doorways and gates.

My sister, with an energy that surprised me, turned an area in front of our house into a garden, where organic vegetables now proceeded to grow on broad terraces interspersed with beds of herbs and flowers. I had never suspected her of being the gardening type, and I remember how naturally it came to me to disdain her efforts, to imply that she was succumbing 'just a little too enthusiastically' to the reigning ethos of that time and place, which held that we were all but children of Mother Earth, and that salvation lay in return to a soiled simplicity. I, myself, was embarked on a similar gardening project, but the secrecy and illegality of it excused it in my mind; I had a great need to feel selfish in those days, to believe myself cynical and greedy, and my pot gardening was therefore done in a highly commercial spirit, with little breath wasted on the beauties of nature, or on the supposed virtues of working 'outside the system.' In my first year or two, I was haphazard in my methods, and my harvests were small, sufficient only to underwrite another period of subsistence. But being more or

less 'Mexican' in my growing style, I had casually imported a
common horticultural technique, whereby the female plants
(marijuana is male and female—dioecious), those which bear
the most potent flowers, are purposely kept from being polli-
nated, which results in a final product much stronger and
better-smoking than normal. My seedless 'thunderbuds,' as
they were called locally, were soon a tremendous hit in the
market, and I was inaccurately, but usefully, credited with
having invented the entire *sinsemilla* style of homegrown pot.
By 1976, when I had been cultivating for about three seasons, I
was making excellent money, probably as much as I'd ever
made in a year in Mexico. I marketed my product through
some people I knew in San Francisco—who had had nothing to
do with my previous importing business—and I started to
appreciate the 'good thing' that I had fallen into.

My relationship to that silly weed, marijuana, can be of no
interest to anyone other than myself, but I feel a need to
record—for reasons of historical curiosity, no more—that I was
anything but the typical, pot-smoking longhair of those days. I
hardly ever indulged, and I was only casually a believer in the
doctrine that held that marijuana was a 'better' intoxicant than
alcohol, which led to violence, was identified with the death
culture, ruined your liver, etc. Marijuana made you dull and
forgetful, and for me this was a terrible quality, an excellent
reason to shun it; unlike many of my fellows, I felt no need to
subvert whatever brainpower I still had, and I would sample
my own products only when I absolutely had to, say while
entertaining prospective buyers, or when forced to act conviv-
ial at a party or other gathering. But though not much of a pot
smoker, I did become, through years of close contact with that
remarkable plant, a true aficionado of cannabis, an amateur
expert on the various strains, their propensities, genetic peculiarities, etc. Years of growing it in the national forest behind
my farm—always at a considerable distance from the house, in
case of a police raid—led me to know it in the loving way that

any dirt farmer knows his crop, and I must say that, to the extent I could pretend to be a simple, nonreflective peasant, I was fairly happy with my situation.

My sister, who had planned on becoming a doctor, had no complaints about being a nurse; the side of her which I had always found unaccountable, her *compassionate nature*, now took over, and she followed it (if it makes sense to speak of 'following' one's own nature) to the very brink of self-destruction.

In occasional moments, I reflected on the waste of her intellectual capacities, that someone with so unusual, and forceful, a personality, someone so lovely, and so otherwise gifted, should merely be emptying bedpans, inserting i.v.'s in wasted arms, pushing pills, etc. For some time she worked in a coronary care unit, and it was my misfortune to visit her there once, to see the poor devils who, temporarily, had been resurrected, whom she was keeping alive with strange chemical nostrums and outrageous mechanical devices. The intensity of her concentration, her remarkable skillfulness, made a strong impression on me, but I couldn't help hoping that she would soon 'get over' this, outgrow her need to mortify herself, to serve suffering humanity at its most painfully abject.

Then she transferred to a different job, in a worse hospital, at less pay. She was in an intensive care unit now, and the day-to-day parade of sad cases, the constant air of fateful crisis, began to wear her down, undermine her spirit. After every few months of work she would repair to our ranch, where, with the blank countenance of a bombing-raid survivor, she would dig silently, remorselessly in her garden for days. Then, after about a year and a half of this, she became so depressed that she couldn't go to work anymore, and she resigned. I happened to be in L.A. at about this time; I actually helped her move to a new apartment (the end of her job had coincided with the end of a stormy affair). I remember feeling, probably for the first time, slightly concerned for her mental well-being, which had never before seemed at all precarious (despite my occasional doubts about her rationality). But she managed to right herself in due course, to find another lover, and then to get hired on at a less stressful position, as the health-plan administrator at a small suburban clinic.

I need to remark—since it strongly influenced my impression of her at this time—how beautiful she had become, how uncannily she now resembled our late mother. Despite her continuing attempts to 'de-feminize' herself, always to dress in an unappealing style, to seem somehow sexless, she was the most female of women, someone from whom emanated a concentrated warmth, an attractional feeling of great, delicious power. The fact that she was basically inclined toward others of the same sex (although, in this period, she had her first 'ordinary' relations, if I'm not mistaken) in no way interfered with this emanation of hers, and various friends of mine, who got to know her at the ranch, were severely taken with her, became intensely devoted. But her heart, I think, could be engaged only by another woman. I had always felt something 'perverse' in this orientation, had suspected that, but for the interference of her conscious mind, hers would have been the usual order of urges and impulses. I imagined that the era to which she had been so finely attuned—our slack age of righteous resentments, self-conscious liberations, and so forth—had determined her course, and but for her early, unnatural turning against our father (and with him, against all 'oppressive mechanisms of patriarchal authority') she would have ended up much different. But if a horse had wheels, as someone's grandmother once said, it wouldn't be a donkey, and even I had to admit that what she had self-consciously chosen, or somehow forced herself, to become was what she truly was, now and forevermore.

At the end of 1977, she bought a small house in West Hollywood with a friend, and I was given to understand that this signaled a sort of matrimonial commitment on their parts. 'Margie,' my sister's lover, was an X-ray technician with a strong interest in women's motocross racing and the raising of Welsh corgis. They lived together for three years, until Sylvia, as I understand, began to fool around with someone else, and Margie reluctantly kicked her out.

OURS HAD ALWAYS been an uneasy relationship, but at some point during these years we quietly turned a corner, and my sister was forever after someone I trusted, someone I basically enjoyed and wanted to see. Prison had changed her, making her at once drier (in her humor) and somewhat wetter (in her affections), and I got the feeling that all charges had been dropped against me, that I was henceforth to be given the benefit of the doubt. When I think of how truly different we were, fundamentally unlike in our approaches to life, it seems miraculous that we had even kept in contact for so long; over the years, she had had many occasions to write me off (and I, to give up on her as a prig, an insufferable 'disapprover'), but somehow we always stopped short of a final break. Now I was glad just to have her. I liked knowing that in this wide world there was someone with whom I shared the mysterious 'blood' tie, that strange connection which overrides all others, persists sometimes against monumental odds.

Despite my doubts about her own behavior in the matter, I had somehow ended up as distanced from our father as she was. I had always thought it a serious, portentous mistake on her part to have stopped seeing him, and her ideas of him were now so odd, so fundamentally distorted, that probably nothing could have brought them in line with reality. Her friend Franklin Howard, for instance, who had disappeared some years before, had almost certainly been murdered (she believed). Gerson had arranged this death (she believed further), as he had arranged Howard's catastrophic accident, out of motives that were ultimately unfathomable. When I pointed out that the pathetic Howard had a history of sudden, protracted absences (he had been lost in the Arizona desert, by his own account, for seventeen years), she accused me of denying the painfully obvious, and she referred to the various 'suspicious' circumstances of his disappearance: no farewell note; no telltale changes in behavior just before the sad event; substantial sums left in his three bank accounts; etc. I had made the mistake of telling her I had mentioned her involvement with Howard to Gerson, and for her this was sufficient reason to believe in an act of 'bloody revenge.' It was in vain that I pointed out the contradictions in her own argument: if Gerson really cared as little for her as she thought, then it was absurd to think he would go to such trouble, have someone 'removed' just to protect her from a baleful influence, or whatever he might consider Howard to be.

I have to admit, however, that ever since my own experiences in Mexico, I had been sensitive to the idea that he worked in strange ways, that our father's hand might indeed be upon us, even as we imagined ourselves independently launched in life. I hadn't gotten any explanation out of him of the events of those days, and after a while I had stopped asking, seeing that his opinion of me declined the longer I remained confused. He had always said that a man not in control of events, one who failed even to *pretend* to be, was deserving only of scorn; that one with so little respect for himself was pathetic and in some situations even dangerous. I hated to think he was categorizing me this way, and so to avoid further censure, having suppressed my natural doubts and curiosity, it became necessary for me to avoid him personally.

In these years, he retreated even further into his curious retirement; he stayed home a lot, collected oils and acrylics, married younger women (two or three), divorced, had a prostate operation, etc. Never one to sit on the boards of large corporations, for fear of state and federal disclosure rules, he had become even more shadowy in his connections to certain business entities, among them the famous Parkman-Dorkman conglomerate, which succumbed to an SEC investigation in 1978. As a sign of his waning powers, perhaps, his name was actually mentioned in press reports of the Parkman downfall. In years past, while his involvement might have been widely suspected, never would it have been officially acknowledged, and I remember the peculiar thrill, the odd sensation, as I read the press accounts, almost of a momentous profanation having been perpetrated. (The journalist responsible for another series of articles, first published in *The New York Times*, about my father and the supposed role of organized crime in Hollywood has since retired; the book that was to have been based on his articles has yet to appear.)

Along with the rumors of his demise, of the dissipation of his legendary influence, came certain counterrumors, that something 'big' was afoot, that the forces which he continued to represent were only extending their infiltration, while he, yet more thoroughly disguised than before, was approaching that condition of perfect invisibility to which he had always aspired. I had no way to evaluate such bold contentions. My various Gerson experts, to whom I still made occasional recourse, were about equally divided between those who felt one way and those who felt another, but I must say that if he was 'pulling' something, he was doing it in great style, with a truly convincing impersonation of someone I had never expected him to become. One was sorely tempted now to take him for what he seemed, a soft-spoken, courtly old fellow, well preserved, well dressed, with an abiding interest in his art collection, his golf game, a few Jewish charities and not much else. There was hardly a hint anymore of that daunting force of personality which had been so remarkable, of his mysterious, ineffable 'presence,' which had made him loom large in the hearts and souls of all who encountered him. This *haimisch* old gent, with his still-athletic gait ("He could always hit the long ball"—Sid Feldman), his perpetual tan, bony, age-spotted hands, resembled nothing so much as a retired wholesale businessman, who had done quite well, gotten away with a bundle, and now was living out his days without remorse.

I saw him for the last time—unaware, of course, that this was to be *adieu*—in September of 1982. A new wing was being dedicated at his temple, which is called Beth Tamid (some wags still refer to it as 'Beth Gerson,' on account of his formidable fund-raising efforts). I had come to town specifically to accompany him to this dedication, but now I learned—false, nonobservant Jew that I am—that Rosh Hashanah was to begin that evening, and that he expected me to go to services with him.

"No, Dad," I said with a smile. "I've got somebody I have to see. Over on the other side of town."

"Who's so important that you can't go to services with your father? I haven't seen you in a year and a half, son."

There was something truly delicious in this exchange—I hoped he was hearing it the way I was, that the irony of it, the rare comedy, didn't escape him.

"I know, Dad," I replied, hardly able to keep from laughing out loud. "I've been real busy, you know. I keep meaning to get to town, but it's not like I live in the Valley or something. Maybe next year. 'Next year in Jerusalem'—isn't that what they say?"

"No. That's just for *Pesach.*"

That afternoon we drove to the dedication. The new wing—to be called the "Sandra Styles Education Center," a huge billboard announced—loomed before us like a gigantic suburban library, and as we entered the circular drive-around, the old rabbi himself rushed forward to open my father's door. Gerson stepped out like a king entering the company of his entourage, and I vaguely recognized various faces in the crowd—they were the usual Bel Air types, but a special sampling, only the highest of the high, the juiciest of the juicy. If any group was likely to have contemplated—perhaps even to have comprehended—the true nature of my father's remarkable career, this was it, and they gave way before him, as he approached the door of the new edifice, with a kind of worshipful reluctance.

I, however, had a hard time making myself go indoors. It wasn't the crowd that kept me out; my mother's name, so prominently displayed, had had a perverse effect on me, and after skulking in the entrance for a few minutes I sneaked outside, to smoke cigarette after cigarette standing against the synagogue wall. I dimly heard the phrases of the rabbi and other dedicatory speakers inside, and it seemed to me laughable, and then absurd, and finally pathetic that my mother should be memorialized in this fashion—her interest in Jewish education had been hard to make out, but more to the point, my father's affection for her had been questionable, at best, an inconsequential datum in the long and murky history of his emotional life. That he should finally choose to settle this monumental honor on her frail, forgotten, inappropriate shoulders bespoke a kind of confusion, or an ultimate poverty, of that life, and I was angry and even embarrassed on his account.

"You're his son, aren't you?" I heard someone say. "You're

Gerson's boy. There's a resemblance—yeah, a strong resemblance."

Someone I didn't know—a big, heavyset fellow in a shiny Italian suit—was addressing me. He had come outside to smoke a cigar.

"Pardon? What did you say?"

"You should be inside, shouldn't you? I mean—they're just about finished."

"I can hear fine from out here, thank you."

A minute or two later: "I didn't know he had a son. I knew about a daughter, but not a son. You live around here too? Are you in the business?"

"No. What kind of business would that be, anyway?"

"Okay. I understand. Say no more. Very good."

A sudden eruption of applause interrupted us. I turned, in undisguised irritation, to face the blank wall of the synagogue, from which the sounds seemed to be emanating.

"I'm Bernie Zilbergeld," my newfound friend continued. "Maybe you've heard of me. I'm a friend of your father's. Well—not quite a friend, but we've done business together. He's an amazing fellow, your father. When they come to write the history of these days, of this industry, there'll be a big hole in the center of everything, and your father is the guy they should stick in there. Believe me—right in the middle."

"I do believe you," I said dryly. "I'm sure you're correct."

"Yeah, when they finally get around to telling the truth— the *real* truth—about things in this town, he'll be right there. Up with the big boys. Up in the penthouse apartment, you might say. Looking down on it all. And—laughing."

To get away from him, I went indoors. There I saw my father, with the notes for a speech in his hand, just now walking down the center aisle, with well-wishers smiling upon him from either side. He mounted to the podium. The auditorium was surprisingly handsome seen from within—a series of skylights, large and artfully placed, gave a pure, gratifying illumination to the scene, and there was a sense of wholeness, of a group of people gathered for a respectable purpose, animated by one spirit which, when all was said and done, reflected credit. My father cleared his throat. For a moment I saw him not as himself, but as a stranger, just some handsome, gracious elder figure, serene and powerfully magnetic. I leaned forward, eager to hear what he might to say.

NOTHING IS EVER really buried, or forgotten; yet we make our way by the necessary expedient of selectively forgetting, suppressing those memories that could cripple us, and the other side of this phenomenon is that ideas that come to us at the wrong time—say, when we're too young or too weak—reappear at regular intervals, sometimes when we're finally ready to understand them. And we jump on them (these ideas) with that special spring appropriate to something really new, with that devouring energy that alone allows us to grasp, to comprehend completely. And this is the real gift of faulty memory: without which, nothing ever advances.

I had occasion to muse this way early in 1983, when my sister, without even a phone call to announce herself, suddenly appeared at the Boneyard for a visit. It was with a feeling of deep amazement, really of disbelief, that I shook the hand of her traveling companion, who, laughing at my discomfiture, said that it looked as if I had finally "gotten my growth, yes, all of it." It had been twenty years since I last saw Marcela, and my response to her was indeed that she, too, had finally grown up, become a woman; now she was someone I could only abstractly, theoretically relate to the tough-talking, manipulative teenager and girl I remembered. I took her suitcase (a Samsonite locking bag) and led her into my house, already half intoxicated with her, dizzy with the feeling that something important was happening, something unexpected and signal.

"No, I didn't want to come," she said almost at once. "I feel bad forcing myself on you like this, just say it if I should go away. The good news is that I have to be back in Mexico on the fourteenth. So, I'll only be ruining your life for a few days. I have a friend, too—a quiet, appealing type, who's supposed to meet me here. When he finds your ranch—*if* he can find it—I'll take him back to Mexico with me. He has to be brought across the border."

This friend, who appeared three days hence, had paper troubles of a familiar kind, and I gathered from this that Marcela was still of the same mind about many things; if not still a fugitive herself, then certainly an ally and protector of such people. I had lost track of her some time ago, and I think that even Sylvia no longer followed all the twists and turns of her subterranean career. I assured Marcela that she was welcome to stay at our place as long as she wanted, and that her friend, whenever he showed up, could stay too.

"Thank you. Thank you. Sometimes we have it in our minds that someone will stand by us, and we believe that very strongly. But we don't want to turn his way, fearing that this idea may not be true. But sometimes—it is true."

I smiled at her, confused by her beauty. "You can always stay with me, Marcela. I hope I could stay with you, too, if I was ever down that way."

"Of course you could. Certainly."

✳

It was the off-season for me. I had been doing little for the last few months, outside of working on the house, reading, and entertaining the occasional marijuana buyer who drove up from San Francisco to sample my product. In years past I had found the wintertime pleasant, useful, but now all the major projects for the house had been either completed or abandoned, and I was left with a tremendous amount of time on my hands, quiet, accusatory time. I had tried to write various 'books' in years past, to occupy myself that way, but this one in your hands— these crude, hurriedly penned pages now before you—was all I was really suited to write, ever destined to compose. My girl-friend of some duration, who had been highly supportive of my attempts to literize, had recently left me. As a final test of my imperfect devotion, she asked me to accompany her on a long trip to Asia, but as I was unable to conceive of a change in scenery producing a corresponding change in mood, I declined. It was her opinion—voiced subtly, caringly, which only made me resent it the more, somehow—that I was 'blocked' as a writer, as I was blocked as a man, because I had yet to come to terms with the dilemma of being my father's son, and that I would have to 'work this out' before I could really start to live.

Oh, but how rich I am now in such opportunities—I write and write, all the time 'working out' in mysterious psy-chological fashion, yet I feel none of the relief that she told me to anticipate. These several weeks, as I've waited for the person I need to kill, I've done nothing but compose and reorder the story of my regrettable past, and I come to see how little I really know of it—how faulty and incomplete is my grasp of the telling, presumably crucial details, for example, of my father's business dealings, or of his relations with the Señora, or with Franklin Howard. The problem is that I am too close to my material, that I've assumed that because it's indisputably mine, I actually comprehend it, can call it forth as needed. A compe-tent journalist, I think, would go about my project much differently; he would begin, for example, with a massive amount of plodding, purposeful research before ever daring to set himself up as another 'Gerson expert,' with claims to authoritativeness.

My only defense (if it counts as such) is that the fog through which I've always seen my father, the ignorance he somehow induced, is the most important thing to know about him. Though someone else, someday, may descry him by means of an accumulation of demonstrable 'facts,' he will have disappeared at just that moment into greater obscurity, and his enduring secret will be lost forever. This is why, toward the end of his life, when he became 'just himself' to me, I was baffled and a little repelled, unable to accept the connection between this comfortable, conventional old guy and the mysterious force which had determined my course in life. He was more real, in other words, when I hardly felt his ghostly hand upon me at all, when his manipulative powers were most subtly, penetratingly deployed, and it took every ounce of concentration just to begin to make him out.

Marcela, as if without a care in the world, proceeded to seduce me, and we entered upon an idyll whose consequences I will never escape. The weather at the ranch was very stormy at first, requiring us to bundle up and stay indoors, huddled round the wood-burning stove; then it turned harshly, bracingly clear, and we were drawn outdoors, enticed to go on invigorating walks together. Behind our ranch, beginning about a hundred yards to the north, is a series of canyons, where from time to time I had planted marijuana gardens; through these canyons runs a stream, or system of streams, whose destination is the Trinity River, and Marcela led me down into this scrub-jungle, rejoicing as of old in having a 'field' to play in, a semi-wild ground on which to enact our little mating game. As Marta, at the time of our first trysts, had toyed with me in the garden at Las Casuelas, so did her twin make use of the local woods, like some brown nymph whose powers of enchantment activated fully only out-of-doors.

"Do you ever think of her?" she asked once, as we were sitting on top of a steep escarpment, resting. "I mean, do you ever remember how she *really* was—what was distinctive about her, and how, for example, she differed from me?"

I had been thinking of Marta almost constantly since Marcela's arrival, but the truth was, I'd previously come close to forgetting her. Only very occasionally did thoughts of her come to visit, and they had been, till recently, comfortably vague, almost empty of emotional component.

"Sure, I think of her," I pretended. "I think of her a lot. I've never forgotten her, no, not for a minute. There was something special about Marta and me together—I've often wondered how it would've been if she'd lived, if we'd gotten married, say. In all these years, I've never met anyone who could make me feel the way she did. I think she was the 'one' for me—the real one, the big one."

Marcela nodded, very solemnly. "I felt bad for you. I was sorry I couldn't speak to you then, to tell you how it happened. Somehow, knowing the events was a small consolation. It was awful, but at least it made sense. It could be understood."

Marta died at a time of great tumult in Mexico; in the fall of 1968, in the capital city, a student strike had been long under way, a strike made more serious, from the point of view of the government, by the imminent commencement of the Olympic Games, which were to show to the world how progressive was the modern Mexican republic. Apolitical down to her toenails, Marta had been neither a university student, nor a strike sympathizer, but her birthday, as it happened, fell on the very day when a tremendous *manifestación* was planned for the Plaza de las Tres Culturas in Mexico City. As it had always been her custom to spend her birthday with her twin, she had traveled up from Cuernavaca the day before, and it was agreed that they would meet in a certain café following the rally.

"I was the reason she died," Marcela now declared, in a simple, straightforward tone that I somehow admired. "I've always known that this was the case, and I accept it, I live with it. I was the 'bad' one, always the dangerous one, the wild striker, and if she wanted to see me on our birthday, then she had to come to where I was. The thought of going to my mother's house in Cuernavaca for the festivities was impossible—I never even considered it.

"Sometime before, I had planted some stories in a magazine about my mother. These were about her business practice, her cheating. As a result she now hated me deeply, but also I was now known to the public, and when there was an action at the university, I was often asked to give an opinion on it, for publication. On 2 October, I went with the thousands of other students to the plaza, prepared for a big, noisy demonstration. I warned Marta to stay away—there was always a chance of some police violence, because the government, as the Olympics came close, wanted to prove to the world that no bunch of dirty students could get in its way. Maybe some strikers would be beaten a little—that was the worst possible, we thought.

"At six in the evening, as we were giving speeches, the soldiers began to arrive in the plaza, in tanks and trucks. They blocked all the streets and paths going out. Then a helicopter flew back and forth above us, and we could see some soldiers in the belly of it, at the open doors, holding rifles. At just seven, a bright light appeared in the cabin of this helicopter—a green light, a sort of flare, really. At that same moment, down on the ground, they began to kill, with wave after wave of shooting into the crowd. The people went back and forth, back and forth, caught inside the plaza. The heavy firing went on for one hour, maybe more.

"You know that I survived—how, I can only half explain. Let's just say that some friends had prepared for this event without telling me, and when it happened, I was taken away and hidden outside the city. My wounds were treated, and I was protected and kept away from the police. But on about the third day of my protection, a good friend came into my room with a newspaper. It was a publication of the right, a newspaper owned, in fact, by my mother. There was a picture of me on the cover, looking very dead; and underneath it said, *'Ella Prueba—La Violencia.'* ['She Tastes It—Violence, Her Own Thing.'] Something like that. I had been caught in the plaza, it said. I had been carrying a bomb, and I was shot. Along with about thirty-five other 'terrorists,' it said—according to the government, these were the only victims of their butchery. I had simply suffered the consequences of my own 'fanaticism,' you see.

"I began to cry—I became crazy, and they had to give me medicine to calm me. For some weeks I was sick, knowing who this was—that this was really Marta, that the picture was of her, that against my wishes she had gone to the plaza, been in that unlucky crowd. Despite what the government claimed, there were actually hundreds, maybe thousands of victims. In the morning of October third, when the Red Cross finally was allowed to come, they say they loaded bodies in trucks for hours. Some died immediately, but most bled to death during the night. This was because the soldiers wouldn't allow the doctors to come earlier.

"I mourned my sister, but things were hard for me at this time—after recovering from my wounds, and from my mental disturbance, I had to leave Mexico. When I came back, I found that I was wanted by the authorities, and to this day my status is incorrect, and I live under false conditions. But let me tell you the strangest part, the saddest part of the whole story. Several years later, when I was living in Saltillo, I met a young man—a *chilango*, a Mexico City boy, who, as it happened, had known me at the time of the strike. He had also been a 'trouble-maker,' a student rebel, but not so serious as me, not really serious at all. Anyway, on the day of the plaza, instead of going to the protest like everyone else, he went to the Café Pintada, the place where I had told Marta to wait for me. At around seven o'clock—so the *chilango* swears—Marta came into that café, and like everyone else, he noticed her, because she was very pretty, but also because he mistook her for me. And this puzzled him—he knew where I was supposed to be at that hour.

"He watched her, and it seemed to him that she was nervous. Looking at her watch, smoking cigarettes. At about nine o'clock, a few students rushed into the Pintada. Something tremendous had happened, they said, an awful event at the plaza. They spoke loudly, and the news swept around the café. Now the *chilango* was sure that 'I' was who he thought—the news made me look even more nervous, and several times I jumped up, as if to run away somewhere. He was on the point of coming over to my table, to say that, if needed, he would drive me somewhere, help me get out, when two men entered the café. They looked very suspicious—they had the way of the *ganaderos*, the federal security police. They looked all around, and the *chilango* was sure that they were looking for student rebels, people who had escaped the strike. Then when they saw me—saw Marta—they came over to that table. After speaking to her for a few minutes, they dragged her away."

As Marcela spoke, she removed her overcoat. The little ridge we were sitting on, high above a brushy canyon, was suddenly illumined, as the winter sun broke free of some clouds, and the tangible warmth combined in me with a certain agitation resulting from this impromptu confession of hers. She looked at me closely now—for the first time in several minutes—probably to judge the effect that her words were having, to see whether she should continue.

I had felt almost nothing, to tell the truth, but now—imagining that I ought to feel 'something,' have some sort of response—a dim emotion stirred in me, and I thought that I knew what it was like to be really hurt, to have suffered an inconsolable loss. When Marta died, all those years before, it had touched me only distantly; I knew that something momentous had happened, that I had lost someone 'important' to me, but my actual feelings were radically subdued, suppressed. I remember that at the time, I went through the motions of seeming to be hurt—I lost no opportunity for affecting an attitude of romantic desolation, which I thought becoming to me. But my actual inner experience was of a kind of nullity, or stupor.

Now, though, I felt a glimmering of something—something certainly real. This was so unusual for me, so unexpected, that I paid the feeling a great deal of attention, and I almost wanted to grab hold of Marcela, to tell her what was happening, to thank her for this 'gift' of feeling. She must have sensed my agitation, because she drew back at that moment; then, as if mastering her nervousness, her reluctance to meet me on such intimate terms, she carefully moved a little closer.

"That's all right—I can see in your eyes what you felt, that she was really the 'one' for you. That after all these years, something still lives in your heart for my Marta. I won't talk about it anymore, no, I don't think I should."

"On the contrary," I said, "I want to know everything. Tell me, please. You were saying that they picked her up. That she wasn't at the plaza. But then what?"

They had picked her up, Marcela now added, and after driving her downtown, probably to the Procuraduría de Justicia, the central police terminal in Mexico City, they kept her overnight, maybe well into the next day. It was better not to imagine what had happened to her in the course of those hours; other survivors of the Procuraduría, which is used, even to this day, as a detention center for political suspects, speak of the awful conditions there, of the tortures meted out routinely, especially to women detainees. But maybe Marta's experiences were a little different. A strange 'operation' had been set up at the Procuraduría that night: only those students were brought downtown who were the sons or daughters of important people, of big powers in the government or in national business. Such 'bad' children were roughed up just a little, and then phone calls were placed to their parents, who, for certain considerations shown the arresting officers, could secure their children's release. Marcela was almost certain that such a call was made that night, to her mother, at home at Las Casuelas. But the response to this message was most unusual.

"I believe that she laughed at them—laughed when they said they were holding Marta. This was so exactly the kind of trick that I, in my desperation, would have played (she thought), that she wasn't fooled for one minute. She told them to go ahead, to do their worst. When news of 'my' death finally reached her, a day later, she still didn't know that Marta had visited me in the city; and she arranged for the picture of me, along with the ugly article, to be printed in her paper. But this act was later hailed all over Mexico as an astonishing, a formidable gesture. The great dragon lady, you see, who had been insulted by her bad daughter, had now had her revenge. From exactly this moment, in fact, dates my mother's return into the highest circles of power in Mexico, where such 'strength' is admired. Not only had she let her own daughter die—actually arranged her death, it was rumored—she had publicly rejoiced in it, as a kind of warning to her other enemies."

What response could I make to this? How to answer this frank, straightforward confession, which was followed, a half a minute later, by something I would never have expected of Marcela—a pouring forth of hot, girlish tears, a crumbling of the tough, resigned, equable façade? I wanted to hold her, and I even made a gesture in this direction; but she pushed me away. It was as if she wanted to experience this, her own authentic sorrow, without any props, to meet the desolation head-on, as she had possibly not done in many years, if ever. I remember that she cried in this undefended, childlike way for quite a

while, with me sitting decorously by her side. My own feelings
of loss were wholly eclipsed, entirely washed away—over-
whelmed, like some tiny puddle in the path of a raging winter
freshet.

It was the low position of the sun, which was directly
opposite us, that finally made me face her; I had been sensitive
to sunlight for some years now, probably as the result of my
experience in Mexico, when I had once been left out to bake too
long, and I needed to protect myself—my eyes, especially. The
shy, or wincing, way that I moved seemed to catch her attention, and she impulsively took my face in her hands. Mistaking
my sun sensitivity for something else, she murmured some
words in Spanish, and then she put her face next to mine, not
really kissing me, but placing her lips in the right vicinity.
After a few seconds, I kissed her lightly. The smell of her tear-
washed skin was like a drug, a sudden, overwhelming jolt to
me. I felt dizzy, disoriented, and then a tremendous urge awoke
in me, and I pulled her forward, dragged her straight onto my
lap. She gasped, breathing into my face a breath of weird,
musky sweetness. I put my mouth over hers, to absorb more of
that sweetness; and in seconds we were making love, right there
on top of her overcoat.

Sometime later—maybe half an hour—as we hiked up
out of the canyon, she asked what we were supposed to 'do'
now. Should we tell Sylvia, or should we leave it to her imagination, that something important had happened while we
were away in the woods? I said that I didn't know. It would be
obvious, I thought, that something had happened, and if not,
then it didn't really matter, as Sylvia was unlikely to feel
strongly about it one way or the other. Marcela seemed to
accept this, and we continued on up to the ranch.

I WAS ENCHANTED, I was entrapped. It was years since I had made love to someone I really wanted, and I went for the 'whole experience' with an appalling eagerness, like some teenager in the grip of his first grown-up passion. I was more like such a teenager, in fact, than I'd ever been before, than I'd been in my days with Marta, when, more concerned with the outward aspect of things, locked in a sort of power struggle with her, I had kept a fairly tight rein on my behavior. Now, though, I felt that there was nothing to lose. Fate had conspired to put Marcela and me together, to give me a second chance with one of the twins, and I was determined not to hide my feelings or to settle for anything less than complete and exhaustive satisfaction. Marcela, as if carried away by my exuberance, went along with whatever I wanted—she, too, seemed ripe for some shameless experience, some wild and uninhibited episode at odds with her normal mode of life.

If it occurred to her—beyond that one time, as we were hiking back up—to show concern for my sister's feelings, she made no sign; and I conveniently assumed this meant that they were no longer involved, had stopped being lovers years before. If they had, in fact, been making love up to and through the very morning before our fateful walk, I'm not sure it would have made much difference, but Marcela, I think, would then have had to act in a more cautious, diplomatic way. We were helped with our problem, luckily, by the arrival of Marcela's friend, who, only a week or so late, finally figured out how to get to my ranch from San Francisco. 'Lalo,' an Argentinian by birth, had a sprained back, and Sylvia immediately began to tend to him, prescribing bed rest and isometric exercises that required her to wait on him in a moderately nurselike way. I remember meeting this strange-looking, well-mannered visitor and even sharing several meals with him, before his presence had any real impact on me, before I accepted it as an evident (albeit unimportant) fact of our situation. Marcela also had little to do with him—we both, by tacit agreement, assigned him to my sister's care, hoping the two of them would entertain each other.

Those were thrilling days—I say this even knowing what was to come, even ruing them now as I do. My first feeling upon meeting Marcela after so much time, that something significant was about to happen, a momentous turning in the course of my life, seemed to be borne out, and I was carried along by a feeling of ever unfolding discovery, as if some great mystery were being revealed by degrees. She had never really hated me (she now confessed), but her 'twin-thing' had gotten in the way, had prevented a full expression of her true sentiments. When you had a double, she explained carefully, an actual duplicate in the world, someone with all the thoughts, tendencies, and moods that you had, down to the least signifi-

cant, you sometimes got into strange behavior. This was how
she now understood her early life, as a sort of reaction to the
'monstrous' fact of being twinned. If there was someone in the
world who was *exactly* like you, then the choice was either to do
everything the same, be like Tweedledee and Tweedledum, or
to split your one common personality down the middle, and
then seize one side—never mind which—and carry it forward,
usually to a point of extreme exaggeration.

"Thus, Marta could become the feminine," she explained, "the subservient, the conventional one, in love with a
gawky American boy. While I, modeling myself on our awful
mother, became hard, political, ruthless. No time for love, not
love of the ordinary type. But I felt the other side in me all the
time: always dying, suffering. I had a Marta in me—I could
have been her, my sister."

"You seem to understand it so well," I observed earnestly.
"I guess in all these years you've had the chance to think it
through—to analyze the mechanism fully."

"No, I don't 'analyze' anything," she answered with some
heat. "I only *feel* things now—as I never did before. I *feel* Marta
in myself—just as if she'd come to live in me, and had never
really died, and now I could finally be the whole person, for us
both. When I had the chance to visit you here, I immediately
knew the two things I had to do: one, to see your sister, because
it's a long time now that we don't talk, but two, to see you, see
the boyfriend of my dead twin. I had a feeling that there was
something I had to express to you—some secret, tender feeling."

Oh, it was indeed sweet to be with her—not that 'tender'
is the word I would have chosen, to describe how she was, what
she seemed to feel. I remember that for a few days I was almost
uncertain which one I had; whether she was not, in fact,
'Marta,' my true love, my chosen life companion, miraculously
preserved and returned to me. She was surely Marta-like in her
yielding, accommodating way, her willingness to meet me
wherever I might want to go (speaking romantically and sexu-

ally); she was Marta-like, too, in her delicious, slow-limbed physicality, reminiscent of a paradise of sensuous warmth and welcome which I had once visited, but without then appreciating its value, its fearsome rarity. In this life, there could be but one place for me, one 'home' where all my yearnings found satisfaction, where my particular breed of passion felt itself appropriate, and could therefore emerge. If it was in Marta— or in a memory of her, expertly suggested by her twin—that I alone found this paradise, then so be it, and all power to nostalgia, to necrophiliac *amour.*

She was not like Marta, however, in some important respects. There was her English, for a start: precise, fluent, and less accented than I remembered, as if she had spent the last few years working for the UN, rather than hiding out in a basement in Saltillo (or wherever). With Marta, I had always ended up having to speak Spanish; not that Marta's English wasn't serviceable, but Spanish somehow became our private language, our way of being immediately in rapport. But I couldn't imagine speaking Spanish to Marcela. The few times I tried, the words somehow died in my mouth; nor was she encouraging, and I even heard her speak English to Sylvia, who, from working in hospitals, where she saw Latins every day, had retained much of her old fluency. But the most telling difference—what really convinced me, beyond any doubt, that this was Marcela, she and only she—was her 'programmatic' way, her distinctive thoughtfulness in all things, as if every turn of events, every development in our companionship had occurred to her before, had first taken the form of an idea in a series of related, carefully considered calculations. Never mind whether this was really the case, whether she was actually so mad for 'planning' as Marta and I (and even Sylvia) had often joked that she was; she inevitably gave this impression, and it amused me to see how this quality, strange to encounter in a ten- or fourteen-year-old, had persisted even into the adult, marked her as strongly as would a scar or other deformity.

It was an integral part of her personal power. Though

probably just as confused, just as ill prepared as anyone else, she always seemed on top of things, composed, secretly satisfied by the way they were falling out. Thus, though our little walk in the woods, on that day when we first made love, had almost certainly not been 'planned,' I felt somehow that I was playing a role, performing just as expected, and that Marcela, perhaps even unconsciously, had 'seen' the events of our immediate future and then exerted her will to bring them about. I kept remembering how she spread her overcoat on that rocky ledge; a casual, natural-seeming thing to do, perhaps, but it came to haunt me, as it seemed to imply that she had known, twenty minutes before we lay down, that we would soon be needing its protection, madly rumpling it.

I had a warm, rustic bedroom on the second floor of the house, directly above the wood-burning stove in the living room. On an afternoon about a week before the end of her visit, as we were lying in bed, resting up from amorous exertions, the fire in the stove began sending gouts of heat straight up, through the galvanized pipes that I had purposely routed through my room. I got up to open the window, as I was feeling stifled, and when I turned back to face her, Marcela, propped up in some pillows, smiled at me in a way that reminded me painfully of her sister—just so, on afternoons fifteen years ago, had Marta gazed at me, conveyed the fullness of her heart without a single word.

"I thought that I didn't like to see a man," she said plainly. "That I disliked their bodies. But I don't dislike you, not at all. I don't fear you. You look to me just like a boy, like a boy who to his surprise has become a large man. Something still is youthful in you. Come over here, please."

I walked obediently back to the bed, expecting some kind of ordinary embrace. As I got closer, though, her smile faded, her gaze descended, and with an anxious gobble she suddenly took me straight in her mouth, swallowed me whole. I had never been 'taken' with quite that degree of alacrity before, and my first thought was of being eaten by some ravenous fish, one whose feeding impulse had unluckily focused on my tenderest part.

"There," she said, breathlessly spitting me out again. "You see . . . ?"

I didn't see; but this act seemed to have significance for her, and she reapplied herself, almost with an attitude of desperation. We stayed in these unnatural positions for some time, Marcela on her knees, crouched at the edge of the mattress, myself posed stiffly before her. Probably as the result of too much recent stimulation, I could feel almost nothing; I imagined that my woodenness, the deadness of my organ, was slowly spreading into the rest of me, turning all my cells into stiff, ungiving compartments, each having nothing to do with the rest. Finally I pushed her head back.

"Please. Take a break."

"Why—don't you like it? Is something wrong?"

"No. It's very nice. But let me get in bed beside you. I'd rather be fucking you, I think. Yes—I really would."

There—I was happy again, 'home' again. I could do this all day, maybe all my life. To be so far inside her that I hardly had to move, had just to go on breathing and absorbing, so it felt, some sweet, juicy radiance from within her, this was my true preference, my own particular fanaticism. As I lay subsumed in her, almost motionless, engulfed and mesmerized, all manner of half-grasped thoughts and intimations played over and within me. I almost felt that I knew what my 'purpose' in life was now—that if I could but hold on, persist in this for a while longer, some momentous revelation would be mine, a final truth conjured up by our mystic, motionless sex.

"Bastard. You . . . don't do that. Don't hurt me . . . not now. Wait—WAIT—"

A violent, twisting orgasm resulted—at such moments, she would often grab my shoulders, seem to be pushing me down, out of her, but any movement away on my part was greeted by curses, angry commands. I felt that I was just her 'instrument' at these moments: that by some process of reversal, I had become, not her ardent, half-punishing lover, but a mere helpmeet, one whose role was simply to remain, to assist at her transport across dark, cataclysmic waters.

"Sweetheart," I might murmur afterwards, "my dearest darling. You're so beautiful now. Your face is like an angel's. Truly—a saint's. Let me kiss it . . . all over."

On this particular afternoon, however, as soon as she had had her hard 'crisis,' she turned away from me. I had the impression she was angry, that something hadn't gone quite according to schedule (when thwarted in her own interior program, she often became resentful, and one had to pull back, knowing that in a minute an alternate plan would be put into effect, that her experience then would again correspond to an internalized 'schema'). After a few seconds, she rolled onto her other side, facing me again. The sensitivity and warmth that I had always associated with Marta, the same miraculous, undefended full-heartedness, which had meant so much to me, was again in her face, glowing in her dark, protuberant eyes.

"But you're—not fair. No, you're not. You don't let me please you. This is something that I've never done to a man before. I haven't been with so many, you know, not many at all."

"No, I know that," I said sweetly. "And I appreciate it—believe me, I really do. But I like it straight up with you—or any other way, for that matter. You don't have to do any special 'tricks' for me."

Once again, despite my protestations, she took me in her mouth. This was what we men 'really' liked, she seemed to believe, the prize that we secretly sought before all others. Again, I felt made out of wood, as if what were being done were happening to some artificial extension, something stuck through a wall, being acted on by persons unknown. I had been lying on my side, but now, for convenience's sake, I rolled over onto my back, and Marcela pushed me up onto a mound of pillows. It was a long, strenuous effort on her part—on mine, too—but by furious fantasizing, with Marcela herself as the object of my imaginings, I brought about the outcome she required.

"There. It's done. It's finally done."

"Sweetheart, what's the meaning of all this? Why do you feel you have to do this?"

"I . . . don't know. Just—to please you. In every way I can."

"But—you *do* please me. I told you that. Just to be lying next to you is a supreme pleasure—if I was any happier, I'd evaporate. Ascend into the stratosphere."

"I know this, but . . ."

"Marcela—I'm in love with you. Being with you these few days—it's so wonderful, it's like I've been aiming for this, destined for this my whole life. I've never felt better. And I thank you for it. I thank you—so much."

I remember how she looked at me then: gravely, almost uncomprehendingly, as if for an instant, I had stopped speaking a language she could understand. Years before, Marta had sometimes looked this way, when something I did (or failed to do) brought about a momentary retreat, a lapse into a different kind of consciousness, what I used to think of as her 'pre-Columbian' state. At such times, she always reminded me of a graven image, something carved on a temple wall somewhere, daunting, aesthetically perfect, but beyond all simple, personal appeal.

"I know that. I know that you 'love' me. It's just . . ." But then she suddenly gave up the effort to speak. Light was now returning to her eyes, which were half closed; leaning forward, offering her lips to be kissed, she loomed above me, crept upon me, wholly eclipsing my outward view.

WHEN NOT ACTUALLY making love to her, sometimes I simply adored her, lay beside her and marveled at her physical beauty, now at point of greatest effect, of a ripeness and generosity not to be encountered in someone of fewer years. She had lived a hard life (she claimed), yet she was wonderfully youthful, with thick, fragrant skin not stretched by childbirth, not at all scarred or roughened by time in bad weather. If she had led a pampered, inactive existence, as the wife of some Mexico City billionaire, she could not have looked any better, and in fact, in that case the vitality I so treasured, that made all her physical movements of great interest to me, would have been less, diminished or extinguished by lack of employment.

"But . . . where have you actually lived," I asked her once, "what have you done? Even Sylvia doesn't know. She says you taught school once. That's all she remembers hearing."

Marcela seemed perplexed: how did Sylvia know even this much, and was it wise to answer frankly, to open up this can of worms? At first she seemed troubled, but then she smiled at me, and with a manner of making a clean breast of things, she said:

"I used all my talents just to stay free. It doesn't sound like much, and maybe I've wasted my life. I don't know. But yes, I was a schoolteacher. I lived in a little town in Sonora, away from everything. High in the mountains. You know how it is there, the backwardness, the quietness, and if you can do anything, make things any better for the people, you just do it. I gathered money and founded a little school. I taught them how to read, first. But unfortunately, our efforts were considered political, and we had to leave. The school was purposely burned to the ground."

"That doesn't sound like a 'wasted life' to me—that sounds like something good to do. I'm sorry it ended so badly. Have you been on the run the whole time—have the police stayed after you? Why wouldn't they leave you alone, finally?"

Again, she seemed confused. Her 'plan' had failed to account for this curiosity of mine, for the problem of deciding how forthcoming to be, in respect of both her need for security and mine as well. A little more guardedly, she now explained:

"Some people have kept an interest in me—I don't know why. Through changes in government and other big developments in my country, and now my generation is as legal as it wants to be, and nobody has to hide anymore. But I have to say: I continue to commit some 'outrages.' It's right that they keep after me, I guess. They don't know where I am, or that I do them, but it's right, I haven't become safe yet. Maybe next year, now that I have this wonderful happiness. Now that I have you, all these good, ordinary feelings."

Why didn't I press her, ask her for examples of the 'outrages' that she liked to commit? I suppose that I was under her spell, or more likely, I was responding to her subliminal message of needing—demanding—privacy in this regard, and I wanted badly to please her. I was convinced, though, that if she had spent time living in the mountains somewhere, it was but an atypical, short-lived interlude, and that her life since I last saw her had been a thing of complexity and sophistication, a real, grown-up existence, involving residence in cities, international travel, etc. There was something palpably urban about her, which could only have come (I felt) from years of social and sensual stimulation of a high order, the exercise of her mind, the constant meeting of new challenges. By way of contrast, I felt a mere rube—I had never before been so conscious of the cotton that occupied my head, of the extreme thinness of my 'culturation,' of my essential backwardness. I had spent the last fifteen years in a kind of retirement, I now saw, managing to learn as little as possible, to have as shallow and circumscribed an acquaintance of the world as possible.

"I know you don't want to talk about it," I said once, as we were headed downstairs to dinner, "I know you wouldn't say anything that might compromise someone, but I'd like to hear more of your story sometime. I bet you've been lots of places. And you've come through it all in great shape, with all your faculties intact. Sylvia and I must seem like we haven't amounted to very much, if you look at it that way—she's a nurse, which is good, but we live such small, private lives. I'm just a criminal, like my father. And not a very interesting criminal, either. Just a peasant. A dirt farmer."

"Oh," she answered quickly, "but I *respect* how you've become. I *admire* what you've done for yourself. You live with nature, in privacy, simplicity, and this is a real accomplishment, I think. You've put the whole world behind you, all that confusion. Think how it was for you in Mexico that time. The danger, and how upset you were."

We had never talked, I remember thinking, about my times in Mexico; yet it seemed perfectly natural that she should know about my experiences there. Maybe Sylvia had said something, had alluded to the painful collapse of my illusions of efficacy and independence. Then again, I had never really talked to Sylvia about that time, either, feeling it to be so confused, so embarrassing an episode that my ends were better served by dwelling on it as little as possible.

"Sylvia has her work," I now said morosely, "but I just live here. Doing nothing, getting nowhere. I guess someone can spend his whole life this way, never accomplishing anything, never even trying. At least there's no one around to tell me what a big failure I am. It's better that way—less painful."

I expected some sort of consoling response, and I wasn't disappointed. "No—no one should call himself a failure, not who lives the way you do. Who hurts no one, exists peacefully with nature and his friends. You only hurt yourself with such talk. Think of where you come from: that you could have been one of the others, one of the powerful ones, the cruel ones. You could have been like your father. You and your sister, you have this great victory: that you put him behind you, escaped him. Believe me, I know what it's like to be in the influence of a strong, evil person. You go your own way, always thinking you're free, but you're not. Every breath you take—it first goes through the monster's mouth."

I nodded, and then I asked if she ever heard from her mother. Was it possible that her legal problems had to do with the Señora's influence, that her status would have changed if only her mother decided not to persecute her, no longer sought after some bizarre 'revenge'?

"Oh, yes," she assured me, "yes, without a doubt. My mother is completely insane, I know this now, and her need for revenge is an abnormality, something horrible. Beyond the human range. Anyone who disappoints her can never be safe again, not in this world. She blames me for Marta's accident, which I understand, but it was her own need to hurt that led to our tragedy. But she hasn't forgotten about me. No matter where I am in the world, I think of her, because I can feel her thinking of *me*. She needs to use me, and then destroy me. This is her desire."

"So—I take it you haven't been in touch with her? Not since all those years ago?"

"No. If I ever meet her again, I'm finished right at that moment; I have to keep away, pray to be protected from her."

❋

In my rustic kitchen, my sister had prepared a delightful meal for us: we sat around for hours, in mellow candlelight, sated, comfortable with one another. The agreeable Lalo smoked cigarettes called 'Disque Bleu,' and he compared the wine we were drinking, a semi-sweet white I normally cooked with, to *"vin ordinaire* of the Vendée, a little oily, but tasting of the earth, reminds of times in France." Lalo had been an exchange student there, he said, in the mid- to late 'sixties. His mother was French on her father's side, and he had experienced a kind of awakening abroad, as if part of his soul had been asleep before.

"Understand me—I'm a man without a country," he explained. "I don't go home to Argentina. My father was a victim of Perón. Okay, but my mother took us to Brazil, to Uruguay. To Chicago, Kentucky. I speak German with an accent of Stuttgart, where we lived sometimes. I don't speak good Spanish, either—Marcela says I'm sounding like with a 'bird' in my throat, or something."

"No, not a bird"—she laughed—"a croak. Not a 'crow,' but a 'croak.' "

"Okay, okay. A 'croak,' then."

He had been in France during *les événéments du mai*, he said, the popular uprising in Paris, in 1968. As a foreigner, he attracted the attention of certain agents of the police, who, following a riot at the Palais Royal, arrested him. But he couldn't be deported to Germany (which the police had hoped to do), as his mother no longer lived in Stuttgart; nor could he be sent back to the U.S. To his horror, he found that they were going to send him to Buenos Aires, where he had never lived, had no friends or relations.

In a peculiar breezy, good-natured tone, he then proceeded to recount his experiences in the land of his birth; at the time of his unwilling return, he said, some student groups were making a serious opposition to the government, and the military therefore declared war on all 'terrorists' (that is, on all who opposed it effectively). As the son of an anti-Perón organizer, who had been murdered in the 'fifties by right-wing thugs, he was considered suspicious per se.

"The Argentines don't like me—everything about me was wrong. The way I spoke, like a 'Negro,' they said. The color of my skin, which is too yellow. My hair. Even the newspapers I read, in French or German. When I tried to get work, people asked me if I was a Jew, and if not, then what kind of foreigner, what sort of bad stranger? A man with such qualities is scary to them—probably dangerous."

Ultimately, he said, he traveled inland, to the little town where his father came from. Chanbuco, in the untamed southwest of Argentina, turned out to be a crude, desolate place, with a population of only a few dozen families, none of them called Fiñon (his family name). However, he was immediately recognized on the street; friends of his father took him in, fed him, promised to get him work. They asked him many questions about his years in Europe—and, since he saw no reason not to be honest, he told them all about his police troubles.

"One night, a car drove into town. I saw it myself—four men got out, wearing good clothes. They went into the tavern and ordered dinner. I was on my way home, to the house I was staying at then. When I arrived, I found the door locked, my bag of belongings thrown out in the street. I sat on my bag for about an hour.

"When my friends still didn't come, I returned to town. I

went to some other friends, people who had kept me before. When these people heard me knock, they looked down from the upstairs window. I could call up to them, but they didn't answer. Not one word. Finally, the men from the car appeared. They had had a good dinner. They put me under arrest."

Back in Buenos Aires, he was beaten and thrown in prison; never formally charged with a crime, or allowed to speak to attorneys, he languished for months in a filthy, un-heated basement with many others. Over the course of about a year, everyone else in the basement was either taken away or beaten to death, but he, somehow, always survived, a puzzling exception to the prison wisdom (which held that no one could last in the basement for more than a week).

"I was lost, you see—more lost than the others. Exactly because I had no friends, no family to worry about me, I could disappear. If no one was making trouble, going to the police, always asking to have me back, I could stay alive. Then in 1974, the newspapers discovered the basement. We could go, and a few days later I crossed the border into Uruguay. Ever since then I've crossed many borders. This is my whole life now—always leaving a place, always looking for another place to live, to be. . . ."

This intriguing story—which I, for one, believed implic-itly, avidly—had a strange effect on my sister, who had also been listening to it closely. She was staring down at her plate, looking rather grim; at first, I assumed that she was deeply upset, resentful that such injustices could be visited on anyone, let alone on one whom she now counted as a friend. In years past, of course, her sympathies had always been with the 'oppressed'—with anyone, no matter who or where in the world, who had suffered mistreatment at the hands of jack-booted authority. But now, after an interval of silence, she happened to glance my way; and it seemed to me she was almost smirking, as if his story struck her, not as some egregious tale of woe, but as the wildest of bald-faced inven-tions.

"Here," Marcela said, with a commiserating shake of the head. "Take it easy, my friend. Have more wine." And she filled Lalo's glass, meanwhile making a sort of cooing, or consoling, sound.

"Thank you," he replied sadly. "It's a good wine, yes. Let us all drink—drink to this place, to these beautiful mountains. To the pleasure of this night, in such good company."

As he toasted my sister, who was sitting to his left, she smiled back at him blankly, expectantly; but as he turned to toast me, as well, I felt her gaze fall upon me, and there was a 'meaning' in it, a decidedly dry and insinuating flavor.

"You don't like our unlucky friend," I said an hour later, as we ran into each other on the way to the bathroom. It was the first time I'd spoken to her, I think, in ten days or more; the discomfort of our situation, of my odd, indiscreet involvement with her old lover, stood between us like some immovable impediment, monumental and incredible.

"Why—did I say anything?"

"No. It's what you didn't say. What you haven't been saying. Has he been bothering you?"

"No. Not at all. In fact, I'm glad he's here—otherwise, I would have had to leave."

This simple statement—made without accusatory hints, in an unemphatic tone of voice—surprised me, shocked us both. I was so used to expecting, when it came to matters of feeling, a stoic, nearly wordless reserve on her part, that I could hardly credit what I'd heard.

"But I didn't mean to . . . that is, I—"

"Never mind," she said firmly, cutting me off. "I just want you to think about what you're doing. Think who it is who you're involved with. Who it is you're getting in bed with these nights."

There it was, I reflected—raw jealousy, envy. I had almost convinced myself that this couldn't be the case—that by some convenient evolution of feeling, she no longer cared for Marcela, had only the most casual thoughts of her.

"I'm sorry. You don't know how really sorry I am. I didn't want it to happen this way, really I didn't."

"I'm not talking about that." She looked at me in disgust. "Sometimes I forget how dumb you are—how big, and dumb, and lost in your stupid self. Do you think she enjoys making love to you? Are you the 'man' she's always wanted, do you think? Who do you think she is—not Marcela?"

I was flabbergasted. I really didn't know what she was getting at. Standing there in my comfy flannel bathrobe, I furrowed my brow as if I really were this stupid, self-absorbed character she described. Then somewhere upstairs, a door opened quietly. I was aware of a sudden change in the atmosphere, of another consciousness coming into play, attending to our little dispute.

"Really," I continued, "I don't know what you're getting at. And you don't have to call me 'stupid,' either. This whole thing is just an unfortunate mess. I would've given anything for it not to have happened—or for it to have happened somewhere else."

"Do you think she likes you?" Sylvia persisted. "Is she in 'love' with you, do you think?"

Above us, a floorboard creaked. The landing gave onto a short hall, which led back to the bedrooms, where Lalo and Marcela were resting. But in a house like ours—just an old, drafty cabin, with thin wooden walls—voices carry alarmingly, and even feelings have a way of broadcasting to every distant corner.

"I don't know. That's for Marcela to say, I should think. But I do know how *I* feel. And I'm going down to L.A. with her. We may even go into Mexico, I'm not sure yet."

"Yes, I've heard all about your 'plan.' That means that I'm supposed to keep him company—drive him down myself. But what if I say no? What if I won't do it?"

I saw her point. I had, indeed, been counting on a little trip, just Marcela and myself, the two of us alone together. It would take us six or seven days to get to the border, and we would disport ourselves in various garden spots I knew of along the way. I couldn't imagine that my sister—who, despite her evident jealousy, supposedly cared for the both of us—would want to thwart so innocent an intention, which grew out of our straightforward attachment to one another.

"Now that you put it that way," I said dryly, "of course not. That would be 'inconvenient' for you, wouldn't it. No, I'll take him down myself. We'll leave tomorrow. Or maybe on Saturday. I'm not sure yet."

"Yes, why don't you leave tomorrow. That would be good."

Somewhere above us—not on the landing, but a little farther back, closer to the bedrooms—someone cleared his throat. I was fairly sure it was Lalo, innocently listening in. I almost stepped back, away from the bathroom alcove, to call up to him, to invite him down to join us. Anxious that his feelings not be hurt, that he not get the wrong impression, discover our hospitality to be but a shallow, two-faced sort of thing, I said clearly:

"Anyway—I'd prefer it like that. I'll get to know him better then. He's got a fascinating story, don't you think? Anyone who lives through experiences like that—why, it takes a lot of character. Real guts."

My sister looked at me as if I'd suddenly taken leave of my senses, and I continued, in the same 'carrying' tone:

"Anyone who suffers through such things—who really learns about political repression, firsthand—well, you just have to admire them. You wonder how they ever came out of it alive. An ordeal like that leaves you devastated, emotionally destroyed. And he seems so cheerful, so solid. . . ."

Realizing, at length, that I was speaking for the benefit of someone above us, Sylvia replied, in an equally clear tone:

"Some people tell all kinds of stories—they make up all sorts of lies. You have to be careful. The idea that he's from

Argentina, for instance, is just ridiculous—you only have to hear him speak a little Spanish to know it. It's not that he has a 'crow' in his throat, like Marcela says, but that—"

The bedroom door slammed shut; to judge from the sound, it was the one farthest back, to the room where I'd been staying with Marcela. Sylvia glanced up, as if to see through the floorboards; then, as she looked my way again, her expression underwent a remarkable, wholly unexpected change. Instead of the dry, disinterested 'honesty' of a moment before, there was almost a kind of pleading, a depth of sisterly concern and sympathy.

"Why—what is it?" I said, utterly nonplussed. "What's the matter?"

"Nothing. It's just that . . . well, I just want you to be a little careful. To be—"

But she failed to continue; somehow, she couldn't find any more words to express her misgivings. After a pause I said, "Well, I hope you're proud of yourself. How could you say that? When you knew he was listening in? Now you've probably hurt the poor guy's feelings. I don't see the point of being rude, no, I really don't, Sylvia. . . ."

Two DAYS LATER—my discussion with my sister notwithstanding—I left her behind at the farm, taking Marcela with me. Marcela, and Marcela alone. Sylvia and Lalo were to follow in a day or two, in Sylvia's car; my need was such that I wouldn't permit any obstructions to my plan, and I drove off with hardly a backward glance, convinced that things would work out, that our travel plans were nothing to be too concerned about.

Now I blame myself for what was to happen, for the disaster soon to befall us, but I also have to admire the rigorous simplicity of the trap they had set, into which I didn't so much blunder as rush eagerly headlong, dragging my sister (and my father) behind. A life of dry circumspection, of emotional restraint and vague moral debilitation—which I blamed, in secret, on my 'upbringing,' on the supposedly baleful paternal and maternal influences—had prepared me for just such a stumble, which someone less inclined to feel sorry for himself might have avoided. That point had been reached, in other words, in a blighted life when an irrational gesture seems in order: when some kind of wild, uncaring behavior seems the only antidote to burgeoning self-disgust.

I can't believe, though, that Marcela knew all this about me. That she had been able, in just our few days of reacquaintance, to take my measure so accurately. What she was about to do speaks, rather, of a higher order of cunning, of a mind accustomed to calculation, adept at deception. I had once been a raw, impulsive youth, a silly, self-deluding teen; once I had been so foolish as to commit indiscretions under the very nose, the very roof of the one I had most to fear. Without knowing this one as the one to fear, I proceeded as most others do, hoping that my youthful vagaries would go unnoticed or, if noted, would be taken for expressions of 'high spirits,' nothing more. Never could I have conceived of the idea that I was being observed, that an 'impression' was being formed, a final, definitive judgment made. That in the mind of my enemy—the enemy of my father, my family, of all our hopes—my character had been ruthlessly, conclusively analyzed.

I have to resist, however, too deep a development of the idea that everything was 'planned,' that my whole life, going back to our days in the childish garden, had been but a preparation, that someone had been steering all along for this inevitable outcome. Then my first days in Mexico, including even my affair with Marta (which the Señora, in that case, created, urged upon us), my debacle in the desert, when some 'second power' seemed always to be struggling for control of my fate, indeed, the whole odd, disorderly trek that I've made through my times, my regrettable 'personal history,' would be primarily the work of others. But if that were true, then the small component that I've managed, through close husbanding and self-deception, to claim as my own, as the expression neither of heredity, nor of my father's benign interference, nor of chance, would be taken away, and I would be less of an 'I' than I could continue to support—hardly of sufficient weight or moment to justify such orthography.

No, I have to deny that idea. The simple need to go on, to tell what remains of my story requires it. But I'm almost convinced that my experience in Mexico that time—my few days of suspended animation and terror—was a crude attempt by the Señora to exact a premature revenge. She had decided that she would get at Gerson through his children; this happy thought, which was to prove so clever in the end, led her to commit energies and materials to the battle before it was ready to be won. I slipped through her fingers that time. But no matter; a better day would dawn, a set of circumstances more favorable to her. The idea of arranging his destruction through his offspring owes something to Marta's death, maybe, to the personal pain—if we see her as being capable of experiencing pain—that befell the Señora on that occasion. Though she would never have put herself at risk, she could see how other, lesser mortals might do so, might be encouraged to compromise their own security in the interest of saving a child, for instance.

At about this time, indeed, my father's well-being was becoming a matter of some concern to him: there were now bodyguards, round-the-clock surveillance experts, drivers trained to take evasive action in traffic, electronic devices, etc. In the days of his true glory, when his enemies had been many and the threats to his safety substantial, he had been famous for his unconcern, his blithe indifference to danger, but now he relied on physical barriers, on tall gates, triply locked windows, signs on the lawns of his Bel Air mansion promising, "IMMEDIATE ARMED RESPONSE." Indeed, he hardly ventured out of the house on Dolores Court anymore. My few remaining Gerson experts, in the interest of staging an eventual father-son rapprochement, all now drew a picture of a man who, for want of alternatives, was slowly succumbing to a sort of benign dementia, a paranoia by default. Some of them even think that he knew that the end was near. I think he probably felt just the opposite: that it wasn't—although it might as well have been— and that he needed, through the erection of this series of laughable physical barriers, to invite it.

On the twelfth of April, he took a phone message (he had been out for the first time in weeks—lunching at the Century Club). As Ray Narciso reported, a girl identifying herself only as 'Sylvia' had called from a motel in Meiner's Oaks, which is a few miles southeast of Santa Barbara. This girl said simply that she wanted to speak to her father. And she promised to call back that evening.

It had been more than twenty years since he last heard from her; I like to think that he awaited her call, the evening call, in a state of some eagerness. I have only Ray's description of his behavior to go on, though: "He went straight into his room. When I went in there a little later, to see if he wants somethin' to eat, he told me to get the hell out and shut the door." That's all. At six o'clock she called again. Now I have Sylvia's own report of their conversation, which she recalled with some discomfort, physical and otherwise, at my insistence:

"I couldn't really talk. I wasn't supposed to say anything, just what they told me. His voice sounded real weak, detached. I had to listen hard, and then he said something that I remembered, used some old phrase, something from when I was a kid, and I knew him. I told him to come straight to the motel. I wanted to see him real bad, I said. I was leaving on a foreign trip, I think they had told me to say.

"He asked if I wanted him to bring me money. I said no— it didn't matter."

In violation of all the rules of professional 'security,' he then drove to Meiner's Oaks by himself. My sister can't recall if she stipulated this, or if he supplied this crucial component of their plan himself. (I think this was probably a crucial stipulation and that, for abundant good reasons, she has forgotten making it.) Maybe there was even an odd feeling, a sense of the fateful hour's having arrived, the end drawing near. The prospect of seeing a daughter thought lost to him can account for only a certain portion of his uncharacteristic impulsiveness; underneath this, lurking within it, was a less sanguine stirring, I'm sure, a sort of cold admonition of fate, which he doubtless savored with his customary detachment.

He arrived in Meiner's Oaks at about eight.

In a room on the bottom floor of Roy's Days-Inn, a man with slicked-back hair probably watched him arrive. My father went upstairs, to Room 23. The door was unlocked. He went in, saw his daughter sitting there, on the edge of a bed. She looked thin, distraught. The resemblance to her mother wasn't even so marked anymore—though present, spookily sensible—smudged by fatigue and by years of occupying her body in ways her mother never even considered. She rose from the bed, turned to face him, but didn't approach. He understood immediately that she had something 'important' to say: indeed, something appeared to be tormenting her, demanding immediate, unequivocal expression. Despite himself—entirely unlike himself—he walked right up to her. He took her hand, kissed her.

"How are you, dear?"

"Dad, I— I'm fine. I—"

"You said you were going on a trip. Where? Why?"

"Dad— Dad—"

The door opened behind them. The man from downstairs

stood there, holding a gun: maybe he made an apologetic face, then began firing. My sister interposed herself, took three rounds herself. My father fell a second later. The gunman shot him once in the back of the head, to make sure of success; then dropped the gun and left.

I REMEMBER AN ARGUMENT we had—we had just crossed the border, at Tijuana. She inexplicably wanted to drive down to Ensenada, where she said she had a friend, while I more reasonably wanted to head east. I hated Ensenada—I remember sleeping on a beach there once, around a campfire, and waking just before dawn to find myself surrounded by hundreds of rats. They appeared to have been creeping in closer and closer as the fire died.

"Ensenada is just a pit," I said in Spanish, "a scumhole. People die there and they throw their bodies in the ocean. I've seen it myself."

"You've had your way so far," she replied in correct, somehow remonstrative English. "I've come along with you, I've done everything you wanted. Please, just grant me this wish. You surprise me sometimes with your selfishness. It has to do with how big you are, I think—that you assume people will just make way, let you roll over them, like a truck."

I laughed at that. We were still laughing at each other then—enjoying one another. Still, a corner had been turned, in that moment. The facts of the case were so entirely otherwise—I had been so accommodating to her, so uxoriously yielding in every way—that I assumed that she was joking, that in a minute she would smile, and we would continue on our journey, undoubtedly toward Ensenada.

"No, I mean this," she repeated. "You don't know how you push me. Always I feel your mood; then, I must respond. If I don't we don't get anywhere. And they say that the woman is the one with the moods. . . ."

"What are you talking about? What in the *world* do you mean? All I said was that I hated fucking Ensenada. Anyone who's ever been there can tell you that it's a cesspool. I'd rather go almost anywhere else. And the fact is, I've done exactly what *you* wanted; I've driven you down, been your loyal servant. Now I'm awaiting further orders. That's all."

We had driven straight over the border, without waiting for friend Lalo. I remember being slightly curious at this unexplained change of plans, when the whole purpose of her trip, I had thought, was to connect with him and then usher him into Mexico. Apparently she had decided that there was a greater chance of trouble, of his being detained, if he were accompanied by someone Mexican-looking—indeed, by someone who might herself ring bells with astute border officials.

"I have a friend," she said now in her cool, 'planning' tone of voice. "A young woman. She lives in Ensenada. I just want to see her a bit. I'm with her . . . the way I once was with your sister, you understand? If I don't stop for her, she'll think that something's gone wrong. She knows I went up to the States. She expects to see me, you see."

"So you're saying: I should take you to Ensenada so you can see your girlfriend? And then what—I should just disappear? Quietly exit?"

"No, you don't understand me, as usual. I just want her to meet you—she has to know who you are, see you, so it makes sense to her. She has to see what's happened to me. This important, wonderful change."

"You're dreaming," I replied. "If you throw it up in her face like that, you'll hurt her feelings. I say we give Ensenada a wide berth, then write her a letter from Mexico City. Do it more gently."

We went on disputing in this crabby, unreal way—we were parked outside a Pemex station near Route 2, the main highway east—for about an hour. Finally I just put my car in gear and pulled out onto the highway, leaving Ensenada decisively behind as an alternative. Marcela sulked for the next half-day, but I think she was really glad not to have to have killed me then (or in Ensenada, when we reached the home of her friend, as had probably been planned). No, this sulking was actually a display of moral sensitivity on her part, I now understand, and I was aware even then of an odd quality of self-congratulation, as if she had suffered for my sake in a way that she could never reveal. When we reached Horcasitas, a town where, in my *contrabandista* days, I had often eaten good *enchiladas verdes*, she was suddenly desperate to make a phone call, presumably back to her Ensenada friend. (This may have been the time when she phoned Sylvia, explaining in a few choice phrases the case, the situation, what the program had to be. Sylvia has said that she insisted on this phone communication with Marcela, and that Lalo had anticipated her demand, and that they spent two days in an apartment in San Francisco waiting for the phone to ring.)

"We have to hurry now," said my lover, returning from the phone. "They expect me by Tuesday. In my absence, everything has gone wrong. I'm like a businessman, you see—when I'm absent, everything happens, and when I'm present they don't need me."

"Where are we hurrying to, exactly?"

"I told you. Cosales."

I recalled her mentioning something about this remote, unprosperous farming village, where another friend, or group of friends, was supposedly holed up. I had said on the occasion of her mentioning it that I hoped she didn't expect me to stop there—or anywhere else in the state of Sinaloa.

"I don't want to go to Cosales. As I told you, it's too close to where I'm known. I spent seven years in those villages buying pot every few months, and I don't feel like making a display of myself again."

"We won't make a 'display,' Luis. And there's simply no arguing with me on this point. We *have* to go to Cosales, *have* to. It's essential. Please don't be a bully again."

"I'm *not* being a bully, for Chrissake. . . ."

"If you'd rather, stop here. I'll get out. I can take a bus. We've driven this far, we've had a good trip, now maybe it's time to say good-bye. You forget that I'm not just the woman who wants you—I'm someone else, someone with requirements. It doesn't seem like much to you, what I do, and maybe you've never thought it had any value. But I bring many people together. I can't fail these people, not even for you."

It was so absurd—I couldn't believe we were having this discussion, and I had a strong, perverse urge to say that I was sick of hearing her speak English, from now on, it would be Spanish or nothing. I started the car, and in a few hours we were almost to Sinaloa. I had a peculiar sensation just as we crossed the state line, but nothing happened, no 'nemesis' suddenly appeared to take me into custody, and I remained deeply pleased to be in the only landscape I've ever really loved, whose very sky somehow rings true for me, touches my very soul (indeed, makes me feel I have one). The weather was good, and we passed through Culiacán on the evening of April 3, a mild, pastel-colored day. We could have driven straight on for Cosales, to reach it by midnight, but Marcela demanded a stop. She was suddenly very hungry.

"I thought we were in such a big hurry."

"Yes. But now I want a good dinner. Then, to sleep in a comfortable hotel."

"There are no comfortable hotels. Not in this part of town."

"There—see the place with the red window? I remember this from a meal I once had. *Calamar en su tinto*, seafoods like that. Please—stop right here."

A kind of effervescence marked her all that evening, and after dinner, we took a room nearby and made love—not really passionately, since our 'intimacy' had been compromised somehow, but avidly, with a physical rudeness that I liked. I remember thinking at the time that it was just as well that human beings had this way of expressing themselves—otherwise, all these urges, these odd combinations of desire, repulsion, devotion, tenderness, vengefulness, would have gone unknown, never showed forth. I had no idea what was going on in the mind of this other person, I felt, this one to whom I was so closely connected, nor could I have expressed what was in my own heart other than through this series of blunt, hectic movements and gestures. Marcela kept grabbing me by the hair, staring baldly into my face; then she would roll her eyelids down and her eyeballs up, throw her head back and curse. It was ludicrous, maybe, but I had the feeling that I was finally seeing her as she was, coming to know her directly, without pretense or reserve. For her part, it was an experience, I imagine, that she would afterward remember with mingled excitement and loathing—a kind of failed exorcism, a sort of daring, deadly disgrace.

"Put your hands over here, and then . . ."

"Like this? You want it like this?"

"Yes. But harder. I want to feel the life going out of me. Yes—"

I was rough with her—but carefully, guardedly. Then I became afraid—my hands seemed to have an affinity for this, to know exactly what she was after.

"Go on. Be a man. Pretend that you are, if it helps you. Do what a real man would. . . ."

"Oh, shut up. Just shut up. . . ."

As she started to kick and thrash—gone slightly red in the face, and in the throat—I felt a tremendous access of power, and in my mind I raced forward to the outcome of this act, to the veritable end of her. For an instant, that seemed the only thing that I had ever really wanted in life; I hurried through my emotions just to do away with them, to put them safely behind me, so that I could return to the gentle, rational being I preferred to identify as myself. Her orgasm was long, wretched, unending. I drew away in my thoughts, repulsed by the power that derived from this cruel charade, which suggested that the actual behavior, if I could have dared to undertake it in earnest, would have transformed us, brought us to some final, unspeakable glory.

"Your face is just like—"

"Oh, please. Don't speak. Don't spoil it with your sickly words. Your 'full heart.' "

"But Marcela, I only wanted to say that—that I feel for you a kind of . . ."

Later on, as I entered her in a way she hadn't previously permitted, she made unholy, anguished sounds, and I almost reached a new plateau, a place beyond all concern, where any thought of her discomfort disappeared, and I took pleasure in every square inch of my being. I felt myself, in that flash of a half-second, swelling to ten times my normal size, becoming a virtual giant of strength, a bursting, prolific titan. But afterward, she said simply that she hated me, and I contrived to act contrite. Then I could see that she really *did* despise me—not for my lust, my physical greed for her, but for my need to show remorse.

❋

I can't make sense of what happened that night except by referring to what was to come, and even so I'm puzzled by her

behavior, which suggests that she never truly made up her
mind, never took that final, definitive step. I awoke early to find
her gone. I assumed she had gone down to the bathroom (we
were in a private house near the restaurant, to which we had
been sent by the cook/proprietor). I waited some time, fell
asleep again, then dressed and went down myself.

The old lady downstairs seemed uneasy to see me, and to
my questions about Marcela she responded with a look of
bafflement. I ate a big breakfast and walked over to the restaurant. No one was around, and as I strolled off to check on my
car I felt myself attracting the sort of attention that I dreaded,
that peculiarly Mexican kind of scrutiny to which someone of
my size, of my evident bad character, is always subject. (Odd
how in all those years of 'ignorance' I had either welcomed this
attention or been immune to it, yet how sensitive I've become,
how cringing and fearful of life's intentions, as if there could
never again exist for me a benign field of play, a human world
without an evil motive.)

I checked my car, even got in and started the engine. I was
thinking how it would serve her right if I drove off, just left her
there, how she would regret her pettiness, her peremptory
demands, and at just about that moment, Lalo and Sylvia were
arriving at the motel in Santa Barbara, and he was explaining
that the time had come to do it, to pick up the phone and get the
ball rolling. Just as Sylvia was dialing my father's number, and
getting Ray Narciso on the horn, I was settling into an incon-
spicuous back table at the Ninfa Marina (The Mermaid), order-
ing black coffee, and considering for the first time the
possibility that I had actually been abandoned. I couldn't understand why Marcela would do such a thing—I waited for her
puzzling absence to begin to 'speak' to me, to reveal its mysterious inner logic.

"Señor," said a young man with blue eyes. "Can I ask you
a favor, señor? Are you leaving Culiacán soon, by chance?"

"Why? Why would you want to know?"

"If you're heading north, señor, I don't want a ride. But if you're going south, on the road through Cosales, I'd like to be your companion."

"Why—do you live in Cosales?"

"No. I work there. I maintain the telegraph lines thereabouts."

"Are there lines through Cosales? I remember it as a kick-the-pig sort of town, nothing but five or six houses, chickens and scurvy dogs always underfoot."

"Yes. But everything runs through Cosales, señor. All the lines of communication. All the people come together there. . . ."

I realized suddenly that we were speaking in 'code'—that his phrases were almost the same ones Marcela had used, and I paid for my coffees and we left. On the road leading south I noticed the new building that had been going on, all the half-erected factories and apartment blocks, projects begun in the late 'seventies, when Mexico was awash with oil earnings. The construction crews were few, though, and they looked somehow dispirited, and my companion, as if reading my thoughts, described the cruel dashing of hopes that had begun, as Mexico came to realize that her oil reserves had been grossly overestimated, and as the price of crude fell worldwide. We entered a region of rich farmland. It was late in the season, and the profusion of crops in the broad fields seemed astonishing, almost bogus. It was odd to think that this dustiness, this palpable aridity, under so blank and searing a sky, could produce anything alive and green, let alone this magnificent, picture-book harvest.

"You haven't been in Mexico long, señor," said my young companion, again intuiting my feelings. "You don't understand the miracle of her production. In our country, there is a special power, something in the earth, that can't be explained in terms of soil chemistry, water supply, scientific techniques, and so forth. Here a magical 'something' combines with an intense reality, and the result, as you see, is a phenomenon."

"That's a very interesting theory. Metaphysical. Are you a student of philosophy?"

"No. I simply repair the telegraph lines, as I told you."

"But why do you say that I haven't been in Mexico long?"

"Well—there's a certain 'rustiness' to your Spanish. The words don't quite have a shape in your mouth, and then they emerge, making a sound like unoiled metal."

"Let me say something more clearly, in that case. I wonder why we are going to Cosales. I wonder why you've been sent to accompany me there. Where's Marcela? Why did she go ahead of us?"

"I don't know. I don't really know her very well. Maybe she wanted to prepare your reception. I can't say."

"Are you a terrorist? Some sort of revolutionary? Member of an outlawed organization?"

He smiled. "Yes. All of that, I would say. And proudly."

We stopped soon thereafter, at a restaurant. It was past two o'clock, and my companion had been looking for La Chicana for some time, the only restaurant, he said, with decent food within a two-hundred-mile radius. I went inside as he detoured for the men's room, which was outdoors, and I felt immediately that I had been here before, that nothing that could be said to me, or served to me, or done to me in this establishment would come as a surprise. The waitress had the look of someone who had been asleep for a thousand years—dark, Asiatic eyes, plaited black hair, rustic airs. She wore an embroidered cotton dress. If there was a tribe of Sinaloan Indians still tied to this country, still taking its sustenance from the local land, despite the overlay of tarmac, gas stations, and body shops, she was its most representative member, its past, present, and future all incarnate in a single handsome, insolent individual.

"Beer, and the plate of the day, please."

"Clearly. With your permission, señor."

"And there's someone else. He's outside right now. He'll be hungry, too."

"At your service, señor. Whatever you desire."

She disappeared into the kitchen. I waited for a few minutes, then my friend returned, followed by two other men.
One of these looked sensitive, philosophical, university-
educated, like the telegraph repairman, but the other, though
still young, had a vengeful sort of face, a bitter aspect. They sat
down at a table in precisely the center of the room. Our order
arrived, and we addressed ourselves to some excellent *platos
típicos*. Here was the very taste of the country, I felt, the true
essence of this Sinaloan land, in the form of tamales under a
dark, heavy sauce; I remembered immediately all my other
visits, other ventures into fly-blown cafés, cheap roadhouses,
dives of ill repute, where, by an alchemical process impossible
to understand, the torpor and distress of the people were somehow turned to lip-smacking advantage, and one savored a cui-
sine without equal anywhere in the New World (in my
opinion). Here, in this floury, glutinous sauce, was contained
the very secret of that magical fecundity, that agricultural intensity which we had previously discussed, and in this ill-
formed tamale was a 'hint' of the whole history of striving,
overcoming, and succumbing, of the eternal infolding and ex-
foliating of Mexico's fate, of that process toward nowhere and
nothing which I had sometimes thought I understood.

"Señor. You seem to be in some kind of pain, señor."

"No. It's only that I'm enjoying myself so much—rejoicing in this superb food. This true taste of old Mexico."

"Ah. It's this place, La Chicana—she's the best, señor,
beyond any doubt."

I ate on, almost in tears. I noticed that the men at the
nearby table never ordered food, and I pitied them their lack of
appetite (or lack of funds). After about three beers, I began to
think that I could recognize the one with the bitter face. Something spoke to me of previous encounters, of a mutual acquaintance going back to my earlier days, to my first years south of
the border. Though I couldn't recall his name, it seemed to me

that I had once known it—even, in a sense, feared it. I stood up suddenly from the table.

"Señor. Are we ready to go now?"

"No. No . . . I only have to visit the *excusado*, I think."

"It's out back. Around to the side."

No one followed me out. No one got up, or even looked at me, but I could feel them restraining themselves with some difficulty, pretending to disinterest. I arrived at the outhouse and shut the door, actually, jammed it closed with my foot. My heart was pounding in my throat, and my hands were as wet as if I'd been groping for something underwater. Indeed, for a horrifying half-minute I felt submerged, half suffocated, unable to greet the world with sufficient force; it was with a desperate intensity that I conducted an 'experiment' to prove to myself that though I might be fifty fathoms down, I could still breathe, still wetly make my way. The disgusting disarray of the privy awoke me to my situation. As my panic receded, I tried to focus on reality, on this very afternoon, this particular place. Probably something in the tamale had set me off, I thought; some herb or other, used in the sauce as seasoning, had had a psychoactive, or adrenalizing, effect, and in my temporary delirium I had seized on that vaguely familiar face, the face of the other man in the restaurant, attributing to it qualities of fearsomeness and evil intent. But now my pounding heart was quieting. I felt myself coming around. I reflected on the absurdity of my behavior, thinking that in a minute, I'd be able to laugh at the whole event.

"I've never behaved like this before," I said to myself. "No, I've always prided myself on being calm, composed. Maybe I've even seen him before. So what? Maybe he was even one of the men at La Perla, or on the back of the truck. But that doesn't mean he wants to hurt me. It doesn't mean he's 'after' me now."

I looked out the privy door. I had a good view of the restaurant entrance, and also of my car, which was parked up on the road. Something told me just to walk calmly to the entrance of La Chicana, glance inside, wave to them, and then make a break for my car. If they followed, I'd know that I was right; and if not, I could drive back in a few minutes, explain my behavior some way or other.

"But what's the matter? What am I thinking of?" I said aloud. "These guys haven't done anything to me. I've got no reason to think that they're my enemies, or that they're 'planning something.' No, I have to calm down now. Recover my sense of dignity."

At that moment, my young companion came out of the restaurant. I jammed the door of the privy completely shut. I heard him talking to someone else—their words were unintelligible, but there was an unmistakable tone of conspiracy, I felt, a hum of dire intent.

"Señor. Are you in there, señor?" he called out.

"No. That is—yes, I am. I'm still busy in here."

"Señor, can we help you? Do you need some paper, by some chance?"

I heard a mumbling, maybe a snickering. Then my friend approached. Someone else also came behind him, moving more quietly.

"Señor, we have to leave now. The time has come to resume our trip, señor. Our destiny awaits."

"Yes, I understand. I'll be out in just a second. I'm just finishing up."

There was a window on the side of the *excusado*. It was just a ventilation hole, a kind of porthole, roughly circular in shape. It was covered over with rusted metal screening. But I didn't think I could make my way through it. My shoulders were too broad, and even if I somehow managed to get inside the hole, my enemies would hear my efforts, and they would hurry around and catch me on the other side.

"Señor. Don't delay us. What waits for us in Cosales can't be put off, señor, no, it must be encountered, now and today."

"I'm not 'putting off' anything, friend," I called back. "And I told you, I'm still busy. Now step back from the door. I don't like hearing you out there, so close."

I tested the metal screen. It came loose in my hands. On the back side of the restaurant I saw some fences, an alley, piles of rubble. A series of vacant lots stretched off in the distance. In the best of circumstances, though, I would have only a few seconds' head start; my pursuers would undoubtedly know the neighborhood better than I, and they would rapidly track me down, trap me without much trouble.

"Señor. You have to come out now, señor. Or we will come in there, drag you out. I promise you this."

I put my head in the hole. It was foul in there, better not to see or smell anything. I got one shoulder in, then jammed the other in as well. I heard a pounding at the door. With all my strength I drove forward, began to force my way through. I landed outside on my hands and face; then, as I rose to my feet, I heard them breaking down the privy door. I set off at a gallop, across the first of the vacant lots.

WHAT HAPPENED to me after this doesn't really matter—maybe I escaped on my own, or maybe someone 'helped' me, let me have my freedom, out of indifference or simple ineptitude. Maybe Marcela's ambivalence—her refusal to do the evil deed herself—had communicated itself to her underlings, and they were primed to be lackadaisical, to give me up at the first show of resistance. In any case, I soon made my way back to L.A. It took me six days to cross the border, because I had abandoned my car, and when you drive a car into Mexico, you must also drive it out (or else pay huge fines). I tried to bribe officials in Mexicali, but they proved uncommonly virtuous, and in the end I had to sneak back over.

To the possibility that Marcela was showing me a kind of 'mercy'—that at the last moment, she scrupled at killing me, out of affection of some sort—I must answer that anyone who could perpetrate such an outrage is incapable of mercy. The explanation, on the contrary, lies in her utter disregard for me. I was of so little consequence, so incapable of mounting a serious counterattack (in her opinion), that she forgot about me as soon as we separated.

I came back too late for my father's funeral. Jews are buried quickly, and in that connection I should mention that the idea was already current, even generally accepted in the press, that he had been assassinated on account of certain vague 'Zionist activities.' Literature of a suggestive sort had been left at the motel, and someone made some phone calls to station KTLA and to the L.A. *Times*, taking responsibility in the name of this or that Middle Eastern cause. My father was, indeed, a board member of the Jewish Welfare Agency, and of other like organizations, and it was just barely plausible that he had been 'targeted' in some new, terrorist campaign against substantial American Jews. My sister says that she believed this explanation for a while—she was still unclear about Marcela's (and the Señora's) motives.

I found her in a room with two other women (hysterectomy, cholecystectomy) in a hospital where she used to work, in bleak spirits. Though I already knew, in general terms, what had happened to her, I made her go over it all in detail, perversely relishing my role as blundering fool, hapless pawn, as Judas. Within minutes of my departure with Marcela, she said, Lalo explained what was to come, and they hurriedly packed and made ready to follow Marcela and me south. Sylvia thought all along that she could just overpower him, run away whenever she wanted, but as each hour passed, she realized ever more clearly how competent he was, how thoroughly prepared. In San Francisco, they stayed in a ratty apartment for about two days, waiting for the phone to ring (adding Marcela's authority to the venture). There were other people in the apartment as well: they hardly ever spoke around her, and always in English, but she got the impression that they were

Latins, Spanish-speakers (certainly not Middle Eastern). After a long, demoralizing wait, during which she began to realize that she, too, was likely to be killed, Marcela finally phoned. Then she set off for southern California with Lalo, driving straight on for Santa Barbara, and eventually, to the motel in Meiner's Oaks.

"I actually wanted to do it," she told me, "I was eager, I wanted to get it over with. I would die if I had to, because I couldn't bear thinking about it anymore. And . . . I wanted to see my father. I just wanted to be with him, if only for a minute or two. I thought that in that time, I'd be able to tell him something. Show him something. Just some affection—I don't know what.

"When I called the house, it wasn't like they were holding a gun at my head, or anything like that. They knew I believed them, believed that they'd really do it. I thought Gerson might be able to tell from the way I sounded that something was wrong, and I was afraid of that. So, I sounded as regular as I could, but still he knew. I'm sure he did. Anyhow, he came. He didn't bring anyone else with him, either. Maybe there was someone down on the street, waiting in the car; but as soon as they heard some shots, they ran away.

"I always thought that they'd let you go. It never occurred to me that she might be worried about you, want you out of the way, too. It was probably the Señora who thought like that— Marcela doesn't think that way, I'm sure. It's the absence of hatred, or love, or any kind of feeling at all with her; that's what's really scary. That's how it's always been. Of course, she didn't care about you. She didn't care about me, either. She only cares about one thing, some idea in her mind, some political thing, that she hasn't even bothered to write down yet. She offered me a straight-up deal—my father for my brother— and I took her at her word.

"I never hesitated, you know. But maybe I was being stupid; now I'll have the rest of my life to think about it, to see if there was some better way."

I told her that there wasn't, there couldn't have been; that she had done everything that anyone might. In my opinion, I said, she had acted with great courage.

"No. Don't say that. Please—please don't say that."

"But it's true. You know it's true. And I *will* say it. I'll say it over and over again, forever."

"No. I just led him there. I just brought him to them, so they could kill him. And I was thinking about myself the whole time. In that minute before they came, I was just thinking how I could get away, how to save myself. It was okay if they killed him—killed my own father."

"No. That's not so. Look what happened to you."

I was thinking about her wounds—her dreadful wounds. I imagined that at the instant Lalo came into the room, my sister had interposed herself, instinctively sought to cover my father with her own body.

"No," she said, when I explained that to her, "I was just trying to get away. When someone starts shooting, you don't behave rationally; and I'd been expecting that moment for six days. I just went crazy. That's all. I was trying to get away, and I ran into the middle of everything. By chance."

"No. You don't know what you did, not even you. You think you do, but something else happened. You're not capable of saving yourself. You've never been capable of that. You have to save the others first—that's just who you are. It's in your heart, Sylvia."

She sank into her pillows. She was sitting up in bed, in a thick web of i.v. feeds, canvas straps, aluminum poles, and so forth, practically suspended from it all, like some beautiful, wasted, miserable marionette.

"No. I know what happened to me," she repeated, weakly.

"No. You don't know. You saved my life—that's all that happened. And you wanted to save him, too. Save your father. But you couldn't. That's all. But look what happened to you. I can't stand it—I can't stand what happened to you."

She sank even further into her pillows. I became aware, at just this moment, of the attention of the other women in the room; they were making no pretense of allowing us our privacy, and I turned to the one nearest my sister's bed, the one who, I think, had had her gallbladder removed that morning.

"Please," I said, "I'm trying to talk to my sister. My sister just saved my life. She would've saved our father, too, but she couldn't. I'd like to talk to her alone, if I could."

The woman stared at me, in silence, for half a minute.

"What am I supposed to do—get out of bed?"

"I don't know what you're supposed to do. Just let us be. That's all I ask."

I went closer to my sister's bed. I touched her. I kissed her.

"I love you," I said quickly. "And I hate what happened to you. I'm going to get you out of here. Then I'm going to take you up to the ranch. And then—I'm going to take care of you."

"Okay. All right."

"I just . . . hate this. I can't ever make it up to you, I guess, but I'm going to try. Just say you forgive me. Please—say it."

"No. Don't talk like that. It's stupid."

"No. Please—say it. Please say the words."

"I won't say it, because it doesn't make any sense. Now stop it."

I continued pleading in this vein for some minutes. I wasn't aware of how much I was upsetting her; then, I suddenly became aware, and I stopped. I kissed her again. I said good-bye for the time being.

THIS LEFT VERY little time—only these past few weeks in which to make all the necessary arrangements, to see my sister launched on her physical therapies, to travel back to Mexico, to pen these pages. I've been writing furiously ever since I crossed back over, and now I find that I'm almost up to date. My sister needs special care, and I've promised to be back in L.A. when they release her. I think she knows where I've gone—in that case, I'm only adding to her suffering, her worry, but I have to finish what I've begun.

It happens that I have two good friends—I've so far managed to keep their names out of this account. One lives on the northwestern coast of Mexico, in a seaside city, and it was a pleasure to visit him, to see him again after so much time apart. Together we drove inland, two hundred miles or so, to the little town of Cosales. But we found nothing there. No sign of

Marcela, nor of her 'group.' I must say that I was relieved, mainly on account of my friend, of what could have happened to him. I drove back to the coast, said farewell to him again.

It was only after this first effort—when nothing really happened, when I succeeded only in scaring myself, on my friend's account—that I became serious about these scribbled notes, and I hurried to the home of my other friend, near Cuernavaca. In the back of his house stands an old *palapa*, an airy little shack, and here I installed myself, gave myself over entirely to this effort to justify myself. Lacking the discipline of a professional writer, I find that I have failed to order my story properly, and I fear that my method has been so oblique as to leave out precisely what I most needed to include. That is—a sense of the inevitability of my situation, of forces acting beyond my control, bringing me, despite my true wishes, to this fateful point of departure. Or maybe my account of my family and of my peculiar personal history has not, in the end, lacked all suggestion of the fated, of the predetermined. In any event, the feeling I have at this moment—as I sit here in my little shack, writing at a wobbly table, by the light of a forty-watt bulb—is of no options out.

On my tenth night in town, I borrowed an old bicycle and pedaled to Las Casuelas, the Señora's great estate. Everything was as I remembered it: the high, deep-red stucco wall surrounding the entire property; the massive, beaten-iron gates; the manifold foliage visible above the walls, and in many places growing down over them, reaching almost to the street. I stood in the Avenida Ramón Hidalgo for about half an hour, trying to sense the human life within. It was that time of evening shortly after sunset, when the night sounds haven't quite begun, and the day, banished with subtropical swiftness, dies categorically in the mind; spooks and swifts were about, pouring out over the walls, and I thought that I could sense an emanation, a hint of evil, a suggestion of the cruel, murderous heart within. I hadn't meant to do anything this particular night, but I found myself

clambering up the wall, using an overhanging vine to pull myself onto it. Then, after slicing my hands on top, where shards of bottle glass were embedded in the stucco, I dropped down into the garden.

Everything was changed; none of the paths led where I remembered, and whole 'environments' had been transposed, I found, so that I was soon completely lost. The forest of date palms, which had once dominated a large sector, was gone, removed; hills had been leveled, and mini-canyons filled in, and I searched in vain, for over an hour, for the magical glen of memory. After vague, punishing wanderings through slimy jungle and fields of cacti, I arrived, almost by accident, at the old house itself. But I was strangely debilitated—almost sleepy, in my anxiety, my confusion—and I turned away from it. Thinking to collect myself, I settled into some shrubbery near the veranda. There were a number of lights on, mostly in the wing where the twins had used to live.

I knew what I had to do, but this was not the night for it; and anyway, I had anticipated so many obstacles, such a complex path leading to my objective, that I was unprepared for what happened next. A part of the veranda had been glassed over recently, to make a kind of greenhouse, or all-weather porch. Now a light went on inside this, only a few yards from where I lay. A young man entered the room. He put a gin-and-tonic glass on a table, switched on a lamp, and retreated. (There must have been a passage from the main house out to the porch, hidden from me by foliage or on account of my position.) After a couple of minutes, the overhead light went off again, leaving only the lamp on the table. I looked in vain, from my position outside, for the person who had done this switching on and off (there must have been a remote control somewhere inside).

After another few minutes, a figure appeared at the outer wall of the enclosure. She was clad all in black, and being so close to me (just inside the glass), she gave an impression of great size, of ominous girth. I was breathless with anxiety,

being only inches away from discovery (although the shrubbery hid me pretty well), and then she turned, pressed one
hand to the glass, and peered beyond me into the gloom. At
just this moment, some lights went on around me. It so happened that my bush, located between two areas of illumination,
still hid me well, but I was sure that if she had looked to her
right, or a little closer to the ground, she would have made
me out.

I held my breath; I couldn't move, and the Señora, partak-
ing of my immobility (it seemed), stayed at the glass for long
minutes, enjoying the view into her nighttime garden. (If I
imagine now her point of view, the floodlit sight of bushes and
trees, my invisibility seems incredible, and I begin to doubt the
entire sequence of ensuing events.) Her face was remarkably
the same, only a little more carefully, more studiedly made up.
Maybe she had had some plastic surgery, but this was surely
the face that I remembered, the one I had recently, in my
fanaticism, been training myself to hate. In years past, I had
always marveled at her innate composure, and in the first
moments of our strange tête-à-tête this night, I again had this
impression; no one could disturb, no event surprise, this visage, this formidable mask, which exposed itself always (and
only) for some unknown, specific purpose. I saw that she had
become almost ugly—thin, withered and weakened—but in
the same instant I felt, as I imagine my father had once felt, her
uncanny, enduring beauty. Then she turned away from the
glass. She hurried back to a chair near the lamp.

The young man reentered the room. The Señora affected
a sorrowful expression, and he came to her side, took her by the
hand. She spoke some words I couldn't hear, and then the
young man, with an insincerity even I could feel, stroked her
shoulder, kissed the top of her head. I understood, mainly by
the insouciance of his posture, that they were 'lovers.' I was
repelled by this thought, by his youthfulness as contrasted
with her age, her painted desiccation, but the vulnerable ex-

pression she wore had a strange effect on me—I couldn't help
being won to her side, sympathizing with what I took to be her
classically untenable position. (They may have been discussing
international politics, or the behavior of some household pet,
but the stark truth of their relation was what I thought I saw,
from my position beyond the glass.) Now the young man,
turning his back on her, stifled a yawn. I felt at that instant a
profound revulsion against him, solely on account of his nonchalance, his unfeeling disregard for her. It was only with
difficulty that I restrained myself from calling out to him: I
wanted badly to remonstrate with him, to correct him in this
hateful callousness toward an older woman.

Rising on unsteady legs, the Señora now took a step in his
direction. The young man, feeling her approach, retreated
casually, staying just inches beyond her reach. Then they
both—and with a suddenness that startled me—turned
around, faced the passage, the entrance back into the house.
(They may have been responding to a sound I couldn't hear, the
ringing of a bell, a voice on an intercom.) With a worried glance
for the Señora, the young man hurried inside. Left by herself,
she staggered over to her chair, sat upon it; she reached for the
gin-and-tonic glass. Her left hand, trembling slightly, moved
upon her breast, and her short legs, inside a dark housecoat, fell
laxly away from each other.

I can't explain the effect this sight had on me. I immediately slipped away, hurried off through the grounds; my state
of mind was of such a dizzy, unsettled sort that I can't remember actually climbing the wall, or even riding my bike back to
my *palapa*.

If I say I was touched by the Señora, moved to find her in
such a weakened, apparently needful condition, I exaggerate
my capacity for experiencing compassion; and I need to add

that I was also gratified to see her this way, to find her dras-
tically reduced. I was not so naive as not to have looked ahead to
this, to have anticipated some such encounter; I knew there
would come a moment when we would have to grapple, when I
would have to approach her, physically, and in a general way, I
had prepared myself for such an eventuality. Certainly, I intended to do her mortal harm. I had even fooled myself with
the thought that there might be some sort of 'release' attendant
upon the murder of this small, undefended, seventyish
woman. But to see her there in a housecoat—in the same kind
of shabby wrap my own mother used to wear—to see her, as it
were, apostrophized inside a glass box, with her frailty on
display, was simply too much. I felt my resolve collapsing, my
murderous firmness of purpose leaking away.

My main feeling, indeed, was one of sadness. This was
possibly the first time, since my father's death, that I had felt
something appropriate to the situation, and I sincerely regretted all that had happened, as well as my general uselessness. I
had always thought that under the right conditions, I would be
able to act with a ruthlessness, with a bloody-mindedness, of
which he might have been proud; but now I had failed him. I
stayed at the *palapa* for about another week, doing nothing,
only occasionally scratching things down in this notebook.

It was on a trip downtown, for the purpose of buying
more cigarettes, that I stumbled on the solution to my dilemma. The casual, remorseless murderer Lalo, accompanied
by the young man of the porch, appeared suddenly before me
in a small crowd, happy, jovial, looking extremely fit and tan.
The two of them were on their way to a juice bar, I found, a
place well-known in central Cuernavaca, called La Única. Here
they proceeded to buy double smoothies and then sit and
drink. I lurked in the doorway of a nearby tobacco shop, unable
to comprehend this stroke of chance, my good fortune. It was
such a shock—to have him there in front of me, only twenty or
thirty feet away—that I fought an impulse to rush up, to thank

him sincerely for delivering me from my quandary. After finishing their fruity drinks the two of them moved off through the square. They looked like a couple of spoiled French playboys, I thought: white trousers, expensive cotton pullovers, identically dark hair still wet from after-tennis showers. I followed them at a discreet distance, up a side street heading out of town.

After two or three blocks, they halted in front of a pharmacy. The young man went inside. I imagined him to be picking up some medicine for the Señora—there was something about the way he had opened the shop door, some suggestion of irritation, disgust. Lalo hummed a happy tune meanwhile, and then he eased himself, rear end first, over the door and into the seat of an old convertible Alfa parked on the street. The young man came out a moment later, and then they roared off, with hoots of laughter trailing behind.

There could be no doubt where they were bound; yet I was seized with a sudden, unreasoning anxiety, on account of my need to have him right then, to hold him immediately in my own, murdering hands. If he should disappear—if his stay at Las Casuelas were just now drawing to a close, for example—then I might never have the chance to profit from this coincidence. I had ridden my bike into town, and now I pedaled furiously uphill, determined to overtake them before they reached Las Casuelas. Just as I was coming up Ramón Hidalgo (the street on which the main entrance is situated), I saw the Alfa halt at the front gate. Lalo hopped out, and he called to someone on the other side of the wall. I continued riding uphill, with no thought for my bursting lungs and tearing muscles, but just as I was narrowing the distance between us, coming within what I considered 'striking' range, the gates swung open, the Alfa scuttled inside, and they were lost to me.

I was sure they'd seen me; even so, I rattled the gates, demanded to be let in. No one responded to my calls. If there was a gateman, he had by now vanished into the thick, purplish

foliage, which gave to the sandy drive, on which the car had
headed up to the house, the look of some wayward path
through a menacing dream. I could have climbed the wall, but I
was belatedly aware of my vulnerability. I was unarmed, after
all, and out of breath, and in the presence of a known killer, a
professional assassin of some kind. I hurriedly retrieved my
bicycle, rode back to my *palapa*.

There followed two uneventful days (three days ago, and
the day before), when I did nothing, just retraced my steps,
waited patiently, hoped earnestly. Then two days ago, I again
saw the tennis players, and I followed them up the same street.
At the pharmacy, the young man again bought something, then
he drove off in the white convertible, leaving Lalo to hoof it up
the hill by himself. I followed at a distance of about half a block.
At a dusty, deserted stretch along the Avenida Benito Juárez,
where a small canyon, a narrow, brush-filled *barranca*, parallels
the road for a bit, he stopped and ostentatiously lit one of his
French cigarettes. I could feel him inviting me—I felt it, I say,
and I wanted to accept, but for some reason, I declined his
invitation. After about another minute, he continued uphill,
and I let him return to Las Casuelas unmolested.

The day after—nothing. No one appeared, and I began to
have doubts, to become anxious again. But I could feel the
'Manipulator' behind it all: I knew that she would give him to
me, I knew that she had decided, in her wisdom, to offer me
this special opportunity, that I could depend on her absolutely.
(Even if she only wanted to destroy me, if he were but her
means toward that end, I accepted her conditions; her plan had
become my own, and we were finally working together, committed to the same enterprise.) At the *barranca* again, just this
morning, Lalo stopped and, almost with a gesture of yearning,
of pleading, he turned to face me across the street. I don't know
why he didn't shoot me right at that moment—the street was
empty, no one could have seen us, or maybe he thought that I
had a gun, too. We faced each other, in silence, for several

minutes. Finally, shaking his head in exasperation, he turned his back to me again. When I still didn't approach, he continued uphill.

Tomorrow, I will respond; I see us grappling on the brink of the *barranca*, and because of my greater size, my longer and stronger arms, I soon overpower him, and we tumble down over the edge. I put my hands on his throat, and by the time we reach the bottom he's almost dead. I quickly break his neck and leave him there in the brush. Only the neighborhood dogs will find him, and I will have my revenge, my precious payback. If I say that this idea—the prospect of such a happy thing, the inspiring thought of it—has already lost some of its attraction for me, I only mean that the sense of acting out a role, of playing a part, a part designed by someone else, has become paramount for me, and at just this moment of delicious and hard-earned victory, I realize how dependent and insignificant I truly am. At just this instant of final, definitive self-assertion, I begin to fade away, to lose my claim on identity. I even doubt that the Señora really cares about me anymore—the working out of my insignificant fate, which has always been but a small, subsidiary part of her story (and of my father's), is possibly the least important thing she'll be dealing with tomorrow.

As I close my hands around his throat, and as we tumble down through the bushes, I nevertheless experience a moment akin to true freedom: all the force that I can command, every reserve of my will and of my physical strength, is present in my grip, and I play my part with a fierce concentration, as if I believed in it absolutely.

About the Author

ROBERT ROPER was born in New York in 1946. Educated at Swarthmore, Berkeley, and Stanford, he has lived for some years in northern California. He is the author of the award-winning novels *Royo County* and *On Spider Creek*.